Cayman Heat

by

Connie Reeves Cooke

RoseDog🐾Books
PITTSBURGH, PENNSYLVANIA 15222

The contents of this work including, but not limited to, the accuracy of events, people, and places depicted; opinions expressed; permission to use previously published materials included; and any advice given or actions advocated are solely the responsibility of the author, who assumes all liability for said work and indemnifies the publisher against any claims stemming from publication of the work.

The characters and events in this book are fictitious. Any similarity to real persons, living or dead, is coincidental and not intended by the author.

All Rights Reserved
Copyright © 2012 by Connie Reeves Cooke

No part of this book may be reproduced or transmitted, downloaded, distributed, reverse engineered, or stored in or introduced into any information storage and retrieval system, in any form or by any means, including photocopying and recording, whether electronic or mechanical, now known or hereinafter invented without permission in writing from the publisher.

RoseDog Books
701 Smithfield Street
Pittsburgh, PA 15222
Visit our website at *www.rosedogbookstore.com*

ISBN: 978-1-4349-8921-5
eISBN: 978-1-4349-7913-1

Cayman Heat

To Clayton, for everything.

Thanks to my wonderful family and friends for always supporting me and being my biggest cheerleaders – Jacqueline and Gary Reeves, Eleanor and Corbin Cooke, Dawn and Cameron Cooke, Forester Cooke, Jeanne and Pat Simpson, Virginia Reisman, Phyllis Williams, Warner Roberts, Diane Gendel, Susan Krohn, Jeanne Sims, Laura Ward, Margaret Creel, Sherry Sutton, Jan Carson, Carol Sawyer, Mary Rugaard, Mary Ann McKeithan and Joanne King Herring.

Thank you to Franelle Rogers for introducing me to author Sandy Sheehy who helped me through the long editing process, and whose patience, expertise and friendship I will always cherish.

And thanks to my angels – my amazing parents Ruby and W. C. Reeves. There are no words to adequately express my gratitude and love. The world is not the same without you in it. I miss you every second of my life.

Prologue

Grand Cayman
Two Years Ago

Reese Mallory never saw the figure looming below him in the dark blue water, watching and waiting.

The North Wall had his full attention. Even though he'd made the dive eight times, he never got tired of the sheer drop, thousands of feet into water that shaded from true blue to indigo, the giant spotted eagle rays and supple tiger sharks gliding just off the edge, the purple and orange sponges, and plume-like gorgonians waving seductively in the current. He and Lynn had even done their open water check-out dive on the Wall when they'd gotten their scuba certification three years earlier. It was a place that visited him in his dreams.

As the compressed air bubbles from Reese's regulator floated slowly toward the surface, looking much like a school of jellyfish as they rose, the lone figure blended into the Wall's living seascape below and waited for the right moment to make his move.

Grand Cayman's North Wall allowed nothing to detract from its mesmerizing beauty. It demanded undivided attention from its admirers. It breathed its own breath and was alive with violet-tipped sea anemones, an oddly shaped fish boasting every color of the rainbow. Black tip sharks, hawksbill turtles, huge barrel sponges, and bushes of black coral, endangered and strictly protected by Caymanian law, decorated the pristine water as sea whips, plumes, and fans swayed in the eternal currents.

Reese almost never drifted away on his own without a dive buddy, but on the North Wall he became distracted, and the depths of the aquamarine Caribbean Sea beckoned to him. Normally aware of the safety rules governing depth and time, more than once on the Wall he'd strayed from his companions to venture a bit deeper, stay a bit longer, following that ray or that turtle or that grouper another few yards, then another.

One of these days, he was going to push those limits and dive too deep if he wasn't careful. Of course, Reese told himself, he would be prepared for what a deeper dive would require. In his world, power and self-control were assumed, but he also recognized that his life was at stake if he was careless.

Reese checked his dive computer and saw that the limit of his bottom time was approaching. He looked around for the others. They were tapping their watches and pointing upward, indicating it was time to surface.

As they all began their ascent, a flash of silver caught Reese's eye, stopping him just long enough to fall behind the others.

A huge prehistoric-looking tarpon appeared in front of his mask, diverting his attention from the figure rising slowly, silently beneath him.

As Reese and the tarpon studied each other, he felt something come out of nowhere, grab his mask from his face and tear at his regulator, ripping it from his mouth. Before he could react, water was pouring into his mouth and the salt water was stinging his eyes. He thought a shark or another huge fish must have attacked him, going for his head. He spun around but couldn't see the threat.

Reese instinctively tried to retrieve his regulator amid the angry bubbles of escaping compressed air exploding all around him. But when he reached for it, his hand found only the end of the severed hose. His heart began to pound wildly. He twisted around to find his octopus rig, the spare regulator that allows divers to share their tank with a buddy who runs out of air. Where was the damn thing?

Reese quickly released his weight belt to give him more buoyancy as he struggled to get his bearings and rise to the surface. He knew from all his years of diving that he had to remain calm and ascend slowly.

If he panicked and shot to the surface, the compressed air in his lungs would quickly expand, causing a potentially fatal embolism.

All he could think about now was which way was up.

Up to the surface and precious air.

But something was holding him down. He must have snagged a fin on a branch of coral. As he kicked to free himself, he felt his chest begin to burn from lack of oxygen. He knew he had to use what little air he had left in his lungs to try to get to the surface one-hundred twenty-five feet above. He could see the sunlight filtered dimly through the water, showing him the way up, teasing him, and challenging him to try to reach it, as he tried to kick his fins free.

As precious seconds ticked away, he felt panic begin to take over.

Reese's lungs seemed like they would burst. Thoughts of the safety rules left his mind as he fumbled to find the button to inflate his buoyancy compensator. He'd risk an embolism; take his chances with decompression sickness, the bends. Then he realized what was pulling him down.

It was a pair of strong human hands.

As the hands gripped tighter and tighter, Reese sensed himself being dragged toward the abyss 8,000 feet below. He twisted and jackknifed, but he never got a clear look at whoever was trying to make sure he never made it up.

The only thing Reese Mallory knew for certain was that he was about to learn what death felt like.

Chapter One

Grand Cayman
Present Day

Somebody was knocking on the door. At 10:00 A.M. And on Saturday fucking morning.

Someone better be dead, she thought, kicking the covers off the bed and onto the pale blue tile floor. The morning sunlight was straining to find its way through the closed plantation shutters, but wasn't having much success.

Unceremoniously, Koral Sanders pulled herself up, flung her feet onto the floor and grabbed her robe off the chair by the bed. Throwing it around her slender, naked body, she stalked through the bedroom and living room, giving both a grimace as she headed for the door. She pressed her hand to her forehead to quiet the shooting pain of a fledgling hangover and ran her fingers through her disheveled long brown hair.

Koral scowled at the half empty glass of Jack Daniels sitting on the coffee table next to an ashtray brimming with cigarette butts, evidence of her solitary party last night. In the shape she was in, Zulu warriors could have stormed the building last night and she wouldn't have noticed. The clothes she had worn were slung across the back of the sofa, and one of her sandals was propped up on the throw pillow. She had no idea where the other one was. She wished the strewn clothes had been the result of some wild and crazy anonymous sex, but no such luck.

Koral had been in a foul mood after a bitch of a day. She felt like she'd been running with her hair on fire all week and just wanted to chill out and relax, letting her clothes and shoes land where they may as she tossed them aside, fixed a stiff Jack on the rocks, and plopped down naked on the sofa to watch Jack Bauer catch bad guys on reruns of "24."

What she should have done, she realized, was call her new next door neighbor, Julie, and enlist her in a quick trip to Pepper's, to check out the local action. For a single gal, nothing beat a good girlfriend, and Julie was the first one Koral had really clicked with since coming to Cayman. Julie was a perky brunette with a similar sense of humor and a similarly disastrous romantic track record, though different taste in men. Sometimes when they went out together, they'd laugh themselves off their barstools. But Koral hadn't wanted to inflict herself on Julie last night or on anyone else, for that matter. She didn't even remember what time she went to bed, or how she got there.

God, she just had to find a maid, and soon, she thought. She spied the stray sandal sticking out from under the sofa and kicked it across the room.

Housekeeping wasn't her strong suit. Never had been, never would be. She still hadn't given up on her hope of marrying into royalty and having servants.

As she passed the glass-topped coffee table, she reached down and scooped up a half-empty pack of Marlboro Lights, tied her robe around her waist, and yelled, "Who is it?"

"It's Sam, Koral. Open up!" said the familiar, lilting baritone voice.

Koral unlocked the door and slowly cracked it open.

"Sam what the hell do you want at ten o'clock in the fucking morning? And on Saturday?" Koral growled, taking the night chain off and pulling the door open.

Sam Roberts grimaced.

"Such language for a pretty girl," he scolded her, as he closed the door behind him. Koral pulled a face at him and threw her hands up in the air as she turned and headed toward the kitchen.

"I just thought I'd come by and fill you in on a very interesting case," he told her, following her into the kitchen. He made a quick sweep of Koral's condo and shook his head, laughing under his breath, as he stepped over a sandal in the middle of the room. She really was a terrible housekeeper, he decided.

Oblivious to Sam's perusal of the barely controlled chaos of her condo, Koral lit a cigarette and reached for the coffee pot. Filling it with tap water, she turned, leaned back against the sink, and took a long draw on the Marlboro. Holding the dripping pot in one hand, she took the cigarette out of her mouth with the other and blew smoke toward the ceiling. She knew she should stop the nasty cigarette habit, and drinking Jack Daniels along with it, but giving all that up at once might prove fatal to anyone in her path when she was having a bad day. Hell, if she gave up smoking, drinking, and sex, she could be a freaking nun. That thought made her laugh out loud. Fat chance. She was going to quit soon. Just not today. And not all at once. And definitely not sex.

She asked him in that sexy, raspy Demi Moore voice of hers, "What kind of case?"

Sam pulled out a kitchen chair and sat his ample forty-five-year-old body down at the table. The big, handsome bear of a man had skin the color of *café au lait*, a head full of slightly curly light blonde hair, and riveting blue eyes. Clearly, genes from several continents had filtered down through the generations to produce Sam's strikingly beautiful Caymanian coloring.

Sam was always fussing about his size, knowing that he not only would have better luck with the ladies but might live longer if he could lose about forty pounds. It wasn't easy working for the best and busiest private investigator in the Cayman Islands. Especially if you weighed two-hundred thirty and had to chase people on foot occasionally.

Most of Sam's girth was solid muscle, but he knew he had to quit dropping by the Hyatt Regency's yogurt shop twice a day for a double chocolate yogurt stuffed in a waffle cone. Those things were more addictive than booze. He knew that for a fact, since he had tried giving up chocolate before with no success.

Sam had been working for Koral Sanders for six years. He met her one night at the Almond Tree Restaurant when he and the restaurant owner, Jack Alford, were having drinks. The Almond Tree was popular with good-looking expats and local ladies. Women seemed to love its romantic ambience. Tables hidden among the palm trees, hibiscus and bougainvillea on the patio provided ample privacy for those who wanted it. On those rare occasions when Sam had a special date, he knew he couldn't miss by taking her there. Ever since Hurricane Ivan blew the Almond Tree away in 2004, and Jack moved back to the States, Sam hadn't found a spot with quite that magic.

One table over from Sam and Jack, Koral was bending elbows with Royal Cayman Islands Police Service Chief Aron Ebanks, who just happened to be Sam's distant relative. Sam figured Koral to be about thirty-four, although if she was like most women he knew, she would never admit it. She was pretty in a rough-around-the-edges way with shoulder length brown hair, green eyes, a killer tan, and a great body. Not bad for a private eye. Jack knew everyone on the island and everything about them.

Jack met Koral when she came in the restaurant alone one night. After she'd thrown back a couple of stiff Black Jacks on the rocks, they'd started talking, and a couple of hours later, Koral had told him only what she wanted him to know about herself and her past, which wasn't much. Leaving out the parts she'd revealed later in confidence, he filled Sam in on what he knew from her and what he'd picked up on from the notoriously active, though not equally accurate, Cayman gossip mill.

It had taken some effort for Koral to secure a Cayman Islands work and residency permit and then a private investigator's license, but it had been worth it. Her timing had been just right.

She had strolled into the RCIPS headquarters one day, handed the chief her résumé, and asked how she could go about getting support letters, explaining how Cayman needed her skills. She told the chief there was no local Caymanian who had her particular combination of qualifications. She hadn't known that for a fact, but she knew how to look like she did. If there was a job in the Cayman Islands that could be filled by a Caymanian citizen, no outsider could be hired.

The day Koral catapulted into Chief Ebanks' life, he just happened to be scratching his head over a nasty fraud scheme in which the perpetrators had made use of the honest services of a highly-regarded British bank. The chief was under a lot of pressure to protect the reputation of the bank, especially its local office, by nailing the scammers, but he needed someone with accounting expertise to track the money trail. Koral just happened to fill the bill.

She had been working with Aron as a financial forensics consultant since then. When Aron's office ran a background check on her, Aron remembered a couple of high-profile fraud cases in Houston and Austin that Koral had a hand in solving. He saw a mutually beneficial relationship in the stars for the RCIPS and Koral, and strongly supported her applications for residency and a work permit.

When the police chief put his stamp of approval on her, the rest was easy.

The RCIPS had employed Koral on a case contract basis ever since. She was so good at what she had done, mainly catch the do-badders, that the services she performed expanded beyond the "financial forensics consultant" job description. In fact, they occasionally involved basic martial arts techniques, scaling second and third-story balconies and even marksmanship. Koral was very visible on Grand Cayman, and the locals had gradually come to know and respect her.

She had also been around the block more than a few times. Jack knew of at least two messy divorces in her past, but he didn't share the details with Sam. Jack was good at keeping secrets about his friends.

After Jack introduced Sam to Koral, they ran into each other every once in a while since Sam did freelance work for the police department. The two gradually became friends. Eventually, Koral asked Sam to work for her on a couple of cases, and they had been together ever since.

"You remember the guy who disappeared on a North Wall dive a couple of years ago?" Sam asked her.

Gathering her thoughts, which wasn't easy under the circumstances, Koral said, "Yeah, that rich guy from Houston.

Right?" She plugged in the coffee pot. "I knew of him when I lived in Houston. A hot-shot trial lawyer with family money on top of those mega-contingency fees. Rich as hell. Never had the pleasure of meeting him. We didn't travel in the same social circles," she added sarcastically, stretching both arms toward the ceiling.

She was still trying to stop the high-school marching band parading through her head, which would take most of a full pot of coffee to do.

"That's the one," Sam answered. "And they couldn't find his body. Then."

Chapter Two

Koral gave Sam a puzzled look as she poured them both cups of coffee in happy face mugs and sat down across the table from him.

One of these days she was going to buy a house and have a real dining room, she thought, taking a big gulp of coffee. She was tired of entertaining at the kitchen table, even though she did love the fact that her condo was at the Sundowner, which was smack in the middle of Seven Mile Beach, the most famous address on Grand Cayman. Home to gazillionaires and movie stars. And mega-yachts with spoiled young heiresses in dental-floss bikinis draped across their bows. With miles of talcum-powder-textured white sand and clear turquoise water, it was a magnet for the world's well-heeled.

The Sundowner was no Hyatt or Ritz-Carlton, but it had the same view of the beach and the water as those high dollar places did and for a shitload less money. It also came furnished and decorated in luscious tropical pastels. The white wicker furniture throughout was accented with yellow, coral, and aquamarine pillows and cushions with matching drapes in the living room. The walls were covered with paintings of seashells and inviting hammocks placed strategically between palm trees on stretches of white sand. Koral thought she had died and gone to heaven when she lucked into finding it. A friend told her the owners wanted to lease it since they weren't going to be spending a lot of time on

Grand Cayman, but they didn't want to sell it. She snapped it up and was living large at a dream address.

Koral tightened the sash on her robe. Modesty wasn't high on her list of priorities, but she didn't want to distract Sam.

"What do you mean?" she asked, lighting another Marlboro, her interest now on high alert.

"Well, guess what the cat drug in this morning?" Sam announced.

"Someone found his body?" Koral asked, an incredulous look on her face. "Bet that wasn't pleasant this early in the morning."

"Better than that. They found his skeleton with his dive gear still on it, minus his mask and regulator. And get this. His regulator hose was cut."

Sam had Koral's undivided attention now.

"A couple of divers from Miami went out to the North Wall just after sunrise. They went deep, about 130 feet, and in the few minutes of bottom time they had while they were down there, they found a small cave opening. I can't believe no one ever noticed it before now. Maybe someone did, but was afraid to go in very far. It was pretty hidden by some huge coral."

"Anyway, one of the divers decided to go in a ways and check it out. Bingo! There was a skeleton attached to a piece of coral with some four-ply wire. Somebody had wrapped the wire around the guy's tank so there wasn't any danger of it coming loose. After marking the cave entrance with a safety sausage attached to a weight, the divers high-tailed it up to their boat and radioed the police to get out there.

"Cayman's finest sent out a dive team who took a bunch of pictures and brought the guy up. Of course, he had to be brought up in a bag. They didn't want to lose any of him along the way," Sam chuckled, attempting to inject a little humor. "Imagine what those shots would do for Cayman tourism if they ever showed up on some warped diver's blog."

Koral wasn't amused. Sam stopped laughing when he saw the glare on her face, so he cleared his throat and continued.

"The thing they were concerned about was the fact that his regulator hose was cut. Not torn, cut close to the tank. Tying the body to the reef with wire could have been a prank, but not cutting the hose. Looks a lot more like murder now than an accident," Sam said.

Koral leaned back in her chair and took a big swig of coffee. "How did you find out about this?"

"I just happened to be in Aron's office this morning, shooting the breeze about my auntie's third marriage, when the call came in. Naturally, he wanted you to know about it. I told him I'd give you the news since I was coming this way. Aron said he wanted to bring us in as consultants on the case. You know how they're always short-staffed at his office. And with the guy so rich and a lawyer and all, financial forensics could be in order. Besides, I think he wants you on this one because of your famous delicacy and diplomacy."

Sam paused for effect as Koral rolled her eyes. Delicacy and diplomacy were not words usually used in the same sentence to describe Koral.

"Has the guy's family been notified?" Koral asked, purposely ignoring another of Sam's attempt at humor.

"Yeah, they called the guy's wife in Houston. She's on her way right now. Shouldn't take her too long. She's coming down in her Gulfstream. Must be nice. She owns one of the penthouses at the Ritz-Carlton. Big money. We're talking huge."

"She owns one of those penthouses?" Koral asked, her mouth dropping open. She knew they were talking monster freaking money if the rich widow owned one of the priciest condos on Cayman.

"Yep. Can you believe that? Nothing like this has ever happened here before and especially to somebody like this guy. Hell, you know as well as I do there are only two or three murders a year on Cayman, mostly domestic, sometimes Jamaican or Colombian drug guys who stray off course, but certainly nothing like this. This one's really out there."

Sam paused, looked down at his hands, then up at Koral sheepishly. "The only problem is, I've got a ticket on the evening flight to Miami. You remember. My aunt and uncle's fiftieth wedding anniversary is next week, and we're all getting together to celebrate. Some of my relatives are pretty old. I might not get a chance to see them again. I'll be back in a few days."

"Go ahead and go," Koral told him. "With the case this old and cold, the chances that anything will develop between now and then are slim to none. By any chance did Aron discuss the terms for working on this case?"

"He mentioned it would be more lucrative than our usual missing minors and insurance fraud stuff. This is high-profile, given the players, and you can bet he's under pressure from everyone from the manager of the Ritz-Carlton to the U.S. consul to solve this quickly and quietly. Aron said for you to come to his office as soon as possible and he'll give you the rest of the details. I'd sure like to know who hated the guy enough to do that to him. From what Aron has told me, he and his wife were society darlings. Everyone loved them."

"Obviously, not everyone," Koral said.

Chapter Three

Police Chief Aron Ebanks sat behind his desk in his office at the Royal Cayman Islands Police Service headquarters in George Town. His was leaning forward on his elbows as he frowned at a piece of paper he held in his hands.

Koral Sanders stood in the doorway watching him. He looked tired and older than his sixty-five years. A job like his would do that to a man. He had been chief of police for ten years and was admired and respected for his integrity and fairness by the entire RCIPS. He'd often told Koral that he loved his job, but retirement loomed, and more and more, she suspected he was listening to the siren song of a leisurely lifestyle and more time with his kids and grandchildren.

Koral's friendship with Aron had been an unexpected gift. When she first arrived in Grand Cayman and opened her office, she'd had no friends or family on the island. Her parents had died a couple of years earlier and she'd been an only child. They were such a close-knit family and it had been devastating to lose them both. She'd been through a really hard time trying to deal with it and she hoped the move to Grand Cayman would give her a fresh start.

The only relatives Koral had were a distant uncle and a few long-lost cousins that she hadn't seen in years. Aron had been widowed for two years, and his three children were grown and living in Florida. In a community that valued family above all else, he and Koral had that lack of close connections in common.

Koral and Aron worked together on a couple of cases in those early days. Now they worked together on a regular basis. They were a good fit, and they watched each other's backs. Anyone who even acted like he or she might hurt Aron had to answer to her. She might be a woman, but she could kick some serious ass when the occasion arose, thanks to karate lessons that had earned her a black belt.

Aron's salt and pepper hair framed his gentle face and brown eyes as he studied the paper intently. His skin, the color of milk chocolate, was weather-worn from the unrelenting tropical sun. His short-sleeved light blue shirt was crisply pressed and starched.

Koral knew how hard it must be for Aron to have to take care of himself and a house alone. He had a lady who came in once a week to clean and do laundry, but it was the little things of everyday life she knew he missed with his wife gone. Her framed picture still sat on his desk along with those of his children and grandchildren.

"Find any answers in there, Aron?" she asked him, a crooked grin on her face.

He jumped, startled at the sudden intrusion, and his brown eyes twinkled under a mock scowl as he stood up and said, "Koral, have you ever heard of knocking?"

"Oh, come on Aron, you and I don't have to announce ourselves to each other. Not after all these years, do we?" she teased him. "Sam said you wanted to see me. Is it about that?" she asked, pointing at the piece of paper in his hand. She pushed some files over and sat down on the corner of his desk.

"This is the statement from those two divers who found Reese Mallory's remains this morning on the North Wall. I'm sure Sam told you all about it. He was here when the call came in from their boat and told me he was heading out your way. Want to take a look?" he asked her.

Distantly related somewhere down the family tree, Aron and Sam were close friends as well. They bounced theories off each other when it came to catching the bad guys. Even by Cayman standards, Sam had a remarkable network of cousins, in-laws and high school friends, so he usually knew what was going on around the island before anyone else did.

In Grand Cayman, every local seemed to be related to everyone else somewhere down the generational line. Forty percent of Caymanians were of mixed race, twenty percent were black, and twenty percent were white. The remaining twenty percent were expatriates, some white, some Latino, some West Indian, and some Asian. Koral found the result pleasingly exotic—an island of beautiful people who spoke with a distinctive Cayman version of a West Indian accent, sounding much like a melodic twist on a Scottish brogue.

"Yeah, Sam told me all about it. If I do take a look, you know I won't quit until I find out who killed him," Koral said, reaching out for the printed statement.

"That's what I'm counting on," Aron said, grabbing a slightly dog-eared file folder and sticking the pages inside.

"Guess I'd better do my homework on the merry widow," Koral said as he handed over the folder. "Sam told me she's on the way down here."

"What's your gut feeling?" Aron asked her.

"Without doing any research and snooping around first? Your guess is as good as mine," she winked at him and turned to leave.

"Oh, one more thing." He reached into his desk and pulled out a thick file folder. "When their dive boat pulled up at the Ritz-Carlton that day, I informed everyone that we would need to interview all the people on the boat and take their statements. We did that with one exception. Jeanette Ryker, a woman who tagged along with the Mallory party that day on the dive boat, disappeared. It was as if she had evaporated. None of the others knew her. They guessed from her accent that she was from East Texas. When we checked the number on her PADI certification card, it came up with an address in a town called Conroe, north of Houston. But it had been issued in 2002, and she was long gone. The strange thing was that customs had no record of her entering or leaving Grand Cayman. We were never able to locate her. She probably had a fake passport. I've thought these past two years that possibly she had something to do with Reese Mallory's death, although I don't know what part she might have played. Maybe you could try to track her down," Aron baited her.

"Right up my alley," Koral grinned.

"OK. Go find me a killer," Aron dismissed her, with a playful wave of his hand.

Chapter Four

Koral left Aron's office with the known facts of the Reese Mallory case tucked in a file under her arm. No briefcases for her. Too yuppie. Mostly she kept the facts in her head.

She had an uncanny ability to read people, analyze evidence, and look at the big picture, figuring out "why who did what and where to whom," from beginning to end. When she let the facts percolate for awhile, she'd get a whiff of what was in a suspect's mind. At the start, there'd be several scenarios. Most people had something to hide, and big trouble, like insurance fraud or murder, made more than just the perpetrators act suspicious. But eventually, the aroma one or two gave off would deepen, like strong coffee. When that happened, Koral relied on their weaknesses. Give 'em enough rope and they might not hang themselves, but they'd tie themselves up pretty good. Koral could, and had, outlasted the best of them. By the time they realized what had happened, Koral was waiting nearby with whatever official help it took to haul them off and make the case stick on the stand.

That was what set her apart from the rest.

An only child, she'd grown up in Texas City, a refinery town outside Houston. Her parents told her they named her Koral because her mom loved the vivid sunsets created by the pollution from the refineries, and her father wanted a child so badly he figured even before she was born that she'd be the light of his life. She had, of course, taken more than a little friendly kidding about her name; but she'd handled it. She knew that if she laughed at herself along with the other kids, sooner or later, they would accept her and think she was cool. It didn't hurt to have the features of a Gap Kids model and be good at soccer and softball.

Koral had as normal a childhood as anyone. Loving parents, lots of friends in the popular clique of cheerleaders and drum majors, and boyfriends who were on every girl's dream list. Her solid B average pleased her parents, but she knew she would never be a rocket scientist.

Being a private investigator didn't demand a calculator for a brain, even though math came easy for her. Common sense and street smarts did play a big part, however, and Koral had an abundance of both. Besides, she loved what she did.

It must have been all those Nancy Drew mysteries she read when she was a teenager. Koral remembered when she was in junior high school, as they called it back then, and the school librarian was a cranky old witch with a sour disposition and gray hair cut in the latest Buster Brown style. Every time Koral checked out a Nancy Drew mystery, the old bag frowned at her over her black horn-rimmed glasses and said, "Why don't you read something to improve your mind instead of this nonsense?"

Koral looked her straight in the eye and said, "Why do you have 'this nonsense' in the library if we aren't supposed to read it?" That shut the old hussy up.

After high school, Koral enrolled in the University of Houston. She'd thought about majoring in psychology, but her mom drummed it into her head that she needed a career, not a job, that could earn her a decent living with a bachelor's degree. With her dad a shift foreman at the refinery and her mom a legal secretary, there wasn't enough money to help her through a doctorate. So Koral majored in accounting and minored in psych. Only when she went on to get her Certified Public Accountant designation did her mother relax. Now, her mom said, she had something she could always fall back on in her later years, if she found herself unmarried and fending for herself, God forbid.

At least she wouldn't end up selling jewelry in a drug store if she could read a balance sheet.

Koral gave in to working as a C.P.A. for a small electrical contractor in her hometown, the old college try. That lasted about two months. She hated the work. She had never been so bored in her life. She decided she would save that for her old age. She also decided she would never marry an accountant.

After that, she took off to Dallas and tried her hand in the fashion business, as in selling clothes in a department store. Not a good career move. Her track record with men wasn't one for the record books either. In the space of three months, she met and married the biggest con artist ever to write a hot check. Hell, he'd never even met her parents.

First mistake.

When she caught him cheating on her six months after they got married, she filed for divorce, packed up, and moved to Austin.

One night about two months later at a singles hot spot, she met another fast-talking, good-looking loser who told her he had a big house north of town, a customized Harley, and a high six-figure bank account. A week later, he asked her to run off with him to Las Vegas and get married. So she did.

Second mistake.

On their honeymoon in Vegas, he gave her a black eye and a broken nose. After she hit him over the head with a bottle of champagne, and put him in the hospital with a cracked skull, she filed charges against him and filed for divorce the same day.

Koral decided a change of zip code was just what she needed, so after leaving Las Vegas, she headed back to Houston and, she hoped, better luck in the romance department.

She swore to herself she wasn't going to be a sucker for any man anymore. She was going to learn how to read people and know when they were real and when they weren't. Heaven knew she had enough practice.

True to her mother's word, she had to fall back on what she knew best until something better came along. Looking through the classifieds, she noticed that a private investigation firm was looking for an in-house accountant and billing manager. She went for the interview, résumé in hand, and was told to show up for work the next morning.

The firm did a good business, but the work was relatively easy, since most of the clients were insurance companies and law firms that were professional in their record keeping and paid their bills on time. One afternoon, Koral's boss walked in while she was sneaking a look at the guys on Match.com. Her work was done; her desk was clean; so she gave him what she hoped was a non-defensive smile and asked if she could help him.

"As a matter of fact, you might be able to," he said. "We've got a high-end divorce case—two doctors. My gut tells me the wife has squirreled away community assets, but the financial trail for her plastic surgery practice is so convoluted that I can't find them. Maybe with your accounting background...."

Koral found three million dollars and a new career.

Her boss noticed that she showed a real grasp of what it took to blend in, almost becoming invisible, and find people who didn't want to be found, along with the money they didn't want to give up. He showed her the ropes, got her licensed, and made her an associate.

Koral's first official task was to recruit and train her replacement. Her second made her a favorite with animal lovers. It was a puppy mill case the Houston Humane Society was investigating. When Koral read the facts of the case, she wondered how such evil existed in some humans. She knew of puppy mills, but had no idea of the misery the helpless little dogs had to endure their entire lives.

The general public was usually unaware that those cute puppies in pet stores came from illegal puppy mills where dogs kept in wire cages, sometimes three to a cage with no bedding or protection from extreme heat and cold, were bred year after year in deplorable and abusive conditions. The cages were too small for them to move freely or even lie down comfortably and their feet fell through the wire floor. They never received love, companionship, or affection from a human being and were never taken out of the cages to exercise. In many instances, they had slimy dirty water or no water at all. What little food they had was stale and their cages were sometimes stacked on top of each other resulting in the dogs being covered in excrement. When they were no longer able to reproduce, they were killed, abandoned or sold to other puppy mills or individuals, sometimes to be used as "bait" for training pit bulls to fight. That horrible vision made Koral feel physically ill.

They had no hope of ever becoming part of a loving family.

Over a period of weeks, Koral worked closely with the Houston Humane Society enforcement staff's Sgt. Guerra, a handsome, muscular drill sergeant type, with a zero tolerance attitude when it came to prosecuting offenders abusing animals. They had located the owners of a puppy mill in a small town outside of Houston. The HHS officers also received an anonymous phone call from a neighbor about a minor child in the home, as well as a horrible stench coming from it. Having grown up with a succession of rescued dogs as pets, Koral loved animals and wanted to be there personally to arrest the monsters responsible. But even after reading about them, she wasn't prepared for what awaited her.

When Koral and the officers entered the home, they had to immediately retreat to put on breathing apparatuses due to the stench from animal waste and from dogs lying dead on the floors of every room. Even the seasoned investigating officers were shocked.

The dogs had blood dripping from injuries, pus exploding from festered wounds, and bare, raw skin where hair should be. The smell of death and decay, filth, and toxic fumes of ammonia filled the air. Over one hundred dogs were whimpering, whining and shivering in fear and pain.

In addition to the physical horror, the abuse that was evident in the eyes of the pitiful, trusting dogs broke her heart. Koral had to fight the sudden need to throw up knowing how long it must have taken for those poor mistreated little dogs to become so debilitated.

Koral knew she would never forget the look in the eyes of the dogs as they were rescued from the cages and carried to vans to be transported to safety, freedom, and a loving environment.

It was as if they were thanking her for saving them.

The two officers arrested the owners of the puppy mill and testified at their animal cruelty trial. If only those demons could be sentenced to the same punishment they had subjected the dogs to for so many years, Koral thought. Maybe they would think twice about mistreating animals again if they had to suffer the same fate. Unfortunately, unless every state passed laws regulating puppy mills and the treatment of their animals, this atrocity would continue forever.

Koral quickly established herself as a force to be reckoned with. She had a laser-sharp mind and a tongue to match and a no-nonsense approach to challenges. And she didn't take any crap off anybody. Men she encountered on cases quickly learned what the guys in the office had snapped to in a week. Koral Sanders might be easy on the eyes, but she was no "girlie-girl."

She spent a good deal of her time in the Texas Hill Country north of Austin doing surveillance on errant husbands who entertained their outside ladies in the mega-mansions that dotted the waterfront along the clear, sparkling waters of Lake Travis. Many of them were computer nerds who hadn't been able to get a second glance from a halfway hot chick until they made millions in the dot.com boom. Now, although the crash may have cut their bazillions in half, they still had beauty queens crawling all over them and their money. They could take their pick of the highest-bidder babes and spend a weekend in their playpens on the lake while the little woman was home in the city raising little geeks.

Observing and recording were as close as Koral wanted to get to that scene. No more cheating and abusive husbands for her. And certainly, no screaming brats who grow up to disappoint you and make your life miserable. Not that she didn't like children. She did as long as they belonged to someone else.

She had the life she wanted now, and she wasn't going to let anything screw it up.

When Koral and three women from her office went to Grand Cayman for a much needed long weekend, she fell in love with it and decided on the spot that she was going to move to the island and open her own PI office.

She had always wanted to live in a tropical paradise with white sand beaches, clear aquamarine water, and lots of palm trees to lie under and drink piña coladas with little umbrellas in them. She liked ska and reggae and buff guys in tight shorts.

She loved the island, and she loved the people. And besides, there was hardly any violent crime here. Where would anyone hide? The island was only twenty-two miles long and four miles wide, with a population of just over forty-six thousand on all three of the Cayman Islands.

White collar crime was another matter. Even the primmest British banks could rival the corner wash-and-fold when it came to money laundering. Koral figured that with all those places to hide funny money, the Caymans would have plenty of need for financial forensics.

She could start a whole new life doing something she was good at and loved doing. She always secretly wanted to be in the F.B.I. or Secret Service, but being a private investigator in the Cayman Islands was exciting enough for now.

Before she knew it, she was flying over blue water and freedom.

Those Nancy Drew mysteries were going to pay off.

Chapter Five

Koral's trip down memory lane ended when something hit her from behind, knocking her off her feet and flinging the folder from her grasp and spilling its contents all over the sidewalk jammed with cruise ship passengers bent on cut-rate Irish crystal.

"Hey, watch where the hell you're going, asshole!" she yelled, as a young local bolted away like the devil himself was chasing him. He stopped at the entrance to police headquarters and looked back at her.

Just before disappearing into the building, he shouted, "Sorry about that, miss." And he was gone.

"Stupid jerk," Koral said to herself, as she got up as gracefully as possible and retrieved the scattered papers. She had a good mind to go inside, find that little delinquent, and give him a piece of her mind, but just then her cell phone chimed "It's Raining Men." Fishing her Blackberry from her purse, she barked, "Koral Sanders."

"Koral, it's Aron. Where are you?" he asked.

"Spread out on the sidewalk in front of your office," she told him.

"Excuse me?"

"Nothing. I'll tell you later," she said. "What's going on?"

"I'd like you to come back. A young man, a bit disheveled and short of breath, just appeared at my desk saying he saw Reese Mallory killed."

Chapter Six

Koral hurriedly stuffed all the errant papers back in her folder, threw her cell phone in her purse, and hurried back to Aron's office. As she walked in, the officer at the entry desk gave her a sideways glance, smiled and waved. Koral gave the officer a friendly salute and headed down the hall. She stopped in her tracks in the doorway to Aron's office. The young local boy who almost knocked her down on the sidewalk was standing in front of Aron's desk.

"Who the hell is this guy, Aron?" she demanded, crossing the room in three steps. "He almost killed me out there on the sidewalk." She threw her purse and the folder in a chair and turned on the young man.

"Koral, for heaven's sake, please calm down. James has information that may help us find Reese Mallory's killer," Aron told her, as he motioned for her and the boy to sit down.

Koral studied the boy for a moment, thinking this might be a prank, since he couldn't be more than eighteen years old. He was dressed neatly and his light brown hair was close-cropped. His flip-flops looked as if they had seen more than their share of wear.

As they sized each other up, James said, "I'm sorry I ran into you, miss. When I heard about that body being found, I came straight here."

"Apology accepted," Koral told him, as they both sat down, brushing some invisible dirt off her floral sundress. He did seem sincere, she thought, like he normally had decent manners.

"Koral, this is James Ebanks. No relation," Aron smiled. "At least not that we know."

Another Ebanks, Koral thought. My God, how many of them are there?

"James, please tell Miss Sanders what you just told me," Aron instructed.

James fidgeted in his chair, his hands clasped tightly in his lap. His dark eyes were big and rounded and his voice was trembling as he glanced nervously around the room to make sure no one was listening. He started to speak.

"The day Mr. Mallory disappeared, I was working on my uncle's dive boat, the boat all of them were on," he began.

"Dive Cayman One, wasn't it?" Koral asked softly. She decided lightening up a little on the kid might improve his memory for detail.

"Yes," James answered. "After they all went down, I asked my uncle if I could take a tank and dive while we weren't busy on the boat. My uncle told me I could, but to come back up in about twenty minutes. So I put on my gear and went in."

"I could see all of them, but they weren't together. They had spread out, and one man had gone down deeper than the others. I could tell it was Mr. Mallory, because he was wearing those Razor fins, black with silver stripes. He seemed to be having a good time all by himself and wasn't paying any attention to where the other divers were.

"We had been down about twenty minutes, and then I started back up when the rest of them did, except for Mr. Mallory. I thought maybe I should go get him because I knew he wouldn't have enough air left to do his safety stop if he didn't start back up. I could see his bubbles coming from a place where one of those coral swim-throughs met the wall. I was heading there when all of a sudden I saw this big silver bubble of air, maybe three feet wide, then one a little smaller, not like someone had exhaled, more like something had sliced a hose. I hurried as fast as I could, because I thought Mr. Mallory might be in trouble. But when I got to where I thought he was, he wasn't there. I did see a diver swimming away, alone, maybe sixty feet off. At first I thought it might be Mr. Mallory, but the fins were wrong, and there was something about the way the man swam that wasn't right…I'm only guessing here," James said, pausing.

"Go ahead, James," Aron urged.

"He swam fast, like a professional diver, the kind who repair offshore oil rigs, not like someone who does it for fun. I've seen a lot of videos about diving and that's what it looked like to me. And he was swimming away from our boat."

"What did you do then?" Aron prompted.

"Once I figured it wasn't Mr. Mallory, I started searching the wall. I really looked, but I couldn't find a sign of him anywhere. I thought I must have missed him. As I was heading back up to the boat, I stopped and looked down. I saw that diver turn around and point at me, then he drew his knife across his throat like if I told anyone what I'd seen, he'd kill me. I didn't know what to do so I just started up as fast as I could. Of course, when I got back on the boat, all the other divers were there except Mr. Mallory." James hesitated, took a glass of water that Aron offered, then continued.

"I looked around and saw another boat about two hundred yards from us, so I figured he'd been on that one. I didn't recognize it. It was one of those fast Cigarette boats, not a regular dive boat. I could tell there was more than one person on it, but they were too far away for me to identify them, even to tell how many people were on it. I do remember that it was all white and big, probably over forty feet. I guess there must have been numbers or even a name on it, but it was too far away for me to see. My uncle asked me to go down and help Mr. Hammond and Mr. Andrews look for Mr. Mallory and by the time I came up, the other boat was gone. As soon as we got back on board, my uncle radioed for the police."

James took a deep breath and sat back in his chair, his eyes darting back and forth from Aron to Koral.

"Why didn't you come forward at the time and tell us about this, James?" Aron asked him, a concerned frown on his face. He knew after all this time it would be nothing short of impossible to track down the person responsible for Reese Mallory's murder. It was hard enough solving a murder that had taken place on dry land, but a murder that had taken place underwater, and with no forensic evidence, was going to take a small miracle to solve.

"I just didn't put two and two together, sir. I did mention the big bubbles when the officer took my statement, but I was too scared to mention the other diver. Then, I heard today about the body that was tied in that hole in the Wall with a piece of wire," James said, his voice still shaky. "Why would anyone do that?"

"He probably wanted to make sure the body didn't surface where it could be found," Aron told him. "Why did you decide to tell us about this now?"

James fidgeted around in his chair and then sat up straight. "When I heard those divers found that skeleton on the North Wall, I knew it had to be Mr. Mallory since he disappeared there. Will I be in trouble with the police for forgetting to mention the other diver back then?"

Koral shot Aron a glance, and he nodded. "No son," he said reassuringly. "You won't be in trouble, at least not with us."

Chapter Seven

Two Years Ago

The day Reese Mallory disappeared on the North Wall two years earlier began as another mellow morning in paradise.

Sunny, beautiful and carefree.

Grand Cayman was a haven for sun worshippers, scuba divers, illicit weekend lovers, and holders of offshore bank accounts. It was a wonder the island didn't sink under the weight of more than $400 billion sitting in almost 700 licensed banks.

Of course, to keep an amicable profile in Cayman, some of Reese and Lynn Mallory's nine-figure net worth was snuggled up in the hallowed vaults of several of those establishments. One particularly muggy Houston Thursday, the Mallorys decided on the spur of the moment that these assets could stand a little checking on and, more to the point, that a few days of scuba diving with friends would be an ideal break from the pressure of being outrageously rich and unrelentingly in demand.

On the spur of the moment, Reese called their pilot and told him to have the Gulfstream ready and a Grand Cayman flight plan filed for takeoff from Hobby Airport at 3:00 P.M. Lynn e-mailed the manager of the Ritz-Carlton to prepare their penthouse for them and four guests, lay in a few bottles of Veuve Clicquot, a case of Evian water, a couple of six-packs of Red Stripe, some fresh strawberries and all the usual amenities.

Then Reese phoned four of their closest friends—Dennis Hammond, Susan Alden, Sid Andrews and Tabby Kirk. All were certified divers, trained to dive within their limits, comfortable with each other underwater. The group flew together to Grand Cayman for a long weekend of sun, sand, relaxation and diving, and to christen the Mallory's new penthouse at the Ritz-Carlton Residences.

Lynn and Reese had spent many hours discussing the purchase of the penthouse, especially since they would already be dividing their time between their homes in Houston, the Hamptons and Aspen, and the one hundred fifty-foot yacht they kept in Key West with the crew on permanent standby, to sail the Bahamas and the eastern Caribbean. In the end, they decided it would be a good investment, as well as a beautiful place to entertain.

All ten thousand square feet of it for a cool twenty million.

The Seven Mile Beach oceanfront home-away-from-home even came equipped with a chauffeured Rolls Royce and a white Cigarette powerboat. Not that the Mallorys needed another boat. But the forty-two foot Cigarette would do for weekends in Cayman.

Reese loved taking the Cigarette out, especially when a storm was blowing in and the usually smooth water was covered with white caps. The thrill of racing through rough water and feeling the big powerboat lift totally out of the water wasn't for the faint of heart.

And it wasn't really ideal for diving, either. The tanks rolled around on the way out to the reef and back, someone had to steady you on the edge so that you could make an awkward roll-in entry, and climbing the swim ladder with forty pounds of gear was a struggle. Chartering a proper dive boat with a captain and deckhand made for a better time, especially since the captain's dive masters knew the best dive locations on all of the three islands.

The three Cayman Islands—Grand Cayman, Cayman Brac and Little Cayman—peaks of a massive underwater ridge rising up eight thousand feet from the floor of the Caribbean Sea, were a diver's paradise. Two wall systems surround Grand Cayman and the first dive the Mallory party took that day on the North Wall was not for inexperienced divers. The sheer drop made it one of the most beautiful dives in the world. Combined with fast and wickedly unpredictable currents, it also made it one of the most dangerous. After reaching a depth of one hundred twenty-five feet, they'd relaxed for an hour and a half on the boat to vent the nitrogen in their blood, and enjoyed a light picnic of fresh mango, coconut, oranges and conch ceviche.

Lynn and Tabby stretched their legs out from under the overhang for just a little sun while the men checked the dive gear for their next dive.

After lunch, they did a leisurely dive on the sloping shelf, staying above sixty feet as they hovered around coral heads looking for delicate arrow crabs and bright green moray eels. Lynn found herself skimming along the sandy bottom, chasing stingrays one minute, winding through coral canyons the next, then suddenly flying over the abyss of the Cayman Trench. Looking down, she felt like a speck of sand hanging suspended in space, in total awe, what she imagined an out of body experience would be like. Walls of bright yellow and chrome blue fish undulated like drapes. Two tiger sharks cruised through the deep blue just off the edge. Lynn thought she caught a glimpse of a spotted eagle ray at least twelve feet across, but it sailed out of view too quickly for her to be sure. A brilliant array of plume-like gorgonians, Day-Glo orange vase sponges and lavender fan corals along the jagged Wall swayed as they had for eons in their continuous dance with the current.

She checked her dive computer and realized that she had inadvertently drifted down to eighty feet. Signaling Reese, who was six feet to her left, that she was going up a bit, she kicked her fins twice and let herself rise slowly, reminding herself that the mesmerizing seascape could hypnotize divers so that they didn't realize they were being drawn down into the rapture of the deep, nitrogen narcosis.

All of them were aware that the deeper a diver goes while breathing air under high pressure, the greater the intoxication and confusion from increased levels of dissolved nitrogen in the blood. Euphoria, disorientation, and loss of judgment, and skill start at depths of about one hundred feet, even less on a day's second or third dive.

Lynn and Reese were safety-conscious divers. If you took care of your equipment and yourself, Lynn thought, a serious underwater mishap was unthinkable.

But this time, the unthinkable happened.

Chapter Eight

Even though Reese usually chose Dennis as his and Lynn's dive partner, Lynn Mallory liked to be aware of where Reese was when they were diving. She might be studying a Caribbean lobster waving its legs from under a shelf of coral, but she almost always had him in her field of vision in case something went wrong.

One minute they were all floating weightlessly in an undersea wonderland, and the next, Reese had disappeared.

When the group started for the surface, no one noticed that Reese wasn't with them. Lynn thought he was right behind her.

Everyone broke the surface of the water around the dive boat and waited to take their turns removing their fins and climbing up the ladder. One at a time, they handed their fins to Captain Albert Ebanks, a weathered sixty-something, slightly-built man with mahogany-hued skin, who was standing on the swim platform, then they climbed a second ladder to the main deck.

Captain Ebanks noticed that his nephew and deck hand, James, was nowhere in sight as he was trying to get all the dive gear secured. He gave an exasperated sigh and made a mental note to have a stern talk with the boy.

Sitting down on a bench, Lynn eased her air tank back into the four-inch-deep hole that would secure it for the trip back. Then she unbuckled her buoyancy compensation vest to which the tank was strapped. That's when she missed Reese. Usually he was there to help her with her equipment. She looked around the boat, then in the water.

As the last diver boarded, Lynn asked, "Where's Reese?"

"I don't know. He started up with me," Dennis Hammond said. "Something must have caught his eye. I keep telling him he needs to give me the high sign if he plans to stay down awhile." Dennis shook the water out of his hair and began to unbuckle his equipment as the other divers did the same. He stood up and quickly scanned the surface of the water.

"I don't see him," he said. "He's usually the last one up, but he should be running short on air and bottom time by now." The concern in Dennis's voice was not lost on Lynn.

Dennis was Reese's law partner and best friend and had become one of Lynn's closest friends as well. Dennis and Reese had been fraternity brothers at UT, and Reese had introduced Lynn to Dennis a few days after she and Reese started dating. The three of them were together constantly after that.

Somewhere behind her, Lynn heard a woman's voice. "I saw him below as I was doing my safety stop. It looked to me like he was going back down."

Lynn turned to look at the woman. She wasn't part of their group. As they'd assembled at the dock, Captain Ebanks asked if they'd mind if she came along. Her boyfriend had gone out tarpon fishing, he'd explained, so she had no one to dive with. Reese had glanced around for consensus and when no one objected, quickly said, "Sure. Why not?"

Jeanette Ryker kept to herself, not that Lynn had minded. There was something tough about her, cheap even. Although she appeared to be in her twenties, she looked hard.

Lynn and Reese always dove with Dive Cayman and specified Captain Ebanks. He was professional without being stiff, congenial while still a stickler for safety. And his nephew James was attentive to the customers' comfort, if a bit shy.

The Mallorys were open to having a few other divers share the boat with their party. Most divers made interesting company. Take the landscape architect from Bermuda and his wife, who was an expert on island cuisines. Lynn had bought three of her cookbooks, and the couple had joined them for a delightful week in the Bahamas on the Mallorys' yacht.

But Lynn knew immediately that she wouldn't be issuing any invitations to Jeanette Ryker. Jeanette had trailer park trash written all *over her, starting with her overly-bleached blonde hair that was in dire need of attention and her oversized breasts sporting a spider tattoo on one and a web on the other. Her pudgy body was squeezed into a bikini that was made for a fifteen-year-old and did nothing to hide her considerable cellulite. Lynn wondered if the woman had ever looked in a mirror. She also wondered where on earth she had gotten the money for a vacation in Cayman. Maybe she'd won big at one of those Indian casinos in Louisiana.*

"He wouldn't have done that," Lynn said sharply, shooting Jeanette a disdainful look. "He knows better than to dive without a buddy, especially at the depths we were diving."

Dennis and Sid had just dropped their weight belts and air tanks. They exchanged a quick glance, found full tanks and started putting their gear back on. There seemed to be an unearthly silence on the boat as each diver kept their thoughts to themselves, afraid to speculate why Reese failed to surface.

"We're going back down and find him," Dennis said finally, hoping he sounded more positive than he felt. "I'm going to kick his ass when we do. Be right back." He gave Lynn a wink.

Dennis and Reese were so much alike, Lynn thought, yet so different. Reese was six-feet two inches tall with sandy blonde hair, intense blue eyes, and a year-round tan. Dennis was six-feet tall with dark hair, brooding brown eyes under a prominent brow, and a rugged olive complexion. Sid fell a bit shorter, about five-ten, with red hair, green eyes, and lots of freckles. All of them were pit bulls in the courtroom, and opposing counsel was more than a little intimidated when they faced off with any of these three young guns.

Mallory, Hammond and Andrews, P.C., which they formed immediately out of law school, quickly ranked among the top litigation firms in the country. The ambitious threesome was always in the news, winning mega-settlements from drug companies with a less-than-rigorous approach to safety, computer makers whose monitors emitted bursts of nasty radiation and other manufacturers who were casual about the well-being of end users.

Lynn introduced her friends, Susan Alden and Tabby Kirk, to Dennis and Sid on a blind date, and luckily, they'd hit it off. Susan was from an insanely rich Houston family. She was tall, with thick raven hair, blue eyes, a Phi Beta Kappa key and a doctorate in clinical psy-

chology. She also had a penchant for gambling. Tabby was the short, cute scatterbrain with auburn hair who kept everyone in the crowd laughing. She also wasn't lacking in the wealth department.

Both women turned heads, but neither of them was in Lynn's league. Her sun-kissed long blonde hair, aquamarine eyes and delicate and perfectly-balanced features made her a magnet for society photographers. She could have been a supermodel and was in fact approached by more than a few agents who scouted college campuses, but she knew that high-pressured career would have meant being away from Reese for long periods. She didn't want that at all. She couldn't bear being away from him for even a day and she certainly didn't need the exposure or the money.

Now he was missing somewhere in the depths of the Caribbean Sea.

Dennis and Sid stepped off the swim platform holding their masks in place on their faces and disappeared into the clear turquoise water.

"James!" Captain Ebanks called, looking around the deck.

James appeared from the front of the boat as his uncle gave him a disapproving glance. "Get your gear on and help look for Mr. Mallory. He may be in trouble down there." James scrambled to obey, ready to help find the missing diver.

Jeanette was busy storing her gear, seemingly oblivious to the fact that a fellow diver could be in trouble. Lynn and Tabby stood anxiously next to Captain Ebanks and watched James disappear into the water.

It seemed to Lynn that every third person in Grand Cayman was named Ebanks and in a profession associated with the sea or banking. The exception was Bob Soto, who opened the first of many dive shops in Grand Cayman in 1957, which propelled scuba diving into a huge local industry. Reese and Lynn shared a love of the sea and had been diving in Cayman dozens of times.

Now Lynn wished she had never heard of scuba diving.

After what seemed like forever, bubbles from compressed air began breaking the surface of the water, jolting Lynn from her thoughts. She jumped up and leaned over the side of the boat, gripping the rail and straining to see beneath the water. She breathed a sigh of relief when she saw the divers rising to the surface. She was going to read Reese the riot act when he got back on the boat. He knew better than to go off by himself without letting anyone know.

When only three divers appeared, no one on the boat spoke a word. Instead, they waited anxiously for the fourth to surface. When Lynn saw Dennis, Sid and then James in the water, with no sign of Reese, she felt as if her heart was slipping from her body.

Treading water, Dennis pushed his mask back over his head and yelled, "He's not down there. We looked everywhere, and he's not there."

"What do you mean he's not there?" Lynn screamed back at him. "He's got to be down there."

She leaned further over the side of the boat, straining for any glimpse of another diver rising beneath the water.

There was none.

Dennis started up the dive ladder with Sid close behind him. James emerged last, eyes down, shaking his head.

"We need to radio for help right now and get some divers out here to search for him," Dennis told them, as he shook off his equipment. "Maybe he got disoriented and headed for shore. Wherever he is, he doesn't have much air left. If he's still under, he has five minutes tops. Maybe he surfaced somewhere out of our sight," Dennis said, his voice sounding artificially calm, as if he were trying to avoid alarming Lynn any further.

Captain Ebanks quickly got on his radio and began trying to raise the police department. "This is the Dive Cayman One. Come in, please. We have an emergency situation." Over and over he identified their boat. On his third try, he got a response.

"This is the police dispatcher. Go ahead, please."

"We have a diver down and need assistance at once," Captain Ebanks told the dispatcher.

Lynn felt as if she were in a daze as the boat rocked gently. She listened to Captain Ebanks' voice trail off as he gave the police department their exact location.

Dennis walked over to where Lynn sat and pulled her to her feet, her flawless face a mask of denial and fear.

He turned to face the rest of the group and said, "Let's see if we can spot him. Call out his name."

They all took positions around the boat and began yelling Reese's name as their eyes skimmed over the water, hoping to see him floating in the waves. The minutes seemed like hours to Lynn as they called

Reese's name over and over again, looking for any sign of him in the crystal clear liquid desert.

They saw and heard nothing.

Chapter Nine

Lynn sat on the deck of the dive boat staring at the water. Several nearby snorkelers occasionally looked up to stare at the crowd gathering on the beach.

The boat was tied up to the dock next to the beach club at the Ritz-Carlton. Three search and rescue boats and two RCIPS speed boats, normally reserved for intercepting smugglers, were tied alongside. Curious onlookers walking down the beach were being kept at a distance by the police.

The return trip from the North Wall dive had been made in uneasy silence.

Tabby sat next to Lynn, occasionally patting her knee or handing her a Kleenex, but no one spoke for fear of saying something that would cause her to crumble as the reality sank in that Reese was gone. As far as she was concerned, when they left the Wall, they left her world behind.

The North Wall had taken her husband.

"Lynn," a voice behind her said. She kept staring straight ahead at the clear aquamarine water, as if expecting Reese to appear.

She remembered the first time they had come to Grand Cayman. It was the weekend Reese proposed to her. They had just passed the bar exam, and Reese arrived at her house to surprise her with red roses and a limo ride to his family's private hangar at the airport. The gleaming silver Gulfstream V was waiting with a red carpet leading up the steps. Reese told her that a bag packed by her mother's housekeeper was on the plane. Anything else she needed, they would buy in Cayman.

As they reached cruising altitude, Reese popped the cork on a bottle of Veuve Clicquot, and they toasted their success on the bar exam. Then he knelt down on one knee and reached in his pocket. He opened a small black velvet box and held it out to her.

The eight-carat pear-shaped diamond took her breath away. He looked in her eyes and told her he wanted to spend the rest of his life with her. With tears springing to her eyes, she threw her arms around him, and they both fell backwards onto the floor laughing as he recovered the ring box and slipped the diamond on her finger.

He told her he wanted to propose at thirty-thousand feet so that if she said no, he could hold her captive and spend the remainder of the flight changing her mind.

As if she would say no.

She came back to the present as she felt a hand on her shoulder and turned her head slightly. "Lynn, the police need to talk with you at their office in George Town," Dennis said quietly.

"I don't know if I can leave him, Dennis," Lynn said, her voice breaking over each word as she wrapped her arms around herself and rocked slowly back and forth. "He's still out there somewhere. How can I leave him?" she said again, her face streaked with tears.

Dennis sat down beside her and put his arm around her shoulder. "They aren't going to give up looking for him, Lynn. They're going back out as soon as they can get more boats to cover a larger area," Dennis assured her, leaving out what the grim-looking young cop had said about the odds being slim to none that Reese would be found. Given the strong currents along the North Wall, he could be well on his way to Jamaica by now.

For the life of him, Dennis told Lynn, he couldn't figure out what happened down there. Reese was an experienced diver. This just didn't make sense. Maybe he'd suffered a heart attack or a ruptured aneurysm. He was a fit guy, but even professional athletes died from underlying defects that top doctors missed.

Dennis wondered how they were going to handle the long plane trip home once the police were through with their investigation and they were free to go. He wasn't even sure he could get Lynn to leave the island without Reese's body. She might want to stay in Cayman indefinitely.

Chapter Ten

As they walked down the dock, Dennis took Lynn's arm, and she leaned against him to steady herself. He steered her down the steps and along the beach to where the police boat was tethered.

She felt the warm, clear water on her feet and dug her toes into sand the color and texture of talcum powder. Sid, Tabby, and the others on the boat followed. The Grand Cayman police were waiting for them with the search boat operators.

A stocky, distinguished-looking man dressed in a gray tropical-weight suit and an open-colored white dress shirt held out his hand to Lynn as they all walked up the beach.

"Mrs. Mallory, I'm Police Chief Aron Ebanks," he told her, as she put her small trembling hand in his. "I'm afraid we need you and all the others who were on the dive boat to please come to our office for just a short while. We have some forms we need completed, and we need to take your statements. I'm so sorry to ask this of you at this difficult time," Chief Ebanks said, in a soft apologetic voice.

Lynn looked into his soft brown eyes that conveyed sympathy, but with a hint of unasked questions. "I just want to know that you are going to keep looking for my husband," she said, feeling nothing but numbness all the way to her soul. "I can't go home without him."

"We will certainly continue to search for your husband, Mrs. Mallory, but I don't want to give you false hope. With the currents at the North Wall being very strong, there is little possibility we will find him. But we will search for a few more days. After that, if we find

nothing, I'm afraid we won't ever find anything," he said, with finality in his voice that shook Lynn to her very core.

"I understand, Chief Ebanks," she said, not understanding at all. "Thank you for your courtesy and your sympathy." Dennis stood beside her, supporting her with his arm around her waist, lifting slightly, as if he feared she might suddenly crumble.

"Chief Ebanks, I'm Dennis Hammond, Mrs. Mallory's attorney and her husband's partner and close friend. I'll accompany her to the police station." Since Dennis wasn't familiar with the procedures of the RCIPS, he wasn't about to let Lynn be subjected to any kind of questioning that would upset her further.

"As you wish, Mr. Hammond. I assure you, this is strictly a formality," Chief Ebanks replied.

"Thank you, Chief Ebanks," Dennis told him. "This is a nightmare for all of us, especially Mrs. Mallory."

Dennis led Lynn up the beach toward the Ritz-Carlton. Chief Ebanks watched the couple as they walked away, a puzzled look on his face. From the familiar way Mr. Hammond acted with Mrs. Mallory, he couldn't help but wonder if Mr. Hammond was more than just her attorney.

"Lynn, we'll all change clothes and go take care of this, and then we'll come back and let you get some rest," Dennis told her, as they walked. "I'll call your parents and Reese's parents and tell them what happened," he added. "They will want to come down here, but I'll tell them there isn't anything they can do here and that I'll be with you. You can call later today or tomorrow morning and tell them that we'll be back in Houston in a few days."

"Is there anything you want me to tell them for you?" Dennis added.

Lynn closed her eyes and whispered, "Tell them I died today, too."

Chapter Eleven

Lynn sat on the sofa in the penthouse living room with her long legs curled under her and hugged a pillow to her chest. She gazed out the vast expanse of glass and watched the sun's last rays splashing on the blue water that was so clear it almost seemed to be invisible.

She couldn't pull her mind from the afternoon's horror. She vaguely remembered showering and slipping into the beige cotton sundress Susan handed her. Bless Susan! Crediting a liter of Evian water with her recovery from the morning's nausea, she had set to work soothing and comforting Lynn, reminding her that Reese still might be found alive somewhere along the island's rocky shore.

After what seemed to Lynn like hours at the police station, Dennis had driven her back to the Ritz-Carlton, then taken the others out on the deck to give her some time alone. Lost in her thoughts, Lynn hadn't heard him come into the room with Susan, Sid and Tabby. Everyone made bland comments about the professionalism of the police and the advisability of ordering dinner sent up, and whether the grilled snapper or a salad would be tempting enough to entice Lynn to eat.

"You have to eat something, sweetie," Tabby urged. They all avoided talking about the accident, but it hung like a suffocating fog in the room.

Dennis walked around the sofa and sat down next to Lynn. He motioned to the other three to wait outside. Susan started toward them but Dennis held up his hand for her to stop. She frowned but nodded silently and left with Sid and Tabby.

Dennis took Lynn's hand in his and said, "You get some rest, and we'll be back in an hour. I know you need some time alone, but not too much. Okay? You need to be with the people who love you. We just want to take care of you."

"I know that, Dennis, and I appreciate it. I do just need to be alone for a while," she told him.

As long as he'd known her, he'd never seen that vacant look in her eyes before. Lynn always sparkled. He wondered if that sparkle could ever be ignited again after this.

"We'll be back later, and I'll bring you something to eat." He stood up and bent down to kiss the top of her head.

"I'm really not hungry," she insisted, unfolding her legs and getting up from the sofa. She walked over to the glass wall leading to the balcony and stared out at the water lapping gently at the white sand beach. Dennis walked up behind her and put his arms around her. She let her head fall back against his chest as the tears rolled freely down her face.

"What am I going to do without him, Dennis? He was my whole life. Half of me is gone."

"It's going to be hard for a while, I know, and you have to let yourself grieve. We all do. Reese was like a brother to me. There's going to be a big hole in all our hearts that will never heal. But we'll have each other, and we'll all get through this together." He knew that all sounded so clichéd, but what else could he say that wouldn't?

He couldn't bear to see her hurting this way, and he knew he had to leave before he told her how much he cared about her, which wouldn't do either of them any good. He turned her around to face him and led her back over to the sofa. "You rest and we'll be back later," he said, picking up the sky-blue cashmere throw and tucking it around her as she lay down on the pastel pillows.

She looked up at him and nodded. Giving her the best smile he could manage, Dennis turned and walked to the door, looking back at her small figure on the huge sofa. Shaking his head slightly, he left and closed the door behind him.

Lynn knew there was no way she could make them understand what she was feeling, so she didn't try, and they didn't ask. How could she put into words what she and Reese had had with each other, what they now would never have?

How was she supposed to survive without Reese? How was she supposed to wake up in the morning, any morning, without him? He was her life, the very air she breathed. How was she supposed to leave him out there? How was she going to face never seeing him again, not even knowing for sure what had happened to him?

She didn't even have his body to take back home with her. There would be no place to go and sit and talk with him when she needed to feel his presence.

All of the "how" questions were rushing through her brain, and she wasn't getting any answers. She thought of all the winter nights she had jumped into bed and snuggled up to his muscular chest, burying her toes underneath his legs to get warm. He was always as hot as a furnace, and she was always freezing. A perfect match.

Everything about their lives had been perfect. Even when they disagreed, they could discuss the issue without arguing—although she suspected that Reese gave in occasionally just to show he loved her. They were so privileged to be born into great wealth, but what really mattered to both of them was finding each other. They could have had five cents to their name and been happy just because they were together.

When he was on a case, Reese worked twelve-hour days, six days a week. But when it was done, and almost always won, he had the rare knack of putting the office behind him and focusing on her—for at least a week or two. That meant travel, to avoid the temptation to check up on things at work, but also because it was a passion they shared. That was the main reason Lynn hadn't joined a firm or opened her own practice. At UT, she'd excelled at real estate law, and that was dictated by the client's schedule. You had to be there to close the deal. The non-profits she consulted with were just grateful for the time she gave them pro bono.

Lynn thought of their world travels, just the two of them, and of all the incredible memories they made. They had shared romantic holidays driving the countryside in almost every country in Europe. Once, just by accident, they happened upon the small, quaint town of Ribeauville in the wine country of France and spent two of the most beautiful nights she could remember.

They stayed at Le Clos St. Vincent, a five-star hotel with only five guest rooms that was built on the side of a mountain in the middle of a vineyard. The French doors of their room opened onto a view of the vineyard surrounding them and beyond that a time-forgotten town below. It reminded her of an exquisite painting by a French master and was undoubtedly one of the most memorable experiences of their lives. But to Lynn, each trip they took was more memorable than the last.

She would never forget the week they spent on Mexico's Baja Peninsula at the One and Only Palmilla in Cabo San Lucas. Their suite was nestled among tropical palms and exotic flowers, and with the terrace doors open wide, they made love while listening to the waves breaking against the surf-chiseled boulders along the beach below. Afterwards, they fell asleep in each other's arms, the palm trees singing in the cool night breeze.

She also would never forget their photo safari in Africa where they lived like nomads, staying in Governor's Camp, a tent camp on a river on the Serengeti. They would lie motionless as they listened to the gentle sounds of elephants brushing against their tent as they meandered through the sleeping camp in the middle of the night. They heard hippos blowing water as they rose from beneath the surface of the river, the water red with the color of the earth it flowed through. Even though they had two single cots in the tent, they slept in the same one and made love listening to the distant animal choirs on the night plains never feeling threatened or afraid. The silent, almost invisible guards kept watch over the camp just in case the animals got too close.

They watched Hong Kong harbor from their room at the Shangri-La come alive at dusk like a universe of dancing diamonds, to lend their magic to a perfect evening just for the two of them. They made love on deserted beaches of the Caribbean and Mexico, and skied the jagged mountains of the Swiss Alps. They stood in awe at the base of the Great Pyramids in Egypt and laughed at the antics of robed and turbaned vendors.

They lived a lifetime in just a few years together.

It was all too overwhelming for Lynn to think about. Despite Susan's pep talk about not giving up hope, despite the search boats and helicopters, she knew in her heart that Reese would never be found alive. A sixth sense told her that he was dead. She'd felt it out on the boat—more than worry, even more than desperation, a sensation of total, final absence. He was gone.

Her mind just couldn't get wrapped around what she was going to have to face very soon. People would be expecting her to make arrangements for a memorial service. She would be expected to get through this with a certain amount of dignity, when all she wanted to do was fade slowly down into the water that now owned her husband and be with him.

Lynn's strength had always come from him. Her eyes always sought him out across a room filled with people. That was all she needed, but she needed it like she needed air. Just to see him and catch his eye and see him smile their private little smile that only they understood. She never needed anyone but Reese. Of course, she enjoyed friends and the acquaintances she made at parties, charity balls and horse shows, but she could do without them. Doing without Reese was unthinkable. Now she would only just exist. She would never be really alive again.

As sobs shook her body, she mourned for everything they would never have together. No growing old together, no more long evening walks, no more shared adventures, no sharing the ups and downs of a life together, nothing.

They'd had it all, and now Lynn had nothing. The only thing that had really mattered had slipped from her grasp.

Chapter Twelve

Everything had gone just as planned. No one suspected him, and no one ever would. How could someone blame him if a diver succumbed to the lure of the deep and died for his foolishness? The news media blared the story of Reese Mallory's disappearance and presumed death, calling it a probable drowning and blaming it on diver error due to nitrogen narcosis.

Every television station in Houston, and the rest of the world, was running footage of the golden couple and their posh penthouse, as well as their other megabucks houses and that obscenely huge yacht. They showed the dive site where Mallory disappeared and his grief-stricken wife when the dive boat pulled up at the Ritz-Carlton dock with the police and search boats. It seemed the public couldn't get enough news about the power couple. You'd think they were royalty, he mused.

They don't seem so high and mighty now, he thought smugly. The body hadn't been found, and the authorities on Grand Cayman said they didn't expect it ever would. They were so right. He had seen to that. He'd done what he was told, and soon he was going to be a very rich man.

Chapter Thirteen

Present Day

"Dennis, did you tell Sid and Tabby that we would pick them up at six-thirty?"

Lynn asked, as she came down the floating staircase of her River Oaks mansion, tossing her long blonde hair over her shoulder.

"I most certainly did, and they are waiting with bells on," Dennis told her, as he gave his tux tie one last look in the foyer's ornate gold mirror. He couldn't help staring at her as he turned and watched her descend the stairs.

She was the most exquisite creature he had ever seen, and tonight she looked especially stunning. Her gold lace Versace gown hugged her perfect body, and her hair seemed to float around her face like a blonde mist. She was never one to wear her hair up, unless she was out running errands on a hot day. It was always long, full, and flowing. Other women looked at her with barely veiled envy, but she never seemed to notice. In fact, she was always complimenting them on their hair or gowns. This, of course, took them completely off guard. She had that disarming way about her, and people could tell it was genuine.

There was nothing phony about Lynn Mallory, Dennis thought, which certainly couldn't be said for some of the social wannabes they ran into at these galas. God, some of those women belonged in a circus. Most of them were either too old to wear so much make-up, trophy wives too young to be taken seriously, or so loaded down with every piece of jewelry they owned that they risked neck strain and carpal-tunnel syndrome. Any of the above had the ability to scare small children.

It had been two years since the diving accident in Grand Cayman that took Reese's life. Dennis and her other close friends helped Lynn pull together a memorial service that was as dignified as could be managed, given that it was also an A-list social event and the lack of a body made it tabloid fodder. Afterwards, Lynn gradually seemed resigned to the fact that if she was going to survive his loss, she had to pick up the pieces of her life and put the tragedy behind her as quickly as possible. It took six months for the reality to set in, but when it finally did, she slowly began to come back to life, and back to the Lynn that everyone knew.

She threw herself into her charity work, even accepting the request to chair the Ballet Ball, which was one of the top five balls on Houston's social calendar. The other major balls she'd chaired in the past had been record-breaking successes, as was every event with Lynn Mallory's name on the invitation as chair or co-chair. Tonight's Ballet Ball would be no different.

Except tonight Reese wouldn't be there with her.

She strolled over to the French doors leading to the expansive backgrounds. As she opened them and walked outside, stars were just beginning to decorate the clear night sky. The carved fountains surrounding the pool arched small streams of water into the pool breaking the night silence with their graceful dance.

Please, she thought to herself, not tonight. Don't think about Reese and how much you miss him. How you moved mechanically through the days following his disappearance. How you had to be the strong one for his family when everything inside of you was dead. She had worked so hard to push these thoughts into a private dark corner where she couldn't reach them when she was alone with too much time to dwell on the past.

The only way she had survived during the memorial service was to draw on Reese's strength. He was her rock, and he made her strong. Reese's strength was what had gotten her through the living nightmare she had faced. It would be there with her tonight—just the strength, though, not the longing.

Lynn heard Dennis walk up behind her. He put his arms around her and nuzzled her ear.

"We'd better get going or Sid will be pacing his driveway." He turned her around and kissed her forehead. "You know how the litigator comes out in him when we're late," Dennis laughed.

"I'm ready," Lynn told him, as she untangled herself from his embrace. She knew Dennis was in love with her and had been for many years, but she just wasn't sure she was ready for a serious relationship yet. She might never be ready, she thought to herself. Two years was a long time to grieve for Reese, and she knew that sooner or later she would have to let him go if she was to have any chance at love with anyone again.

"Lynn, when are you going to get it through that beautiful head of yours that I love you and I want to take care of you?" Dennis asked, taking both of her hands in his. "I've loved you since I first laid eyes on you, but you belonged to my best friend. I loved Reese like a brother, and I guess I thought if I could just be close to you in a brotherly way, I would settle for that. But now, everything has changed," he said, his intense brown eyes telling her he meant every word.

She knew that Dennis and Susan had ended their relationship because he wanted to be free to spend time with her. Which one actually ended it wasn't common knowledge. Thank goodness her friendship with Susan had survived the breakup. It could have been a very unpleasant situation for everyone concerned, but Lynn knew Susan wasn't in love with Dennis. Susan had never been in love with any man as far as Lynn knew. Susan was a good friend and Lynn hated to think badly of her, but more than one of Susan's serious suitors told Lynn they had something in common with Susan…they both loved Susan.

"Dennis, you know how I feel about you. You're a very important part of my life, and I don't know what I would have done without you all those months after Reese disappeared. But I'm just not ready to make any long-range commitments yet. I do love you, but be patient and please don't push me," Lynn said quietly, hoping he would understand and drop the subject. She wasn't sure yet what the future held for her and Dennis, but she knew her future would include him in some way. She had known him for so long, but as a good friend, and she didn't want to hurt him. If anything further were to develop between them, she wanted to be sure she loved him the way he wanted her to love him. They had not even made love in all this time. She couldn't believe he hadn't pressed that issue, but she also knew he wouldn't let their relationship go on indefinitely without an intimate commitment.

"Okay," Dennis said, a crooked smile lighting up his handsome face. "I'll settle for whatever crumbs you throw me for now." He laughed when he saw the exasperated look on her face.

"I'm just kidding," he teased her. "Your chariot awaits. Let's go to a ball."

Chapter Fourteen

Lynn couldn't believe someone on the phone just told her that Reese had been murdered.

She was at a fund-raising brunch for the Houston Symphony when she got the call from the Royal Cayman Islands Police Service chief telling her that Reese's remains had been found and that his death had been reclassified as a homicide. Somehow, she had managed to leave the River Oaks Country Club ballroom without breaking down, even though her mind was reeling from the news.

She didn't notice the concerned looks she drew from the room full of people. The only thought in her mind was of Reese and the fact that he had not died accidentally.

Someone had murdered him.

She didn't remember driving home. She left her car in the circular drive of her French chateau mansion and rushed up the floating staircase to her study. She'd called Dennis immediately, as she always did when there was a crisis. And of course, he had been there for her, as he always was, taking over to make the arrangements to fly to Grand Cayman. Lynn kept recalling the conversation with the police, going over and over it in her mind, hoping the outcome would be different.

But it never was.

As the Gulfstream screamed off the runway at Hobby Airport taking her to Grand Cayman to identify and claim her husband's body, Lynn sat curled up in the fawn-colored glove leather seat in a state of shock.

She wasn't sure if "body" was the correct description. The police told her that there wouldn't be anything to identify except the items recovered on the skeleton those two divers found. She just couldn't let herself think about Reese in those terms. He was much too vital a man, and too full of life to be reduced to nothing but a bag full of bones.

It had been two years, and she'd had all this time to prepare herself for what she knew might happen one day. In fact, she'd even hoped it would, so she'd know what had taken him from her. Now it was here. She'd never really let herself believe it would come to this.

The police told her they would use every available source to attempt to find out what happened to Reese. The medical examiner had performed an autopsy pro forma which ruled out any broken bones, but beyond that, there was simply nothing to work with. It was now plainly obvious that Reese drowned after his regulator hose had been intentionally cut.

Who could have been down in that water without any of them noticing? They had all stayed together, even Jeanette, until those last few minutes when Reese had lagged behind while the rest of them surfaced.

My God, she thought, someone had obviously been waiting down there for Reese, knowing that they were on the dive that day, knowing their destination, knowing he would probably be alone long enough to kill him without being seen. The thought made her feel sick.

A killer had been watching them. But why?

Who could possibly have benefited from Reese's death? Sure, he'd been a pit bull plaintiff's lawyer, but big corporations didn't go around killing opposing counsel.

Lynn tried to concentrate on recalling that day. She closed her eyes and attempted to picture where they all were in the water. She tried to remember if there were other people down there other than their group, but nothing came to her. Her mind couldn't get past the fact that a predator had been observing their every move.

And probably had for days.

"Lynn?" Dennis's voice drew her out of her thoughts and back to the present.

She was so lost in the past she didn't notice he'd gotten up and poured her a glass of wine. As he handed it to her, she realized that the one thing she appreciated most about Dennis was his thoughtfulness. He seemed to read her mind and anticipate her every need. There weren't many men who had that trait.

"Thanks," she told him. "I just can't believe after all this time I am finally going to take Reese home. That's all I've wanted all along, ever since he died. I just want him near me, at home where he belongs," she said, taking a sip of the cool Chardonnay they kept stocked on the jet.

That wasn't really what Dennis wanted to hear her say. He was the one he wanted near her, not Reese. He had been so patient with her since the accident, giving her time to grieve, giving her space to get her heart in order, giving her everything. It was his turn now, he thought. Even in death, Reese was still between him and the woman he wanted. Even though he loved Reese like family, Dennis had been fighting the resentment for years that he had always come in second to Reese. Well, not any more. He was too close to finally getting Lynn and he wasn't going to give up now.

Dennis sat across from Lynn, studying her and wondering if she would ever come to terms with Reese's death. He'd hoped that her sessions with the therapist that Susan recommended would have helped her move past this lingering dependency. Maybe, he mused, it would have been better if Lynn had seen Susan. He knew that psychotherapists weren't supposed to befriend their patients, or treat their friends, but at least Susan knew what had happened and how Lynn had responded. After all, she'd been there when it happened.

"Lynn, you've had so much to deal with these past two years, and now, all of this is up in your face again. At least now I hope you can find some closure, and put this all behind you once and for all," he told her, as he got up and leaned over to kiss the top of her head, lingering in the fragrance of her hair. "Can I get you some more wine?" he murmured.

"No, I just want to sit here and remember one last time," she said, looking out the window and down at the deep, dark blue water breaking the reef protecting the North Wall of Grand Cayman.

Chapter Fifteen

Dennis called Sid Andrews from the jet to check in and let him know that he and Lynn might have to stay longer in Cayman than they had expected. There was a lot of red tape with Reese's death being reclassified as a homicide.

"I think Tabby and I will fly down and keep you and Lynn company. I know it's a hard time for her, and for you. She needs her friends around her, and she may need more than one good lawyer to help get her through all of this," Sid told Dennis.

Sid had done his junior year abroad at Cambridge and had obtained knowledge of British law, as well as what was needed to get Reese's body released. His assistance could be invaluable in working with the U.S. Consul on Grand Cayman to expedite matters.

"That's a great idea, Sid, but let's wait a few days and let her get over this shock," Dennis said. "The police want her to identify Reese's dive gear and the personal effects found on the remains. Even though the reef protection laws don't allow wearing dive gloves in Cayman, I guess that knuckle he jammed sailing kept his wedding ring on his finger. At any rate, the police retrieved it, so she'll have to identify that, too. That won't be easy for her. We're scheduled to do all that tomorrow morning. By the next evening, she could really use you two to help distract her. You know how Tabby always has a way of lightening the mood. Lynn loves you two."

Lynn thought of Tabby and Sid as family, and Dennis didn't want to make them feel unwanted. The four of them had spent a lot of time together over the past two years and Dennis didn't want to hurt their feelings. He knew they meant well and that both of them cared deeply for Lynn.

After Reese disappeared, the six friends became four when Dennis stepped in to help Lynn cope with Reese's death. Dennis told Susan that his place was with Lynn as long as she needed him, which could be a very long time, and he didn't think it would be fair for Susan to continue their relationship considering the time he would be spending with Lynn.

The thought of playing second fiddle was about as appealing to Susan as tooth decay. She told everyone that she and Dennis had never been serious about each other, that they had decided to end their relationship amicably, that her friendship with Lynn was not going to change because of a man, and that it was a damn good thing she had not fallen in love with Dennis or things could have turned out much worse. Thankfully, she had saved a little face, and everyone seemed to believe her. It made the sting of being dumped a little easier to bear, not that she really cared about Dennis. She didn't.

Maybe one day, she could return the favor.

"OK, buddy," Sid told Dennis, "we'll wait a few days, but keep in touch. Don't worry about the office. I'll handle things here. I can get Dan and John to split up your cases if there's a crisis with any of them. Otherwise, we'll tell them you had a family emergency to attend to out of the country. And for God's sake, if they find out anything about who killed Reese, call me. I just want five minutes alone with the bastard."

Chapter Sixteen

By the time Lynn and Dennis got to the Ritz-Carlton, the sun was beginning to retreat over the blue Caribbean. There was nothing more breathtaking than the last hours of a glorious day in Grand Cayman, so they had their bags delivered to the penthouse and went out for a drink at the pool bar.

They chose a table close to the beach and ordered martinis. Dennis leaned forward and took Lynn's hand in his.

"Tomorrow is going to be a bitch, Lynn. I'm really sorry you have to go through this nightmare all over again." Dennis said, trying to read her, to see how she was really handling everything.

"I'm fine, and I'll be fine tomorrow. I've had a long time to deal with this. As soon as they catch the person who killed Reese, I'll finally be able to put this all behind me and get on with my life," Lynn told him, a faint smile of resolve on her face. She felt a tug at her heart as she watched a young couple strolling down the beach, their arms around each other, looking so happy and in love.

"They may never find the killer, Lynn," Dennis said.

"Maybe not. I guess I should just be grateful they found Reese," she replied, her eyes following the lovers.

The pool bar waitress brought their martinis over to the table and sat them down. Dennis picked up his glass and held it up to her.

"What are we toasting?" she asked.

"To the end of a nightmare and to new beginnings," Dennis said. She picked up her drink and touched his glass.

"To new beginnings," she smiled.

At last, Dennis thought, after everything I've done, maybe she is finally going to get Reese out of her system.

Chapter Seventeen

The lone figure sitting at the pool bar watched as Dennis and Lynn toasted with their martinis. They were leaning so close into each other. How could she seem so happy when she was getting ready to identify her dead husband's remains? What a heartless bitch, he thought.

The man pulled his Panama hat down further over his face, which was already partially covered by his sunglasses, and downed the last of his frozen margarita. He flicked the remnants of salt from the glass off his mustache and slid off the barstool. Walking toward the beach past Lynn and Dennis, he tipped his hat at them and smiled, showing more than a few yellow teeth.

Yeah, the man thought, as Dennis cut his eyes up at him, better enjoy paradise while it lasts, lovely Lynn. You may not have too many more chances.

Chapter Eighteen

Tabby Andrews sat by the floor-to-ceiling window of her fifty-five hundred square foot condo on the sixteenth floor of The Huntingdon on the edge of River Oaks.

She loved living in the most exclusive high-rise in Houston. She also loved the prestige that went with it. She and Sid had an entire floor of wall-to-wall luxury decorated to the hilt by the same designer who had done Paige and Tilman Fertitta's opulent French chateau just down the street.

Of course, the style was different. Tabby and Sid were into minimalist and international flavors, just short of edgy. Sid had given the designer a blank check to transform the shell of the floor into a showplace of earthen tones with ivory sofas, ivory side chairs with blackwood borders, and accents of white throws in the grand living room. The ivory and black complementing coffee and side tables gave just the right contrast. Sheer ivory window coverings were interspersed with sectioned marble panels below the ornately carved crown moldings and high-coffered ceilings. Sitting areas were grouped over diamond-patterned ivory rugs, which contrasted texturally with the gray marble floor.

The richly-painted ivory walls provided a chic backdrop for the couple's art collection of a few selected Picassos, a small but exquisite Van Gogh, their pair of Monets, and a scattering of Frida Kahlos.

Tabby had made an offer to buy "The Little Deer," Kahlo's self-portrait of pain and suffering, from social lioness Carolyn Farb for five million dollars a few years ago, but to no avail. Madonna had also offered millions for it about the same time, but La Farb just wasn't interested in parting with the magnificent painting back then. Tabby just recently learned the highly-sought after piece was sold by its beautiful blonde owner to an undisclosed buyer for undisclosed millions.

Tabby sat alone watching the ant bed of morning activity and snarled traffic below on Kirby Drive, glad she wasn't down there in it. She had just poured a cup of coffee when Sid called to tell her they wouldn't be going to Cayman for a couple of days. Something about Dennis thinking Lynn needed some time alone to deal with the news of Reese's remains being found. What the hell did Dennis think being alone meant if he was there with her? she wondered.

Dennis had been Lynn's shadow for the past two years. It was blatantly obvious to everyone that he had always been in love with her. Reese's death had paved the way for Dennis to move in on Lynn, but Tabby was convinced that Lynn was not now, or ever, going to be in love with Dennis.

Of course, Lynn wouldn't ever tell him that. She was just leaning on him, leading him on, and letting him make a total fool out of himself. Poor Susan was the one who got left out in the cold. After three years as a regular item, the wedding rumors fizzled out when Dennis and Lynn started showing up together at social events.

Tabby was almost certain that Dennis was after Lynn and all her zillions. Susan was a trust fund baby with her own money from one of Houston's well-established fortunes, but compared to Lynn's, it lacked a zero or two.

When Susan and Dennis ended their relationship, she told Tabby that she thought she could actually see relief on Dennis' face. Tabby knew it stung Susan like crazy to suspect she was about to be dumped by Dennis, so she beat him to the punch and salvaged her pride by breaking it off before he did. At least that was Susan's version of the story.

When Tabby and Sid married after Reese died, Sid naturally asked Dennis to be his best man, which meant, of course, that Lynn would be Tabby's maid of honor. It was only fitting, Sid said, since they were all like family. When Tabby walked down the aisle and saw Susan sitting there, she noticed the look on Susan's face. She'd spotted Dennis and Lynn together, and her expression reflected anything but sisterly affection.

Susan might have told Dennis that she didn't have any hard feelings and that she and Lynn would remain friends, but Tabby knew better. She was certain Susan had been in love with Dennis, even though she'd insisted she wasn't and put up a show of *sang froid* that fooled all but her closest friends.

The cell phone sitting on the table by Tabby's window seat started playing the first bars of "Stayin' Alive," announcing a call coming in. Tabby was a hopeless Bee Gees and John Travolta addict. She and Sid met Travolta and his wife at a society fundraiser in Hollywood a few years earlier, and the four of them hit it off. When Colin Cowie, the master of all master party planners, did Travolta's birthday bash several years ago in Cabo San Lucas, she and Sid were there to celebrate with them. God, it was fun being rich, she thought.

She picked up the phone. "Hello."

"Hi there. Want to grab some lunch?" Susan chirped. "I'm in between patients and need to see a friendly face."

"Sure," Tabby replied. "What are you in the mood for?"

"Martinis," Susan told her, with that infectious laugh of hers.

"A girl after my own heart," Tabby said. "Meet you in the bar at Tony's in fifteen minutes."

"Come alone," Susan told her.

Chapter Nineteen

Susan was already sitting at a table in the bar at Tony's when Tabby walked in and waved at a table of social acquaintances in the dining room.

Of course, the only place to see and be seen in Houston was Tony's, if you were anybody of note in rarified social circles. Tony's had owned that distinction for more years than Tabby had been alive. When it came to social validation, no other restaurant came close.

The table of overdone hussies blowing kisses at Tabby, led by the one and only Lisl Hughes, really had a need to be seen rather than to see. They chirped like chubby parakeets in attack mode around their premiere perch in the center of the room. Tabby had no desire to join their little gathering, which was obviously someone's birthday luncheon, but she still thought it was rude of them not to have mentioned a word to her about it.

"Tabby! We thought you were out of town," Lisl Hughes crowed across the crowded dining room.

God, that woman had about as much class as a street whore, Tabby thought, as she perused Lisl's much too tight, and too short, designer luncheon suit. On anyone else it would have looked stylish, but Lisl Hughes looked like a cheap tube of toothpaste someone had squeezed too hard.

"Decided not to go," Tabby answered, turning her back and walking toward the bar, giving Lisl and her tablemates her best Miss America wave as she went.

"Screw'em," Tabby muttered under her breath. Who needs that bunch of bitches? she thought to herself as she headed toward Susan's table.

Tabby really felt sorry for the frantic little wannabes who were all trying so hard to climb up that social ladder. All an obscure little nobody like Lisl Hughes had to do to become an overnight in-demand socialite was to marry Mr. Big Bucks and start helping him spend his trust fund gazillions on mega-mansions, private jets and top-tier tables at charity balls.

Instant society queen. Instant designer clothes. Instant acceptance.

Tabby knew no amount of money could tempt her to crawl in bed with some of those unattractive old farts, or young ones either, no matter how many millions they had. Some of the stories she had heard over the years about those made-in-heaven-matches would make your hair stand on end.

She even knew of one high-profile couple with who didn't keep the lid tight enough on their jar of dirty little secrets. Turned out the husband wasn't just sleeping with his wife, but with her male stylist as well.

When the new wore off the Bentleys and the nasty separations hit the headlines, all of the temporary trophy wives who were required to sign air-tight pre-nups before becoming Mrs. Big Bucks, disappeared from the society columns, their names forgotten before the ink went dry on the divorce papers.

Of course, there were the legitimate social stalwarts, new and old guard, who were always chairing one gala or another. They all did it for the good of the charity, but there were more than a few new ones who only did it to get their pictures in the society columns or boost their husband's careers. Far be it from them to do the actual work on the event. They figured their names on the invitation would be their contribution to the cause.

It was sad really, Tabby thought, as she spied a few of said climbers in various modes of schmoozing around tables in the dining room and bar. She knew they would never break into the big time social circles even though their lips were permanently attached to the asses of every society columnist in town. The pathetic little creatures really didn't realize the columnists who mattered knew the difference between the pretenders and the real things.

Serves them right, Tabby thought. She would never have to worry about things like that. She and Susan had their own money. They'd been on the inside all their lives. They belonged.

Too bad she couldn't say the same for some of the Botox bitches paying homage to Lisl Hughes and her entourage. What a bunch of cows, Tabby thought with a knowing smile.

Tabby reached Susan's table and giggled as she slid into the chair the waiter was holding for her. Leaning over, she gave Susan a hug.

"Hi," Susan said, returning the hug.

The waiter took her napkin off the table and made a grand gesture of letting it float down to her lap. Tony always trained his staff right, she thought.

"There's our boy," Susan said, as she saw Josh Adams, the gorgeous and deliciously tan young restaurant manager, waving at them as he made his way to their table. His light brown suit, blue shirt, and brown tie, all obviously Armani, enhanced his athletic build and very toned body. They also complemented his brownish blond hair and deep-blue bedroom eyes that made women want to get lost in them.

"I didn't see you two come in," Josh smiled, as he stopped at their table.

God, he was gorgeous, Susan thought, as she looked up at him and wondered why he wasn't a Calvin Klein model instead of a restaurant manager.

"Josh, we need two very dry martinis. Fast." Susan said.

"My pleasure," he answered, flashing perfect white teeth.

Oh, no, it would be my pleasure, Susan thought, giving him her best "come fuck me" look and thinking that one of these days, she would do just that.

As Josh rushed to do their bidding, Tabby looked at Susan and asked, "Are you okay? You look a little flushed."

"I'm fine. It's just been a long day already," Susan smiled.

"Did you see the herd in there?" Tabby asked.

"Oh, yeah."

"What's going on?"

"Don't know. Don't care. But the word on the street is that another divorce might be the hot topic these days."

"Whose?"

"Brianna and Charles Stafford."

"You're kidding."

"Nope. Couldn't happen to a nicer couple," Susan said, grinning. "Word on the street is that good old Charles caught Miss Musical Beds in the sack, or should I say, on the rack, with her Pilates instructor."

"I thought that guy went for the more tall, dark and handsome variety," Tabby laughed.

"Maybe that was just his hetero buxom blonde day." Susan smiled. "Guess Brianna will join the ranks of MIAs when the divorce is final."

"I'll drink to that. By the way, what did you mean when you said come alone? What's up?" Tabby asked.

Josh appeared and smiled at them just shy of flirtatiously as he set their martinis down on the table.

"Thanks, handsome." Susan gave Josh her most seductive glance. Twirling the olives in her glass until Josh retreated, she pressed her lips together into a thin line, as if she was getting ready to divulge military secrets.

Leaning into the table, she rested her chin on hands and whispered, "I never told anyone this when Reese died, but I thought someone should know about it now."

"Know what?" Tabby's interest was on high alert.

Susan proceeded to fill Tabby in on a conversation with Reese that had taken place in her office only a couple of weeks before he died two years ago. Tabby sat spellbound, hanging on every word Susan spoke.

Susan knew she could get into big trouble by divulging confidential therapist/patient information. But hell, this was Tabby she was talking to, and Tabby would wear last year's designer clothes before she would repeat anything Susan told her in confidence.

Susan had known from an early age that she was different from other kids. She was curious about the darker side of people and wanted to know what drove them. The veil that hid forbidden desires, ones that inferior and morality-bound people wrapped themselves in, fascinated her. She wanted to get inside their heads and play with their minds. She wanted to probe beneath their carefully constructed exteriors. They were so different from her that sometimes she couldn't believe they belonged to the same species. She loved living on the edge and never held back from taking chances.

Susan had sex with patients in the past and found the experience to be exhilarating. She fancied herself as their protector and teacher, in total control, while she screwed their brains out. Sure, she had given some thought to violating the strict rules of her profession, but she rationalized that in the end, her patients were much better off after she'd helped them handle their problems…with a hands-on approach. She knew they would never tell anyone what had transpired between them, and she sure as hell wasn't going to.

So, in her eyes, she had first done no harm, as the starched medical oath goes.

Especially in Reese's case. She had waited for that day for a long time and she had definitely made the most of it. She didn't think Reese would forget it anytime soon.

She knew she wouldn't.

Chapter Twenty

Two Years Ago

Dr. Susan Alden was busy dictating from one of her client files when the intercom buzzed. She loved being a psychotherapist. Being privy to the innermost secrets of some very well-known people excited her. She was Houston's answer to Hollywood's "shrink to the stars." Some of the most high-profile people in Houston crowded her client list. People would be surprised at some of the things those people did and thought. Just because you had money or were known the world over didn't mean you didn't have dark secrets to hide.

"Yes, Gloria, what is it?" she asked.

"Reese Mallory is on the phone for you, Dr. Alden," her office manager told her.

"Thanks. Please hold my calls for now, Gloria," she said, as she closed the file in front of her.

Picking up the phone, Susan said cheerfully, "Hi Reese, what's up with you?"

"Hi Susan," he hesitated a moment and then continued. "I know this may sound crazy, but I need to talk with you. On a professional level."

"Sure." What was this all about? she wondered. Sounded intriguing.

"Do you have some time now?" Reese asked.

"Let me check my schedule." Susan put him on hold and checked her appointment calendar. She pushed the blinking line on the phone and said, "My next client isn't due until two o'clock. Come on over."

"Great. I'll be there in fifteen minutes."

Susan leaned back in her chair and smiled. Talk about the spider and the fly, she thought.

She buzzed Gloria on the intercom and said, "Gloria, please reschedule all my afternoon appointments. Tell them I had a family emergency. Then you can take the rest of the day off."

Chapter Twenty-One

Reese sat in the chair in front of Susan's desk with a somber look on his face. God, he was handsome, she thought, as she searched his eyes for a clue as to what was bothering him.

"Why don't you move over to the sofa," Susan suggested. "It's more comfortable, and you'll be more relaxed." She got up and walked around her desk motioning for Reese to follow. She could tell something huge was on his mind. Could there be trouble in paradise? she thought, with a slight grin.

Reese stood up and walked over to the large cushioned sofa and sat down. Susan took a chair on the other side of the coffee table. She poured them each a glass of water from the crystal pitcher on the table and handed him one.

As she leaned back in the chair, she asked him with great concern in her voice, "Okay, what in the world got you so upset?"

"I don't really know where to begin, but if I don't talk to somebody, I'm going to go nuts," he said, leaning his elbows on his knees and putting his face in his hands.

This wasn't like him, she thought. He was always so upbeat and, she'd figured, totally controlled on the inside. She wondered what on earth could have a man like him so distraught unless it was money or a woman.

"I don't know when it began," he said. "It just sort of happened. We never really talked about it, but when I brought it up a few months ago, she wanted no part of it," he told her.

"*Brought what up?*" Susan asked. *For heaven's sake, get to the point, man.*

"*You know Lynn and I have this fairy tale life that everybody envies. She's a great girl and I have loved her unconditionally. We have an incredible life together, or at least we did.*"

"*But?*" Susan asked. "*I assume that is the next word that goes here.*"

"*Yes, I'm afraid it is,*" Reese replied, shaking his head.

"*But, what?*"

"*But when I brought up the subject of having children a few months ago, she said she absolutely did not want them. Ever. I couldn't believe it. I'm kicking myself that we didn't discuss this before we got married, but I wasn't sure then, and I couldn't imagine life without her. Now we've been arguing about this for months. During the course of all this fighting over having a family or not, and seeing this selfish side of her that I've never seen before, we've just drifted apart. Or, I should say, I've drifted away. As far as she's concerned, everything is just as it always was. All she seems to care about are her social obligations. Oh, we put on the big front for everybody, but she won't budge on this subject, and I want kids. I just assumed after four or five years, we'd start a family. That's what everybody does, right? I know she loves me, but I'm at the point now that I'm considering a trial separation.*"

Reese looked so dejected, Susan felt an unfamiliar surge of empathy. She wanted to put her arms around him and comfort him.

"*Have you told her you were thinking about a separation?*" Susan asked him.

"*When I mentioned it to her, she went ballistic. I told her if we couldn't work out some sort of compromise, we should think about splitting up. She accused me of emotional blackmail and refused to even talk about it. Said separation or divorce wasn't even on the table. Neither were kids. She said if I started proceedings, it would destroy her. She said she loves me and always has, that she literally couldn't live without me. She even started talking about the ways she could commit suicide, for Christ's sake. I know she's talking out of fear, so I guess I just need some suggestions on how to get her to change her mind and consider my feelings about this. Do you know what a circus this could turn into? The media would eat it up. I hate to think what it would do to our families. I don't know how everything went so wrong,"* Reese said, running his hands through his hair and shaking his head.

Clearly, the dilemma was tearing him up. Susan had worked with lots of couples, and she knew that it wasn't what you had in common that made for a strong marriage; it was how you dealt with the things you disagreed about. Lynn and Reese had the first part down, but clearly not the second. Lynn must be carrying a lot of deeply-hidden emotional scars.

Ever since Lynn introduced her to Reese, Susan thought he was the most perfect man she had ever met. Lynn had to be crazy to risk losing him, especially over this of all issues. What was the big deal about having children? Lynn Mallory could afford the best nannies in the world. If Susan had been married to Reese, she'd know enough to give the man anything he wanted, or at least make him think she would.

"Lynn acts as if nothing has changed between us," Reese said. "She still tells everyone how happy we are and how much fun we have together, and goes on as if nothing has changed. Everyone calls us the 'golden couple,' the 'power couple,' the 'beautiful couple.' Nothing could be further from the truth as far as I'm concerned. I want our relationship back the way it used to be, when I believed we were all those things. I'm miserable and I don't know how to fix this."

"I'm not the one to help you with this, Reese," Susan told him. "This will take a lot of work with a top-notch marriage counselor. I have a few excellent colleagues I can recommend. I do couples therapy, but I think you'll understand that I couldn't be effective with such close friends. This will probably take individual therapy, as well, to help Lynn get in touch with whatever makes her so set against having a family. There are women who absolutely do not want children in their lives. This is usually based on deep issues, ambivalent attachment to their own mothers, sexual abuse by a close relative, that sort of thing. Lynn needs to find the reason she's deluding herself into thinking your marriage is perfect without kids. It's hard for me to empathize, because there is nothing I want more than to get married and have kids. Of course, I have to find a man to help me with that," Susan laughed, hoping it made her sound self-conscious and vulnerable.

"I can't believe you'll have any trouble finding a man when you're good and ready, Susan. Not with your looks and brains," Reese smiled weakly. *And your family, money and position,* he thought.

Changing the subject, Reese said, "I was hoping maybe you could talk to Lynn. She listens to you. Maybe you could get her to change her mind, or at least get her to consider it."

"I don't think that's a good idea, Reese," Susan told him. "For one thing, it wouldn't be ethical professionally, since you sought me out. For another, I suspect that would only make her defensive, and make her feel like we're ganging up on her."

"It was just a thought," he replied glumly. "I guess my marriage might be in real trouble." He sat looking at the floor and raking his hands through his hair. She'd seen him do that before when he was upset, she thought, which had not been very often.

Seizing the moment, Susan got up, walked around the coffee table, and sat down on the sofa beside Reese. He turned to look at her as she took his face in her hands. She leaned into him and softly kissed him, her lips letting him know that he was a terribly desirable man, and that she was violating every rule in the book by kissing him.

Suddenly his arms went around her, his lips answering her kiss. He pushed her back on the sofa, his hands running up her back and down the length of her body, urgently and silently unzipping her dress. Pulling it down to reveal her breasts straining at her black silk bra, he deftly unhooked it and let it slide to the floor. His lips traveled down her firm breasts, his mouth covering and gently caressing each nipple. His hands felt like fire on her skin. She never wanted him to stop.

He sat up, pulling his shirt over his head as Susan unbuckled his belt and unzipped his pants. He kicked them off and pulled her dress down over her hips, taking her black thong with it and tossing it aside.

Then he was on top of her, pulling her body to him. As he entered her, she arched her back to meet him and gripped his arms tightly as his lips covered her neck and face. With each thrust of his body, she moaned, hoping the moment would go on and on. Much too soon, the passion they were engulfed in reached its peak, and with a deep sigh, he lay heavily on her, wrapped in her embrace.

"Susan," he murmured, his face in her hair. "I'm so sorry. I don't know what came over me. You were there, so close, and so understanding."

"Reese, it's all right. I wanted it, too. I guess I've always wanted you," Susan whispered to him, as he rose and looked at her, his face so close to hers.

This wasn't right, he thought, this wasn't right at all. He had no business doing what he had just done.

He finally managed to tear himself away from her hypnotic gaze as he untangled himself from her arms. He stood up, retrieved his clothes from the floor and started putting them back on.

God, he was hot, Susan thought, as she watched him dress.

"Please don't feel guilty, Reese," she purred with a smile. "I don't."

Never mind her profession's strict prohibition against sex with patients. She knew she could lose her license, but rather than making her feel anxious, that recognition gave her a shiver of added pleasure. Risk added spice to anything in life, she rationalized.

Reese stood watching her as she stretched her lithe body out fully on the sofa, her arms seductively intertwined above her head. He knew if he didn't leave then, his desire might overcome his better judgment again.

"This shouldn't have happened," he told her. "I can't believe what I did. It's bad enough I have problems with my marriage, but I am still married and I love my wife. And she's your friend, for God's sake. This wasn't fair to you. I hope you'll forgive me," he said, his face a mask of guilt. He picked up his coat and tie and slung them over his shoulder.

Susan got up and slowly walked over to him as deliberately as a cat stalking her prey.

"I will never forgive you," she smiled, reaching up to kiss him lightly on his lips. "I'll always be here for you. Anytime you need to…talk."

He turned and walked slowly to the door, leaving her standing there, lovely in her nakedness.

"Goodbye, Susan," he said. Then he was gone.

Chapter Twenty-Two

Koral's cell phone rang just as she turned into the parking lot at the Sundowner. She had been looking forward to a quiet afternoon to study the Mallory case and set up some appointments.

"Koral Sanders."

"Koral, it's Aron. The two divers who found Mallory's remains have come up to give their statements and I'd like for you to be here."

"I'll be there in fifteen minutes," Koral told him. She couldn't wait to hear their account first hand as she wheeled out of the parking lot and headed toward George Town.

When Koral walked into Aron's office, the two men with him stood up and shook hands with her as Aron introduced them.

Jerry Adams was a short, stocky man with jet black hair and a full beard. Koral thought he looked a bit like a pro wrestler. She was surprised when he told them he was a marine biologist from Scripps. In contrast, Ron Curtain was tall, toned, and tan with blond hair and dark brown eyes. His southern accent hinted he was from Texas. When he said he was a surfing instructor in California, Koral decided she'd better brush up on her instincts. She wondered how these two, so very different men, had become friends. As if reading her mind, they said they had grown up together in Ohio. Go figure.

They all sat down as Aron turned on a tape recorder and asked the two men to proceed.

The men said they were making a deep dive on the North Wall and happened to find a cave they had not seen before and decided to explore it. The mouth was so jammed with black coral and vase sponges that they almost missed it. They had gone in quite a ways and were surprised at how curving and deep the cave was. They were just getting ready to turn back when they saw the figure looming in the dark in front of them. Needless to say, they were terrified when they put their dive light on it and saw that it was a diver, or rather what was left of one.

Curtain took hold of the air tank and turned it around to find himself face to face with a skull. As quickly as they could, they got out of the cave. To mark the spot, they inflated Curtain's bright orange safety sausage, designed to help searchers locate stranded divers, and attached the line firmly to a large black coral at the mouth of the cave. Not surprisingly for an engineer, Adams had the latest dive computer with a GPS function, so they made a note of the coordinates and started for the surface. They called the authorities as soon as they got back on the boat, and police boats raced out to the North Wall to meet them.

The recovery divers went down to retrieve the remains, which were taken directly to police headquarters and scrutinized by the forensic medical examiner. The ME's report stated that circling the bone of the left ring finger, below a knuckle enlarged by some old trauma, was a broad gold band. Inside the buoyancy compensation vest were the initials "RM" in black waterproof Magic Marker. It matched the description Lynn Mallory had given when she'd made her statement two years earlier. Because the case had been kept open, the medical examiner's office still had Reese's medical and dental records on file. They matched, too. The ME had no doubt that the remains on the steel table in front of him were indeed all that was left of Reese Mallory.

End of report.

Now, if Koral and Aron could find the missing pieces to the puzzle, like who owned the white Cigarette boat that James Ebanks saw that day on the Wall and who was on that boat, they had some hope they would find the killer.

After the divers left, Aron told Koral, "I've informed Mrs. Mallory. She'll be coming in to identify her husband's effects Monday. I'd let you know when that is set up."

Koral nodded. Then she added, "I'm going to check around the island to see who owns a white Cigarette boat or who might remember seeing one in the marinas or out on the Wall the day Mallory disappeared."

"Call me later and let me know what you find. Be careful," Aron warned her.

"Don't worry, Chief Ebanks," Koral kidded him. "What person in their right mind would want a piece of me?"

Aron looked up over his glasses and gave her a frown. She saluted him and closed his door.

Koral left police headquarters and walked out into the perfect sunny day. She loved the slow pace of life in Grand Cayman. People were always cheerful and smiling, and the sidewalks were always crowded with sunburned tourists from cruise ships, which meant that business was good for all the restaurants, souvenir shops, resort boutiques, tax-free purveyors of British bone china and jewelry stores in George Town. Today, it looked like nobody had a care in the world. Lynn Mallory did, though, and Koral planned to watch her every move, her every expression, when she arrived for the sad occasion of identifying her husband's effects. Maybe Mrs. Mallory could also shed some light on the white boat James Ebanks saw that day.

Koral knew the type of men who owned those Cigarette boats were high-rollers surrounded by all the silicone sweeties money could buy. She had seen enough of them on Lake Travis when she worked in Austin. A big-busted Barbie Doll bimbo in a thong bikini was the *de rigueur* accessory every time one of those boats was sold to an old buzzard, or young stud, with money to burn. The boats were definitely chick magnets. But somehow, she couldn't see one of those aging playboys doing Reese Mallory in on the Wall.

Koral crossed the busy street along with all the tourists and walked to her Jeep. She always had the top down on it and loved soaking up the warm tropical sun while she drove, but she always tried to be close to cover in the afternoons when a sudden shower arrived like clockwork.

Driving along Seven Mile Beach on the way back to her office, Koral made a mental list of the marinas close to town. She knew the three largest ones could accommodate boats up to one hundred fifty feet in length. There was also a privately-owned smaller marina that could house the larger boats. She would start with those four and hope she could find what she was looking for fast.

As she drove, Koral couldn't help but marvel at the beauty of the aquamarine water lapping at the white beach. She also couldn't help looking, with maybe just a touch of longing, at the hotels and homes along the most luxurious address in Grand Cayman, knowing how much money it took to live in some of those places. People with bottomless pits of cash lived there, and most of them only used the pastel palaces a few weeks a year. Maybe one of these days I'll get lucky and meet a man who can afford me, Koral thought, laughing out loud.

Koral pulled into the parking lot of the shopping center where her office was located just west of the Hyatt Regency complex. She shared the L-shaped strip center with a dive shop, a grocery store, two hole-in-the-wall restaurants, a liquor store, and a night club. It was pretty convenient to have everything you needed within a few steps. Thank goodness there wasn't an ice cream or yogurt shop in the center. Koral didn't have many weaknesses, but ice cream made up for all the ones she didn't have.

She parked the Jeep and grabbed the files out of the front seat. Unlocking her office door, she crossed the room, which was about the size of her bedroom growing up in Texas City, and opened the blinds behind her desk. Her office was as big a mess as her condo, but she knew where everything was, so she didn't worry too much about it.

She sat down, pushed some papers aside and jotted down the names of the four marinas she'd thought of in the car. She looked up the phone numbers and called each one, making appointments to talk to the managers the next day.

Of course, finding the white boat after all this time would be like looking for a virgin in a Solid Gold nightclub. Oh well, she thought, stranger things have happened. All she needed was one lucky break.

Chapter Twenty-Three

Setting a clean ashtray to the right of her keyboard, Koral lit a Marlboro Light and booted up her computer. Yahoo wanted her to know that the death toll from the recent mudslides in the Philippines had topped two thousand, that Congress had approved a new spending bill, that a televangelist had been caught having sex with his underage niece, and that there was something better than Botox.

"What did private eyes ever do before the Internet?" she asked herself, answering immediately: "They sneezed through dusty court records, got newspaper ink on their chinos and couldn't do shit from twelve hundred miles away."

At this point, Koral wasn't looking for anything arcane hidden away in subscription databases. Google would do. She typed in "Reese Mallory" and got over fifteen hundred entries. Shit! If there was anything worse than too little info, it was too much. Trying "Reese Mallory" combined with "Lynn," she got one hundred twenty-eight. That was more like it. She scrolled down four years, figuring some fawning Houston social rag might have done a major gush-fest around their wedding. Voila! A full profile of Houston's young golden couple in *77019*, the slick tabloid named for the zip code of the city's poshest neighborhood.

The article began with a list of Reese's most recent scores—three class action lawsuits in which the amounts of the settlements were officially confidential but pegged at two hundred million each minimum, by the grapevine. That would be some major cash in contingency fees. Even among Houston's legal eagles, Reese Mallory was in a class by himself. He named the game and everybody played. Koral wondered if one of the defendants in those megabucks lawsuits might be pissed off enough to kill him but quickly shunted that notion to the "highly unlikely" category. The defendants had been huge publicly-traded companies. Boards of directors didn't tend to hire hitmen.

So even if Reese had to wait tables to put himself through law school, he would have been raking in millions three years later. His last name alone would have opened any door, even if it was bolted shut. As it was, he and Lynn had the moon and stars at their feet. Coming from two of the wealthiest families in the country gave them just one more cozy little trait in common.

As a result of his grandfather's real estate and banking zillions, and his grandmother's concern about cancer, Reese's family name was on several buildings in Houston's famed Texas Medical Center. For her part, Lynn was a Saferty. Her great-grandfather had been one of three founders of the second-oldest oil company in the country, and her grandfather and father had multiplied the fortune through good management, good luck and a penchant for marrying women from wealthy families.

The article featured the typical sepia-tone historic photos—a gusher coming in while three men threw their hats in the air, a lawn party at a mansion to rival Tara, and a man with his suit coat slung over his shoulder going over blueprints with a guy in a hardhat. But the opening shot was of Lynn wearing a sleeveless black number and pearls sitting on a sofa in her parent's living room. Leaning over the back, Reese had one hand on the sofa, the other cradling her shoulder protectively. Both smiled at the camera, but their expressions were different. He looked proud, like he'd won a big case. She looked happy, but there was something else, like a faint cloud across her brow. Surely it couldn't be insecurity, Koral thought, not with those looks, those brains, those bucks and that guy. Maybe she was worried about having to pull off what would be the wedding of the decade, to say the least.

The story went on to note that Reese had graduated at the top of his class from the University of Texas Law School, and Lynn had followed right behind him. ("I plan to use my degree to help small non-profits incorporate and get on a solid legal footing," she told the reporter. "For every need in the community, and there are many, there are people who have excellent ideas and loads of dedication; but they don't have the resources to hire the legal help they need.") So, Koral concluded, Lynn planned to play the twenty-first century version of Reese's grandmother.

They'd announced their engagement the Christmas before graduation, with the wedding that October. He'd given her a pair of five-carat pear-shaped diamond earrings for Christmas, tastefully echoing the rock on her left ring finger; and she'd given him a gold *ankh*, the ancient Egyptian symbol of eternal life, on a gold chain. "It means our bond will last into eternity," he told the reporter. "I never take it off, even in the shower."

"You won't find a nicer couple," one of Lynn's sorority sisters declared. "But frankly, they are living proof that life isn't fair. I mean, how can any two human beings look like they do and have the brain power to match, be really nice people, and have those buckets of money? There are countries, dozens of them, whose gross national products are smaller. Lynn happens to have the "Killer Bs...beauty, brains, body, and bucks. And Reese is right up there, too."

One of the city's leading socialites, a regular at the Court of St. James, compared Lynn to New York's legendary Park Avenue princesses, only without the attitude.

Noticing that her computer pegged the time at 5:03 P.M., Koral got up and poured herself a double shot of Jack Daniels from the bottle she kept in the credenza. Someday, maybe she'd spring for one of those little bar refrigerators; for now, neat would have to do. This was shaping up to be a long evening, but not a boring one. Returning to her computer, she saved and closed the *77019* story and began scanning other Google entries.

In an article titled "How the Rich Stay Rich," *Vogue* called the Mallory-Saferty wedding a "merger." The result, the author noted, was "a combined fortune with more zeros than the distance from Earth to Mars."

They'd both grown up as only children in River Oaks, the fairy tale Houston neighborhood. Koral knew it from the annual spring Azalea Trail, when her mother and every other garden-fancier within a hundred miles of Houston, shelled out for tickets to gawk at the shell-pink, fuchsia and white blossoms filling the otherwise off-limits backyards. The Saturday night before Christmas, her dad would treat her and her mom to dinner then drive them up and down the storied streets with the eye-popping holiday light displays. The streets were lined with huge oaks standing like sentries guarding the faux Taras and Tuscan villas draped in red, green, blue and her favorite all-white lights. The December electric bills for each of these mega-mansions could have supplied power to a comfortable three-bedroom house for a year.

Reading on, Koral learned that even though Reese and Lynn had known each other and lived only three blocks apart, they had attended different private high schools. Lynn had gone to St. John's in River Oaks and Reese attended Kinkaid in the almost equally exclusive but newer Memorial Drive neighborhood to the west. Their parents clearly traveled in the same social circles, but their moms, heaven forbid, wouldn't have run over to borrow a cup of sugar. Living in River Oaks wasn't the same as living in Mayberry. The estates in the section where the Mallorys and Safertys lived were so large, it could take ten minutes just to walk across the manicured lawns to the next house, and then you'd have to get past the high brick fences, security systems, and uniformed guards. Maybe that was why Lynn and Reese hadn't started dating until their freshman year at UT.

As the Style columnist for the *Washington Post* put it, the minute Reese and Lynn were married, they were "wooed" to attend, and support, every charity ball in town. In their first four years of connubial bliss, Lynn chaired three of Houston's top balls—the Houston Grand Opera Ball, the Museum of Fine Arts Grand Gala Ball and the Winter Ball. On countless occasions, they hosted charity ball kick-off parties and underwriter dinners for the see-and-be-seen society crowd. The Mallorys ruled in the A-list stratosphere of Houston's social and charitable scene, opening their River Oaks French chateau mega-mansion to host royalty, presidents, and Hollywood celebrities.

Just reading about all those parties made Koral's feet ache. Of course, she'd heard the Mallory's name when she lived in Houston. You'd have to reside under a rock not to know who they were. But she was shocked at just how many social events they attended. Didn't they ever take a night off, curled up with a bowl of popcorn and a rented Tom Cruise movie in what Koral imagined would be the most lavish home theater east of L.A.? Apparently not.

From the local and national society coverage, it looked like everyone who wasn't their friend wanted to be, and everyone who was wore it like a badge. The Mallorys' names were at the top of every invitation list, and they rarely disappointed a host by declining. And if *you* weren't on *their* invitation list, you invented reasons to be conveniently out of town the night of their party.

In one article, an Oscar nominee for best supporting actress gushed to *W* that "everybody loves Lynn and Reese." The funny thing, the "next Julia Roberts" explained, was that unless you followed those columns, you'd never guess that Reese or Lynn were more than merely well-to-do if you met them off their home turf. "They're both so warm and genuine," the actress declared. "No airs, no aloofness, no grabbing the spotlight. Just nice people."

Apparently, Lynn Mallory made you feel like you were the only person in the room when she was talking to you. She wasn't one of those socialites looking over your shoulder to see if there was someone more important she could be seen with at an event. Someone even spotted Lynn at Target, her long blonde hair pulled up with a clip, looking like a teenager in blue jeans and a polo shirt.

When they weren't visiting Hollywood chums on the gilded beaches of Malibu or cruising the Caribbean on their yacht, Lynn and Reese escaped Houston's sultry summers at their homes in Aspen and the Hamptons. Their penthouse in Cayman was their latest *pied-a-terre*. The interior designer, best known for his redo of two landmark Art Deco hotels on South Beach, must have loved the spread in *Architectural Digest*.

Koral stood up, stretched and lit another Marlboro Light. Thank God she didn't have to worry about hiring and firing staff for four households and a yacht, or choosing just the right haute couture gown for the Ballet Ball.

On a whim, she put Lynn Saferty's name in Google. Only seventy-six entries came up. She went twenty-five years back to a May photo feature on mothers and daughters in *Town & Country*. There was the lovely Marjorie Saferty with her four-year-old only child. Both were wearing cloud white Oscar de la Renta numbers with sweetheart necklines and puff sleeves. Marjorie, a waterfall of shimmering blonde hair cascading forward over her left shoulder, sat on an apple green loveseat in front of a wall the color of daffodils. Little Lynn stood at her feet, gazing up adoringly, her hand reaching toward her mother.

But instead of looking down at her daughter, Marjorie Saferty was staring straight ahead, giving the camera a model-perfect smile. Her right hand was in her lap with her left gestured toward little Lynn's, not as if she were about to grasp it, but as if she were about to keep it from grabbing, and rumpling, those yards of de la Renta silk.

It made Koral think of a course she'd taken as a psych minor: Attachment Theory. She remembered there were three kinds of attachments between mothers and children. The best, of course, was secure attachment, which resulted in secure kids. To Koral's surprise, the worst wasn't avoidant attachment, where the mother rejected the child, who grew up having trouble forming close ties. It was ambivalent attachment, where the mom was warm and loving, but then sometimes and cold and distant at other times. It didn't have anything to do with whether the child misbehaved or was a little angel, but the poor thing didn't know that and kept trying to win mommy's love. Children of ambivalently attached mothers could grow up to be exceptionally charming and sensitive to others; but when they formed adult bonds, they needed constant reassurance and couldn't stand competition for affection.

The *Town & Country* photo looked like a textbook illustration of ambivalent attachment.

Koral decided to check out early stories on Reese. She found one of him as the dashing captain of the Kinkaid tennis team, then as the guy who'd won the University of Texas a major victory at Lacrosse. She hadn't even known UT *had* a Lacrosse team. A three-inch piece in the *Texas Lawyer* announced his choice as editor of the UT Law Review, a position traditionally awarded to the top student in the class. Did she really expect him to be second?

The Houston society columns featured dozens of photos of him escorting beautiful girls to one charity gala or another. Seemed Mr. Mallory was quite the man about town.

Make that towns. Houston wasn't the only place he was in high demand. He also appeared in slick rags focused on Aspen, the Hamptons and Monte Carlo, always with a different celebutante on his arm.

But Lynn was the star. Lynn Saferty had been paparazzi fodder from the moment she was born. There were magazine photos of her from her birthday debut at St. Luke's Hospital to her marriage to Reese and all points in-between.

She was in *Town & Country* at ten years old modeling a two thousand dollar *Alice in Wonderland* dress; in the *New York Times Sunday Magazine* in her cheerleading uniform at St. John's when she was sixteen; in *W* at her debut at the International Debutante Ball at the Waldorf Astoria when she was eighteen; and in *Vogue* at the dual deb balls, one at the Ritz Hotel in Paris, the other at the Plaza in New York. Then, in every major newspaper and magazine in the country, there were photos celebrating her engagement to Reese Mallory. God help her if she ever had a bad hair day. Some photo jock from *People* or the *Enquirer* would have been there to snap the evidence.

Every shot of Marjorie Saferty confirmed Koral's initial impression: Little Lynn didn't get to crawl up in Mommy's lap for a cozy bedtime story. Marjorie looked about as warm as a frozen margarita. There was even mention of her having a problem with Valium dependency. Koral wondered if this had anything to do with the fact that Lynn's father had a reputation as quite the ladies man, according to a catty blog.

Funny how a man with money could get away with just about anything. It must have been pretty dirty underneath the Persian rugs at the Saferty house with all the nasty bits they swept under there.

Being an only child with emotionally distant parents must have been a pretty lonely existence for Lynn, Koral thought. No wonder everyone who described her relationship to Reese called them inseparable. Totally dependent might be more accurate. Koral wondered if the lack of love and attention when Lynn was growing up could manifest itself in murder if she thought Reese might be straying, especially given her father's roving eye. Stranger things had happened.

But nothing Koral could find, not even in the tackiest blogs, even hinted at problems in Lynn and Reese Mallory's marriage. On the surface, it looked squeaky clean and perfect in every way. But was it really?

Koral decided she was going to stop by and have a chat with Lynn, to see for herself if her instincts were right. Lynn was due to come by RCIPS headquarters on Monday to identify what was left of her husband and his dive gear. That meant she'd be flying in Sunday, which it already was, Koral noted. God, it was already 2:38 A.M. according to her computer monitor. She had gotten so caught up in the Mallory fluff, she'd lost track of the time.

She decided that Sunday afternoon would be the perfect time to head over to the Ritz-Carlton for a friendly visit with the widow Mallory.

Chapter Twenty-Four

Koral arrived at the Ritz-Carlton wearing sandals and a turquoise cotton sundress. The building rose out of the white sand and lush landscaping like an ivory stucco temple. She couldn't help but feel a little sad as she remembered all the fun she'd had right here on this spot, although there was a very different structure on it back then.

The Holiday Inn, and its Bullshit Bar on the beach, had ruled the club scene on the island when she first visited Grand Cayman. What a place that had been, she thought. Good times, fun friends, warm nights with hot guys.

But, time marches on, as they say, and the old Holiday Inn had been torn down, along with its famous bar, to make way for this new money magnet.

She wished just once people would leave well enough alone. But she knew good times and memories weren't worth nearly as much for big-time developers as they were for her. Especially when beachfront property on Seven Mile Beach was worth about a million dollars a front foot.

Back in the day, all the locals hung out at the Bullshit Bar at night and watched in amusement as the "harbor sharks" went into overdrive. These were the local guys who picked up lonely female tourists at the bar, after they got a little liquored up, and gave the term "memorable trip" new meaning.

When taxi drivers picked up women from the overnight cruise ships to take them into George Town, they always told them about the Bullshit Bar's reputation for being a fun spot to meet men, have a few drinks, and maybe get lucky. By midnight, it seemed everyone in Cayman was there.

Including Mike.

God, she didn't want to think about him now, she told herself. But once the memories came around again, it was hard not to relive every passionate moment they had crammed into two short months.

Mike Lane shot into Koral's life like a bullet straight into her heart. He walked up next to her at the bar that night, ordered a Jack Daniels on the rocks for himself and one for her. He didn't even ask her; he just ordered as if he'd known all his life what her favorite drink was.

He cocked his head sideways and stared at her with the most mesmerizing gold flecked eyes she had ever seen. She hadn't even known God made eyes that color. But once she looked into them, she knew she didn't want to be anywhere but with him. His light sandy hair was blowing around a tan, handsome face with an anvil-shaped jaw and straight Roman nose. His strong hands wrapped around the glasses of bourbon as he turned to hand one to her. His six-foot two-inch frame towered over Koral. When he smiled, everyone else at the bar disappeared.

Her previous track record with men seemed to wrap itself in a bubble and float out to sea. She knew somewhere deep down in her heart that this man was the one she'd been looking for all along. They sat and talked until well after two in the morning. Mike was thirty-six and had moved to Cayman a few years before Koral. He had captained several large yachts over the years for financial giants from New York and movie studio heads from Los Angeles and was now the captain of a two hundred-foot yacht that belonged to a part-time Cayman resident. He loved the water and the warm tropical islands of the Caribbean and had dreamed of one day living on his own boat.

Mike had had a typical Midwest childhood, growing up on a farm in Iowa with doting parents and four younger sisters, but he yearned for excitement and faraway places. He missed his family but made occasional trips back to see them. Given Koral's string of train-wrecks in the romance department, Mike Lane seemed too good to be true.

Koral told Mike her life story, give or take a husband or two, as they walked up and down the beach the rest of the night, stopping only long enough to sit on the sand for a while and look at the full moon. It was there on the beach, hidden by the huge hibiscus trees and palms swaying in the warm night wind that Koral found out what that "to hell with everything, I want you now" feeling was like. Mike pulled her down to him on the sand, cradling her head on his chest. It seemed they had known each other forever, but if it didn't last past this night, she would have no regrets.

She looked up into his mesmerizing eyes as she and Mike knelt on the sand facing each other. He took the straps of her dress in his thumbs and slowly dropped each one off her shoulders. Koral never took her eyes from his face as his hands slipped around her and unzipped her dress. He tugged at it slightly as he eased it down past her hips, then let it fall to the ground.

She had never known this feeling of total abandonment before. Mike pulled his shirt over his head, and laid it out on the sand beside them. He discarded the rest of his clothes and took her shoulders in his hands, gently lowering her down on his shirt. He slowly leaned over her, covering her body with his own, kissing her face, her eyes, her neck, while his hands roamed down from her shoulders and came to rest on her breasts. His kisses traveled down her neck, and as his tongue toyed with each nipple, she closed her eyes, finally realizing why this place was called paradise.

As Mike lifted her body to him, her fingers dug into his muscled arms, and she held on to him as if she would drown if she let him go. He entered her slowly and wrapped his arms around her, cradling her head in one hand as the other moved her body up to meet his, effortlessly moving in and out of her, while the symphonic sound of the night sea rippled through the rustling palms.

Afterwards, they lay on the sand looking up at the night sky draped with a canopy of stars and talked about a future filled with balmy tropical nights.

After two failed marriages and years spent developing a hard exterior to insure she would never get hurt by a man again, Koral felt as if Mike had melted her iron-clad heart with a blow torch.

Mike was hardly ever gone for more than a few days at a time, so they had all the time together they wanted. When his employer wasn't on the island or using the boat, Koral and Mike would spend long, wonderful nights on the yacht, making love above, below, and on all three decks.

Christening a yacht took on an entirely new meaning for them.

Then one beautiful summer day, Mike took the yacht to Cayman Brac with the owner and several guests aboard. Halfway there, they stopped to swim and snorkel. When Mike started the engines to head to the island, the yacht exploded killing everyone on board.

The police report said a spark must have ignited diesel fumes, and just like that, Koral's new-found paradise was only a memory.

Chapter Twenty-Five

"May I help you, miss?" a voice said. Koral jumped, not realizing she had gotten teary. She wiped her eyes with the back of her hand, hoping the concierge didn't notice. She had an inkling of how Lynn Mallory must have felt when Reese didn't return from the Wall—that is, if Mrs. Mallory hadn't been involved in that disappearance.

"Yes," Koral replied, shaking her head and quickly putting her sunglasses back on. She didn't allow anyone to see her cry. Her memories and emotions were private and hers alone.

"I'm here to see Lynn Mallory," she told the concierge. "My name is Koral Sanders, and I need to see her regarding a police matter." Pull yourself together, girl. You don't have time for emotional displays right now, she chided herself.

The concierge excused himself and picked up the house phone. Koral couldn't hear what he was saying, but in a few seconds, he turned around and told her she could go right up. South Tower penthouse, he told her, pointing toward the elevator.

Koral couldn't wait to see what twenty million dollars bought. God, she thought. Twenty fucking million dollars! Where do people get money like that?

Oh yeah, she remembered. They came by it the old-fashioned way. They'd inherited it.

The elevator stopped, and the doors opened directly into a great room that gave new meaning to the term stunning. It was decorated in Cayman pastels of pale peach, yellow, and seafoam green. You could have a pick-up basketball game in here, but you'd have to watch the windows. The sweeping arc of a sofa, a good fifteen feet long, faced a floor-to-ceiling wall of glass looking out over the aquamarine sea, which gave the illusion of being part of the design. Koral felt like she was in a tropical dream.

She looked up to see an equally stunning woman coming toward her, hand outstretched. She was dressed in a short, pale blue sundress that accented her flowing blonde hair, perfect body and long tan legs. Koral was all set to hate her.

"Hello, Miss Sanders," the vision said, flashing a million megawatt smile, as she shook Koral's hand. "I'm Lynn Mallory. It's nice to meet you. Chief Ebanks told me that you might be stopping by."

Well, so much for hating the widow Mallory, Koral thought. She actually seemed nice. Koral knew that her own looks were a cut above average, but in the presence of this stunning creature, she felt like a piece of old furniture.

"Please call me Koral."

"Okay, Koral it is. Please, sit down," Lynn said, motioning toward the semi-circular sofa that could easily seat an entire baseball team.

"You have quite a place here, Mrs. Mallory," Koral said.

"Please call me Lynn. And thank you. Reese and I bought it just before he died. Actually, he was the one who wanted to buy it. I thought it was a little ostentatious, but he convinced me that it would be a good investment and that I would love it for entertaining. He was right, as usual. He used to send me wild banana orchid plants to fill up this room. They're the national flower of the Cayman Islands, which I'm sure you know, and they looked so beautiful in here," she said, pausing a moment. "He brought me some just before his accident. I mean, his murder," Lynn said quietly. The pained look on her face seemed genuine, Koral thought.

"Do you think there is any realistic prospect of finding his killer?" Lynn asked, sadness haunting that exquisite face.

Koral was surprised how Lynn opened up to her immediately. "It won't be easy or fast since so much time has passed, but things have a way of turning up," Koral cautioned her. "Maybe finding your husband's remains is a good omen," Koral told her.

Koral saw Lynn frown, giving her a skeptical sideways look.

Koral added hurriedly, "Don't get me wrong. I'm not some wacko who believes in the supernatural, and I don't draw pentagrams on the floor and chant three times for spirits to appear. Whoever did this is going to slip up and when they do, we'll be waiting," Koral promised her.

"This whole nightmare still seems so unreal," Lynn told her.

Okay, Koral thought, remember why you're here. Enough feeling sorry for the widow. Koral decided the best way to start this cat-and-mouse game was at the beginning, so she jumped right in with the standard questions.

"Did you and your husband have any marital problems?" Koral paused a beat.

Lynn winced slightly but then shook her head.

A line of inquiry worth exploring, Koral thought.

"Did he have any enemies, anyone have a grudge against him for any reason? Any defendants from whom he won big settlements who might have taken it personally, made threats? Any old girlfriends who might have been lurking around to cause problems for you and Reese?" Koral was watching Lynn's face carefully for additional signs that all was not well in the picture perfect Mallory marriage.

She saw none.

"No, on all counts," Lynn replied tersely. "Reese and I have known each other practically since we were born. Our families knew each other, of course. We went to different schools in Houston, but when we were both at the University of Texas, we ran into each other again. We rediscovered each other, I guess you could say, and have been together ever since."

Money attracts money, Koral thought. Like a magnet.

"Before we started dating, Reese had no serious girlfriends. Oh, there were casual dates, of course. Many of them, in cities all over the world, if you believe everything you read in the tabloids," she smiled wanly.

Koral remembered those Googled photos of Reese with various gorgeous women. What a sea of information that had turned up.

"He was an attorney, as you know, and of course, there are people who might have lost court cases against him and been angry, but not enough to kill him. He prosecuted suits against corporations, and corporations don't tend to get murderous. In the rare case they do, it's toward the plaintiffs and whistleblowers, not the attorneys. Everyone loved Reese. He was an exceptional man," she whispered.

"I'm sorry, but I have to ask these questions," Koral told her.

Lynn pulled a tissue out of her dress pocket and dabbed at her eyes. Koral thought that was a bit odd since she didn't see any tears. Guess debutantes were taught to call on Southern belle tactics when they needed sympathy.

Be nice, Koral thought. Envy doesn't become you.

"I know you do. It's just so hard to have to re-live this," Lynn said.

Clearly, all hadn't been as perfect inside the Mallory household as it looked from the outside, but Koral was becoming more certain by the minute that Lynn Mallory had nothing to do with her husband's murder. Despite all her wealth and connections, she still looked lost without him. Koral decided to take a chance.

"By the way," she said, "we might have a lead in the case. I wasn't going to mention it until I checked it out, but maybe you can help me and save some time."

Lynn's eyes widened with hope.

"The teenage boy who was working on the dive boat with your group that day came forward and told us he had gone in the water with dive gear after your group had already gone down.

"He saw some large air bubbles coming from the other side of a coral swim-through and went to check it out. He didn't see Reese but he did see a strange diver swimming away fast and wondered who it was. As he was heading back up to the boat, he saw that diver stop, point at him, and draw his knife across his throat as if to tell him he'd better keep quiet about what he saw or he'd be dead. The boy was scared to death and never said a word about what he saw, until yesterday.

"When he got back on the dive boat, he was wondering how that diver got out there. He looked around and saw a large white boat, one of those Cigarette boats, about two hundred yards away. By the time he came up from helping your husband's partners look for Reese, the boat had taken off, and he figured whoever he saw below in the water was on it," Koral told her.

Koral was watching Lynn's expression for any hint that she knew about the white boat.

Nothing.

"My God," Lynn said, "that boy could have made the difference in finding Reese's killer if he'd just said something that day."

"Well, you know how kids are. He was scared to death. He was only sixteen at the time, and seeing some maniac with a knife threatening him more than a hundred twenty-five feet underwater put the fear of God in him," Koral said matter-of-factly.

As Koral got up to leave, she said, "I'd appreciate your not saying anything about our young witness. We don't want anything to happen to him. Whoever killed your husband probably wouldn't hesitate to kill again. As you know, I'm working with Police Chief Ebanks, and if you can think of anything that might help us, please call me day or night," Koral said, handing Lynn her business card with all her phone numbers on it. "We'll find the killer. Sooner or later." Koral smiled, reassuringly.

Lynn walked Koral to the elevator door. As soon as the doors closed, Lynn grabbed her phone and dialed Susan Alden's cell phone number.

Chapter Twenty-Six

Susan was just leaving Tony's when she heard the familiar ring tone of "Respect." Handing her valet ticket to the attendant, she fished her phone out of her purse and waved goodbye to Tabby as she drove away.

"Hello."

"Susan, it's Lynn. I'm still in Grand Cayman. Can you come down here? I need you." Lynn's voice sounded urgent.

"Why, what's the matter? Are you okay? Isn't Dennis with you?" Susan asked, her radar immediately sensing trouble. God, couldn't Lynn ever solve a problem by herself without all the drama? she wondered.

"I'm fine, but things are getting a little crazy. Dennis is here, and he's being such an angel. But I just need you. A lady private investigator who's helping the police with Reese's murder is asking all kinds of questions about our marriage. She wants to know if Reese had any enemies or old girlfriends with a grudge. You know, the usual intrusive shit they feel like they need to know. I'm sure she's only doing her job, but I just don't appreciate her insinuating something was wrong with our marriage. And, of all things, that damn white boat we used to have might be involved. I had forgotten all about that boat until now, but she's going to find out that we used to have a white Cigarette boat, and it isn't going to look very good that I didn't tell her about it."

"Lynn, take a breath and calm down. There is nothing to suggest that you had anything to do with Reese's death. That's crazy. She can't blame you for his death just because you forgot to mention a boat you used to have. You're being a little paranoid," Susan scolded her.

"Well, does this sound paranoid? She also told me that Captain Ebanks' nephew who was on the dive boat with us saw a boat like ours out there on the Wall that day. He also saw the person who must have killed Reese underwater."

Susan's sudden intake of breath threatened to choke her, as her voice seemed to die in her throat. "What did you say?"

"Never mind. Just please come. I'll tell you everything when you get here. Will you come?" she pleaded.

Regaining her composure, Susan told her through gritted teeth, "Yes, sweetie. I'll catch the next Cayman Airways flight late this afternoon. Pick me up in front of the terminal."

Of course, I'll be there, Lynn, she thought. Aren't I always there for you?

Chapter Twenty-Seven

Susan handed five dollars to the valet at Tony's and slid inside her black Porsche Turbo. Few things put a smile on her face like her car.

She may not be a teenager any longer, but the looks she still got from men of all ages made her feel like one when she was driving her Porsche. As she headed toward her River Oaks house, she replayed the conversation in her mind that she'd had with Tabby. She had chosen her words very carefully.

Of course, Susan had left out the part about the incredible sex on the sofa.

"My God, you don't think Lynn could do anything to hurt Reese, do you? I never knew there were problems between them," Tabby had said, her eyes wide with disbelief. "They sure had everyone fooled into believing they were the perfect couple."

"You never know what people are capable of when they're threatened, Tab," Susan had replied. "It would be devastating to Lynn to give up being the darling of two continents. Oh sure, she'd still have her gazillions, but she wanted Reese at her side. Just between us, from a professional perspective, she could be a poster child for neurotic dependency. I'm not saying she had anything to do with his death, but it looked a little too convenient that he died not two weeks after his visit to my office. Don't you think? Somehow, Lynn must have found out what he told me. Maybe he even told her himself. We'll never really know unless she tells us, which I don't see ever happening. She has way too much pride to let on to anyone that all was not well in her little playpen of paradise."

Susan had waited for the implications of her words to settle in Tabby's mind, but she wasn't expecting the answer she got from Tabby.

"Susan, you said you and Lynn remained friends when Dennis appointed himself Lynn's lord and protector after Reese died, but how did you really feel about breaking up with him? You told me a long time ago that you could imagine a life with Dennis. It seems to me you gave him up just a little too easily and are just a little too anxious to serve Lynn up on the altar as a suspect," Tabby said.

"That's silly," Susan said nervously. "Lynn and I are friends. We'll always be friends. Just because Dennis acted like a shit and a fool doesn't mean I have any hard feelings against Lynn. It just seemed to me I should tell someone what Reese told me. Professional ethics wouldn't allow me to do it then since he was my client, but he's dead now and that changes everything. Normally, a psychologist would still protect her client's confidentiality; but now that his death has been ruled a murder, the situation has changed. I guess I should be talking to the Caymanian police, but you're such a close friend to both of us that I wanted your feedback first. I don't imagine anyone would think that the fact Lynn didn't want children would be a very good reason to kill her husband. But if he threatened divorce, that would be a very good reason to kill him. I just think the police are entitled to every bit of information that might prove useful."

Tabby looked flattered that Susan had taken her into her confidence. The gambit had worked. The revelation about Reese's visit and his threats to Lynn about a separation had left Tabby speechless. In terms of professional ethics, it had been questionable, but she'd sworn Tabby to secrecy, knowing full well that Tabby's sworn pledge meant she'd immediately spread the word about the Mallory's marital troubles but wouldn't reveal the source.

Satisfied that the conversation with Tabby didn't reflect negatively on her, Susan picked up her cell phone and called Cayman

Airways, quickly making her reservation as she wheeled into the winding driveway of her sprawling colonial mansion on Lazy Lane. People who lived on her street were in the top echelon of society gods and philanthropic giants in Houston. Hell, they even hired their own off-duty city policemen to guard their grounds and park their patrol cars on the street for everyone to see. Kept the curious and nosy public out.

Susan loved her house, but unless she could swing things back in her direction, she stood to lose it along with everything else she inherited when her parents died in an accident.

Other people could have made a twenty-five million dollar trust fund last a lifetime, especially one augmented by a carriage-trade therapy practice, but other people didn't have Susan's fondness for dabbling in aggressive stocks or going on weekend gambling trips to Las Vegas. Besides, Susan Alden never did have a head for business. Her specialty was getting other people's heads straight. She knew her house was way too big for one person, but she'd set her sights on the perfect man to keep her company on long cold nights.

Unfortunately, she'd had to shift to Plan B.

But now, Plan B was looking good.

Chapter Twenty-Eight

Lynn parked her black Mercedes in front of the small terminal building at Owen Roberts International Airport in Grand Cayman and waved to Susan when she emerged from customs. Even surrounded by a throng of tourists in flowered shirts and straw hats, Susan stood out like a swan in a hen house in her yellow Zac Posen sheath and Manolo sandals. Lynn had always envied Susan's dark good looks and her innate confidence that seemed to ooze from her every pore. Lynn had tried to develop some of that confidence during her early years, but she always seemed to fall short in her mother's eyes. Lynn really counted herself lucky to have Susan for a friend, one she could turn to in a crisis and always counted on to help her through rough times. Her mother was certainly never available for late night girl talks, and God forbid she dispense with advice on boys and sex.

After loading Susan's luggage, Lynn wound her way out of the airport complex, careful to keep to the left, British West Indies style, and swung onto West Bay Road for the drive back to the Ritz-Carlton. On the way, Lynn filled Susan in on her visit from Koral Sanders that afternoon.

"She told me that boy on our dive boat not only saw the killer underwater, he saw the boat the killer had to have been on," Lynn told Susan. "It was a large white Cigarette boat just like the one Reese and I kept here. He said he saw at least two people on it and thought there may have been more but couldn't identify any of them. They were too far away."

"Lynn, you can't be sure the people who killed Reese were on that boat," Susan cautioned. "It could have been a coincidence that boat was out there at that particular time."

"They had to have been on that boat. There were no other boats in sight. At least I didn't see any. Hell, I didn't even see the one that kid saw, and the killer had to have gotten out to the Wall somehow. If that boy had just said something to somebody when he got back on the boat, things might have turned out differently," Lynn said, a wistful look on her face.

"Lynn, you can't start playing the 'what if' game. You'll drive yourself crazy. Besides, by the time everyone realized Reese wasn't on the boat, it was probably already too late to save him," Susan told her. "And it's going to be hard to track down that boat after all this time," she added.

"Yes, but Jerome Johnson, the man who owns the marina where we kept it, still has records of it, I'm sure."

"You don't really think someone took your boat out and killed Reese, do you?" Susan asked incredulously.

"I guess that is a little farfetched, isn't it? I don't know. I'm just grasping at straws at this point," Lynn sighed.

"Tell you what. Let's forget all this madness about boats and murder and go out somewhere fun and have dinner. It'll do you good to forget about this for a while. Tomorrow is going to be a very hard day for you. Take my professional advice and put all this out of your mind for tonight. Okay? Let's just the two of us go out and leave Dennis at the penthouse. He'll be fine by himself for a few hours," Susan urged.

"That sounds great," Lynn smiled, glad for a break from all the stress.

Susan picked up her cell phone and dialed a number.

"Who are you calling?" Lynn asked her.

"Oh, just checking in with my answering service," Susan replied.

After a couple of rings, Lynn could hear the voice that answered. It was male but it wasn't familiar to her.

"Dr. Alden's office."

"Hi, it's Dr. Alden," Susan said. "Unless I have any emergencies, I'll be out of pocket for a while. I'm in Grand Cayman and I have a dinner engagement with Mrs. Mallory. Tell my associate to go ahead with that matter we discussed earlier."

Susan ended the call and dropped the phone in her purse.

Chapter Twenty-Nine

It was almost 11:00 P.M. when Lynn and Susan returned to the penthouse after an *al fresco* dinner at Remington's, the popular beachfront restaurant at the Hyatt Regency. Dennis had already gone to bed. The two women stayed up for a while longer, sitting on the balcony, drinking a glass of wine, and admiring the carpet of stars spread across the indigo night sky. A gentle breeze caressed the palm fronds on the trees lining the balcony.

"We've been through so much together, Susan," Lynn said, a faraway look in her eyes, as she stared up at the twinkling dots so many trillions of miles away. "Do you remember the year you, Tabby and I chaired the Symphony Ball?" she asked, a mischievous smile on her face.

"Oh, my God, yes. What a fiasco that could have been," Susan laughed.

"You'd think we were novices at this sort of thing, not noticing the major underwriter's table wasn't on the seating chart and the guest check-in list," Lynn giggled.

"With a thousand guests in the ballroom, there we were having the waiters set up a table at the front of the room for the big cheese and his entourage. If we hadn't caught that, and if we had been anyone other than who we were, we would have been blacklisted by every organization in town from chairing another major ball. Thank goodness nobody ever found out about it."

Lynn and Susan were both laughing so hard, they spilled their wine.

"Tabby was oblivious to everything that was going on that night, and we were about to commit ritual suicide with the steak knives," Lynn pointed out, laughing even harder.

"The decorations committee had done such a stunning job on the ballroom that it took everyone's mind off of our faux pas for that crucial few minutes while we got everything fixed," Susan said, wiping tears from her eyes. "They were all so busy clucking over the table decorations and flowers and the stage, to say nothing of the million and a half dollars we raised, they almost forgot that we forgot them. And do you remember that horrid red gown that Emily Kirksey wore? I don't think she could have gone to the bathroom alone in that thing, it was so tight. Every man in the room was busy looking at her bulging bust, and I swear if she had sneezed, she would have hurt someone when those silicone watermelons flew out of that dress. Old man Kirksey was so proud of those boobs," Susan said, the two of them doubling up in giggles again.

Lynn picked up the bottle of wine on the table beside her chaise and refilled their wine glasses. When they caught their breath, they leaned back against the soft pillows and were quiet again, lost in their own thoughts.

"It's funny how things turn out," Lynn said, stretching out on the chaise and watching the lights of a cruise ship on the horizon.

"How's that?" Susan asked her.

"When you think of everything Reese and I had together, you'd think that would have been enough for him. But it wasn't," Lynn said wistfully.

"What do you mean?"

Lynn hesitated a moment, a little unsure of whether or not to open up to Susan about such a personal matter. Then she continued. She had to get it out.

"For about a year before he died, he had been pushing me to have a family. I told him I didn't want that. Ever. I liked our life just the way it was. I'd never wanted children, and I thought he knew that. We never really talked about it before we got married, and he just assumed we would have them one day. I think if I had told him how I felt beforehand, we probably wouldn't have gotten married. Maybe subconsciously I never brought it up because I knew what would happen. I just don't like kids, and I sure didn't like being one. I would have made a lousy mother, just like my mother was." Susan couldn't believe Lynn was actually talking about her mother after all these years.

"And, besides," Lynn continued, "I didn't want to share Reese—with anyone. I know people wondered why we never had children, not that it was any of their business."

Susan sat quietly, doing her best not to show her feelings, listening to Lynn open up to her like never before.

"You want to know something funny?" Lynn continued. "Everyone thinks I am such a tower of self-confidence. But they're all wrong. It's an act I've perfected over the years to hide how insecure I feel at times. Ever since I was a small child, I've been in the public eye because my family is so goddamn rich and my mother was a famous beauty. I never asked for all the attention, and I never really wanted it. There isn't a time I can remember that photographers weren't chasing after me to get unflattering shots that they could sell to the tabloids for big bucks. They were successful a few times, and I can't tell you what that did to my self-esteem. The ordinary things people take for granted every day, like just walking outside for the morning newspaper or running to the grocery store for a loaf of bread, are things I would be terrified to do. I've been battling panic attacks for several years because of this, and the migraines I get would bring down a Sumo wrestler. Everyone thinks I had this charmed life, but let me tell you, living with my parents was no picnic. My mother was cold and distant and my father was gone all the time, not that I blame him. It wasn't easy living with my mother." Lynn's face was a mask of sadness and at that moment, Susan actually felt sorry for her. But that feeling passed just as quickly as it had gone through her mind. It was hard to feel sorry for someone who had every goddamn thing in the world that money could buy.

Lynn stopped talking for a few seconds, and looked as if she had just given up top secret information to the enemy. "I can't believe I'm telling you all this. You must think I'm nuts," Lynn said, tracing the top of her wine glass with her finger.

Susan sat up and swung her legs off the chaise. She looked at Lynn with feigned concern on her face and said, "Not at all, sweetie. That's what I do. I listen to people's problems and help them find solutions. I'm your best friend, and I'm talking to you as a friend, not a shrink. Why didn't you tell me all this before?"

"I don't know. I've just always been a very private person, and I didn't want you to think I was one of those whining neurotic types who couldn't handle her marriage problems. After seeing my parents' marriage disintegrate in front of my eyes, I blamed myself. I once heard my mother telling someone how horrible and painful childbirth was for her and how she would never have gotten pregnant had she known beforehand. I felt totally unloved and thought I had caused all their problems. I didn't want a child to do that to me and Reese. I just loved him so much I didn't want anything to get in the way of our getting married. That wasn't very fair of me, was it?" Lynn looked so distraught. Susan knew she had more to say, and tried to keep her talking.

"I don't know, Lynn. People sometimes do the wrong things for what they think are the right reasons," Susan told her. "Personally, I can't relate to that because I've always wanted a family. Professionally, I see people all the time who live under the delusion that their way is the only way. I'm not saying you're delusional, but there are opinions, needs, and desires other than your own. You can't always control every situation. You have to decide if your decision was worth the price you paid. How was your marriage that last year? Were you and Reese really happy or were you just going through the motions because it was what was expected of you? Just make sure your memories are accurate when you start planning your future. Especially if your future involves Dennis, which I assume it does. Don't compare him to a fantasy that you created in your mind. One that he can't live up to. He loves you, you know. Think about it."

Susan watched the seed being planted in Lynn's brain. She knew it was only a matter of time before Lynn would give in and agree to marry Dennis. She was too dependent to go through life alone, and he was a link to Reese. Susan was just going to sit back with the rest of the world to wait and see how this chess game played out.

Chapter Thirty

Jerome Johnson unlocked the door to his marina office and walked inside. Early Monday morning was usually pretty slow in George Town, and Jerome thought he might get caught up on some paperwork. He automatically turned around and locked the door behind him, a habit he started years ago when he was in the office alone.

His marina was just past George Town harbor, and even though his boat slips weren't completely full, he did okay. He got a lot of seasonal business, especially from the owners of the larger yachts, because his was one of the few marinas on Cayman that had slips large enough to accommodate them.

While the yachts cruised to Grand Cayman, the go-fast boat owners had their boats shipped over to the island to run around in when they were going to be on the island for an extended visit.

Jerome's secretary, Jasmine, quit a month earlier to have a baby, so he was way behind on his bookkeeping. He hoped he could hire a new part-time girl soon until Jasmine could come back to work, since detail work made him a little crazy. He was the only person who ever came into the office before noon on Monday, which was just fine with him. His two mechanics would struggle in on Cayman time, but since they weren't backed up with work, that was fine with him. He liked the solitude and the quiet. Besides, it was the price he paid for owning the marina. He'd owned the place for twenty-five years and was about ready to sell it and retire to an easier life. Since his wife had died several years ago and there were no kids or family to take care of him in his old age, the money he'd saved up would see him through his final years just fine. The marina would fetch a good price, he thought, so he could sit on a deck chair at a senior retirement home and sip Sea Breezes. He smiled at the thought.

Jerome walked into the small side office that doubled as a lunch room for Jasmine and the mechanics and shuffled through the cabinet for the bag of coffee. Things weren't quite as neat around here since Jasmine had been gone and he had a habit of never putting things back in the same place twice. He filled the pot with coffee and tap water. While it was brewing, he gathered up a couple of files from Jasmine's desk and glanced out the window at some lost tourists on the sidewalk looking at a map. It was hard to get lost on the island, he grinned. They would find what they were looking for, he thought, as he turned back to the counter to pour himself a cup of coffee.

He sat down to sort through the mess on his desk. That lady private investigator who called yesterday asking a bunch of questions about a white Cigarette boat had been on his mind. She explained why she was asking about the boat, and he told her he would dig through his records and see if anything turned up on the owner. He used to remember every one of his customers by name, but two years ago was a long time and at seventy-four, age was catching up with him. His memory wasn't what it used to be.

Jerome got up and opened the well-worn file cabinet. He had his files labeled by year, length, and type of boat, as well as by name. As he thumbed through the files, he wondered why nobody had looked into this when that guy disappeared out on the Wall. Seemed to him like somebody would have noticed that other boat out there and been a little suspicious. Guess they didn't pay any attention to it since nobody knew the guy had been murdered. Everyone just thought he screwed up and drowned.

That is, until that woman, Koral Sanders, told him they'd found the guy's skeleton down there. That sure must have been a quick picker-upper for those two divers, he thought. Not really something you expect to see early in the morning.

Jerome was almost through the whole file drawer when a loose label caught his attention. He pulled the file out and looked closer at the smeared typing on the label.

It read, "WHITE CIGARETTE—42 FEET." Jerome opened the file and scanned the page for a full name. He couldn't for the life of him, understand why a name wasn't on the label. He guessed he'd just forgotten to put it on there.

The owner's signature was, however, on the bottom of the page. Typed under the scrawled handwriting was the name Reese Mallory.

Chapter Thirty-One

Koral and Aron were having an early lunch at the Lobster Pot in George Town, one of their favorite places to eat. The food was always exceptional, and they enjoyed sitting by the water as they ate. There was always a cruise ship or two in port and the people watching was always entertaining. They usually met for lunch at least once a week, whether they were working on a case or not. They just enjoyed each other's company. It seemed they went through the same dialogue every time, and today was no different.

"Koral, you need to find a nice guy and settle down," Aron told her. "I'm sure this life is not what your mother would have liked for you to have in your old age," Aron chided.

"Hey, I'm not that old yet. Haven't seen forty yet and don't intend to for quite a while," Koral laughed. "As for my mother, she learned early that telling me what to do with my life didn't work at all. She always told me I was just like her. Stubborn, headstrong, and willful, with great legs."

Aron laughed out loud and almost choked on his lobster.

"Koral, you always make me laugh. You're like my own daughter, just a few shades lighter," he teased her. "But if you stay in Cayman a couple of more years, you'll even be the right color," Aron joked.

Koral loved Aron's good-natured personality and his genuine concern for her well-being. Since both of her parents were dead,

Aron filled a void in her life and she was grateful for his friendship and wisdom. He didn't get to see his kids and grandchildren as much as he would have liked, so it was good that they had each other, Koral thought, as she reached over and squeezed his hand.

"It's Raining Men" began emanating from her purse, interrupting their light-hearted banter. Picking up her Blackberrry, she said, "Koral Sanders."

"Miss Sanders, this is Jerome Johnson at the Cayman Harbor Marina." Koral sat straight up and said, "Yes, Mr. Johnson, how are you?" She couldn't believe she might already have a lead on the case.

"I think I may have something of interest to you about that Mallory murder case you called me about," Jerome told her.

"I'll be right there."

Chapter Thirty-Two

Jerome Johnson had just finished his second cup of coffee when someone knocked on the door.

"Who is it?" he yelled, getting up from his desk and walking to the window.

"An old friend," a voice answered.

Jerome peeked through the window by the door, but the visitor's back was to him. He thought he recognized the voice, so he unlocked the door and opened it.

"Well, my goodness, this is a surprise," Jerome said, shaking hands with his visitor. "I haven't seen you in quite a while. Come on in," Jerome said, stepping aside as he closed the door.

"It's funny you came by here today. You must have ESP or something. Someone was just asking about a white Cigarette like the one that belonged to Mr. and Mrs. Mallory," Jerome said. "Matter of fact, she also wanted to know if I had one in my marina that anyone had taken out that day Mr. Mallory disappeared. And now, here you are," Jerome laughed.

"Who wanted to know that, Mr. Johnson?" the visitor asked, turning away and looking out the window to see if anyone was around outside.

"That lady private eye, Koral Sanders. Do you know her? I just talked to her a few minutes ago and told her I had some information for her. But since you're here, you can tell her yourself since you're the one who took the boat out that day," Jerome replied.

"I don't fucking think so, Mr. Johnson," the visitor said, turning to face Jerome and shooting him through the head.

Chapter Thirty-Three

Koral left Aron at the Lobster Pot, promising to call him as soon as she talked to Jerome Johnson.

She turned into the parking lot at the Cayman Harbor Marina and parked her Jeep in front of the building. The tropical sun was beating down on her, and she could feel her heart pumping harder and harder with adrenalin. She hadn't expected to get a lead on the case this quickly.

Jumping out of the Jeep, she hurried to the door and knocked.

No answer.

Aron told her that Jerome always kept his door locked when he was in his office alone.

"Mr. Johnson, it's Koral Sanders," she yelled, again getting no response.

She tried the knob, and the door swung open. The lights were off, the shades were closed, and it looked like nobody had been there. That's funny, Koral thought, as she took a couple of steps inside the room. Mr. Johnson had just phoned her from here. Surely he wouldn't be working with the lights off.

"Mr. Johnson?" she called out. Walking around the desk to turn on the lamp, she stumbled over something on the floor and almost fell on her face. Catching herself on the corner of the desk, she turned around to see what she had tripped over.

Jerome Johnson was on the floor in a pool of blood and very dead.

Chapter Thirty-Four

Koral was waiting outside the marina when Aron pulled into the parking lot, followed by a patrol car. Aron and the two officers got out of their cars and walked solemnly toward her.

"The coroner and his team should be here soon," Aron told her. "Were you able to tell from the looks of things what happened here?"

"I don't really know, Aron. I don't think it was a robbery. No sign of a struggle. His wallet is still in his pocket, and his watch and ring are on his body," Koral said, as they started walking toward the building. "I'd say he knew the killer. See what you make of it. All I know is that some son-of-a-bitch shot him point-blank in the head. It looked like he had been going through the file drawers like he was looking for something. It had to be information he found on that white Cigarette boat. I'm sure of it."

She added, "I haven't touched anything but the doorknob and the edge of the desk."

Aron handed Koral and the two officers each a pair of latex gloves. After pulling them on, Koral pushed the door open, and the four of them walked into the office.

Jerome Johnson was lying on his back on the floor, a bullet hole in his forehead, his eyes wide open, as if someone had surprised him. Some papers were strewn around him on the floor, indicating he had probably fallen while holding them.

Koral walked over to Jerome's desk and started shuffling through the papers and folders he had evidently pulled from the file cabinet. Nothing she saw there gave any clue as to what he was going to tell her about the Mallory case. She went over to the file cabinet and thumbed through the folders in the drawer marked "M." There was no folder in the drawer with the name Mallory on it.

Koral turned around and saw Aron kneeling by Jerome's body. He ran his hand over Jerome's face, closing the once warm brown eyes of his friend.

"We have known each other for over thirty years," Aron told Koral, looking up at her, his face etched with sorrow. "He will be greatly missed by everyone. I will catch the bastard who did this," Aron vowed quietly.

"*We* will catch the bastard, Aron," Koral told him, putting her hand on his shoulder. Aron reached up and squeezed it.

The room suddenly seemed devoid of air, and Koral hurriedly turned to leave. It was one thing for Aron to investigate the murder of a stranger, but having to see this happen to a friend you knew and cared about was something else. The pained look on Aron's face was heartbreaking. She took a step around the desk and looked down as something caught her eye. She noticed a small white piece of paper stuck to her sandal, and bent down to see what it was. Peeling the smudged piece of paper from her shoe, she saw that it was a label for a file folder.

"Aron, look at this," Koral said, holding out her hand and showing him the label. It read "WHITE CIGARETTE—42 FEET."

"We've obviously lit a fire under somebody," Koral told Aron, as she placed the file label in a plastic bag and handed it to him. "I think we should have another little chat with the grieving widow. Maybe we can persuade her to fill in some blanks for us."

The coroner and crime scene investigators finished processing the office and were wheeling Jerome's body out to a waiting ambulance.

"I'm thinking the same thing," Aron replied, as he and Koral followed them out. "I don't like what is starting to happen around here since they found Reese Mallory's remains, and I want some answers before I lose any more friends."

"My car or yours?" Koral asked him.
"Mine," he told her. "You drive like a maniac."

Chapter Thirty-Five

Lynn, Susan, and Dennis were sitting at the kitchen bar in the penthouse having coffee when Lynn's cell phone rang.

Reaching over the counter, she picked it up. "Hello."

"Mrs. Mallory, this is Police Chief Aron Ebanks. I wanted to see if you could come to headquarters at 4:00 P.M. today to identify the articles that were recovered with your husband's remains."

Even though Lynn knew what she had to do today, the impact of Aron's words still caught her off guard.

"Yes, that will be fine," she whispered, hoarsely. "May my friends come with me?" she asked. "This is something I'd rather not do alone."

"Of course," Aron answered, thinking to himself that the grief in her voice sounded genuine. "I'll see you then. And by the way, I would like to speak with you about another matter while you're here. It won't take long," he assured her.

"Certainly," Lynn said, a frown forming on her face. What else could he possibly want to talk about? she wondered.

When they hung up, Lynn relayed the conversation to Susan and Dennis.

"What do you think this is all about?" Susan asked her.

"I have no idea," Lynn replied testily. "I thought we'd been over everything several times already two years ago when Reese disappeared. The old coot just won't leave me alone."

Susan glanced at Dennis and he shrugged his shoulders. He couldn't imagine what Ebanks was up to now. Oh well, he thought, he may think he's on to something, but that remained to be seen. That woman investigator, however, was another story. Lynn told him all about Koral Sanders and her nosy questions, but Sanders couldn't know any more than Ebanks knew. And, besides, what was there to know?

Dennis didn't want anyone planting any seeds of doubt about him in Lynn's mind because before they left Grand Cayman, he intended to be married to her. He knew how cops operated. They could make you think even your own mother was guilty of murder before they got through with you.

Well, that wasn't going to happen if he could help it. He had too much at stake.

"Lynn, I think this would be a good time to formally retain me as your attorney. I'm not a criminal lawyer, but these cops won't know that," Dennis explained. "If things progress, we'll need to secure local representation, of course. I've worked with a couple of solicitors on the civil side. They can recommend someone."

The serious look on his face was more than a little disturbing to Lynn as she looked at him, stunned.

"Do you really think it will go that far?" she asked.

Dennis didn't want to alarm her any more than she already was, but he knew he had to prepare her for the worst.

"These cops want to solve a homicide. We have to be ready."

Chapter Thirty-Six

An earnest-looking, young, uniformed officer ushered Lynn Mallory with two others in tow into Aron's office. Koral and Aron stood up and Lynn introduced them as Susan Alden and Dennis Hammond, long-time friends of the Mallorys. Addressing Koral, Dennis added that they'd been in the dive party the day Reese Mallory died.

Clearly recognizing them, Aron stood up, shaking hands with each of them. Then Koral did the same.

When Dennis announced he was present not only as Lynn's friend, but also as her attorney, Aron raised his eyebrows so slightly that Koral thought she might have been the only who noticed.

Dressed in a short black sundress and a black straw hat, her long blonde hair streaming down her back, Lynn looked every inch the gorgeous bereaved widow.

"Mrs. Mallory, I am hoping this will be the last time you have to come to my office for such unpleasant reasons. I know what an ordeal this must have been for you these past two years," Aron told her, his sympathetic eyes never leaving her face.

"Thank you, Chief Ebanks. It has been a pretty rough time for me," Lynn admitted.

"If you'll come with me, we'll get this over with as quickly as possible," Aron said, getting up from his desk and motioning for all of them to follow him.

As she walked behind them down the hallway, Koral studied the three, not entirely sure she trusted any of them at this point.

Aron stopped and held a door open for them to enter. The sterile, refrigerator-cold room with its low-hanging light in the ceiling gave little comfort as Lynn stepped forward.

A table holding something bulky covered by a white sheet dominated the center of the stark room which was devoid of any other furniture.

"Mrs. Mallory, if you would, please look at these items and tell me, if you can, if they belonged to your husband," Aron said quietly.

Aron took Lynn's arm and they walked toward the table while Susan, Dennis and Koral waited by the door.

Aron lifted the sheet to expose a ragged and faded dark blue buoyancy compensator, a pair of neoprene booties, a pair of silver-striped black fins, tattered red nylon swim trunks, an air tank with two cleanly cut hoses, a dive computer on a wristband, an air pressure gauge, and compass, a blue weight belt, a stainless steel Rolex Submariner watch, and a plain gold wedding band in a plastic evidence bag.

Lynn stopped as the sight of the objects seemed to hit her like a physical blow. Swaying slightly, she closed her eyes and reached out to Dennis for support. He crossed the room in three strides and put his arm around her. They approached the table holding the dive gear, and Lynn hesitantly picked up the bag containing the wedding band.

It looked amazingly new for having been in salt water for two years. She took the ring out of the bag, turned it over a few times in her fingers, and then held it up to read the inscription inside. Tears rolled down her face as she read what it said.

"Forever, my love. LM." Lynn read the inscription.

"It's Reese's wedding ring. I had this inscribed myself," Lynn said softly, as she squeezed the ring tightly in her hand and tried to regain her composure.

She picked up the buoyancy compensator and looked at the inside lining. The initials "R.M." printed in faded black indelible marker stared back at her. Lynn's blue eyes reflected a pain with which Aron was all too familiar each time a deceased's effects had to be identified by family members. A part of Aron suffered with them. Death was never easy, especially a violent one like Reese Mallory's.

"That's his dive gear and watch, too. May I leave now?" Lynn asked hurriedly.

"Of course," Aron told her.

Lynn took Dennis' hand and turned to leave, then hesitated. "By the way, Chief Ebanks, was there anything else found with Reese?" she asked quietly.

"No, Mrs. Mallory. Only what you see here. Why do you ask?"

"He always wore a chain with a gold *ankh*, the Egyptian symbol of eternal life, around his neck," Lynn said. "He never took it off."

"I'm sorry, Mrs. Mallory. The only items we found with his remains are here on this table."

"May I take his ring?" Lynn asked, sounding like a small child.

"We'll need to keep it for just a while longer until we finish our investigation. Then you may take it, of course," Aron told her. "There is one more thing I almost forgot. If you would come back to my office for a moment, I have another matter to discuss with you. It'll just take a few minutes."

"Can't this wait?" Dennis asked him sharply. "Can't you see she's upset?"

"No, Mr. Hammond, it can't wait."

The sudden tone of authority in Aron's voice caught Dennis off guard. "This is now a murder investigation and I have some unanswered questions. You and Dr. Alden may wait in the reception room."

Dennis began to protest as he glared at Aron.

"I'm afraid I can't allow you to accompany her, Mr. Hammond," Aron cut him off. "Unless I'm mistaken, you are not licensed to practice before either the Caymanian or British bars, so you have no standing as Mrs. Mallory's attorney in the Cayman Islands."

"Chief Ebanks, I am Mrs. Mallory's attorney, and there is no way you are going to question her without me present. I think we went through this same scenario two years ago," Dennis fumed.

Turning to Lynn, he said, "If he asks you anything that makes you the least bit uncomfortable, refuse to answer until we get you local representation."

"I'll be fine, Dennis. Just go with Susan and wait for me. This isn't anything I can't handle. Please don't make a scene," Lynn told him, as Dennis shot Aron one last look.

Lynn turned and walked down the hall with Aron toward his office.

Susan took Dennis' arm and led him away.

"I don't like this," Dennis told Susan, as they walked down the hall. "I don't like this one bit."

"Dennis, just shut the fuck up," Susan said through clenched teeth. "You'd better get off your ego trip or they'll start looking at you as a suspect. Anyone with eyes can see you had a motive."

Chapter Thirty-Seven

Lynn sat down in Aron's office as he picked up a file folder and took out a small plastic bag. Koral closed the door behind them and leaned against it.

"Mrs. Mallory, I don't know if you are aware, but a friend of mine named Jerome Johnson was murdered this morning."

Lynn's eyes shot up, her expression of recognition giving Aron the fuel he needed to continue.

"From your reaction, I take it you know the name. Am I correct?" he asked, holding up the bag in front of Lynn's face. It held a small piece of paper.

As her eyes focused on the contents of the bag, Lynn said, "Yes, I know the name. What happened to him?" she asked, her voice barely above a whisper as she clasped her hands tightly in her lap.

"Someone shot him in the head this morning in his office at the marina," Aron told her. "This was found on the floor. The file it came from was missing. I thought maybe you could tell us what was in it." His voice clearly indicated that he considered her a suspect.

Lynn leaned across Aron's desk and took the bag from him. Her hands trembling, she read the smeared words on the label and let out a small gasp. She hoped Aron didn't notice. His tight-lipped expression told her he did.

"Chief Ebanks, surely you don't think I had anything to do with Mr. Johnson's murder?" Lynn asked nervously.

"No, Mrs. Mallory, I'm not sure of that at all." Aron could still see the vacant, staring eyes of his friend lying dead on the floor. "Jerome always kept his door locked when he was in his office alone on Monday mornings. His door was not locked today when we went in and found his body. He let someone in—someone he knew—and that person killed him. He had just called Ms. Sanders and told her he found something that might shed some light on your husband's murder. When she got there twenty minutes later, the door was open, Jerome was dead, and this label identifying a white Cigarette boat was on the floor. Would you like to tell me why, Mrs. Mallory?"

Lynn struggled to collect herself. Remembering Dennis' warning, she knew she should refuse to answer until he found her a local lawyer, but she worried that insisting on help might make her look even more guilty in Aron's eyes.

"With everything going on now, I guess it just slipped my mind to tell you about our boat, Chief Ebanks," Lynn confessed.

Aron breathed a sigh of relief as he realized his bluff was working. Lynn Mallory obviously had information she had been hiding, or had conveniently forgotten to mention.

"When we bought our penthouse at the Ritz-Carlton, a forty two-foot Cigarette came with it. We kept it at Mr. Johnson's Cayman Harbor Marina. After Reese died, I sold it. I never used it and didn't see any need to keep it. At the time, we thought Reese's disappearance had been a diving accident. Frankly, he sometimes got a thrill out of taking chances, and I figured he'd taken one too many. None of us suspected murder, even you."

She paused and looked Aron directly in the eye. "I didn't see another boat out there that day, and neither did any of our friends or Captain Ebanks."

She continued. "Mr. Johnson must have kept a file on our boat, and that's the label you found. Maybe he kept a record in it of people who took it out. Maybe that's what the killer was looking for. The first I even thought about our boat was when Koral Sanders told me about the boy on our dive boat seeing a white boat out there the day Reese died. She also told me about the boy seeing another diver swimming away when he went to find Reese. I didn't kill Jerome, Chief Ebanks, and I certainly didn't kill my husband. I was on board the dive boat when Reese disappeared. What reason could I possibly have had to kill either one of them?" Lynn pleaded, her expression one of sincere innocence. "I loved my husband."

Aron had enough experience with human failings to know that married people often had reasons to kill each other, reasons no one else suspected. But Lynn's face told Aron that she was telling the truth. He didn't think she was a good enough actress to conceal a murder. Aron took pride in the fact that he could almost always tell when someone was lying, and he was virtually certain that Lynn Mallory wasn't. If she hadn't killed her husband or been involved in his killing, she certainly couldn't have had a reason to kill Jerome.

"Mrs. Mallory, I would appreciate it if you wouldn't leave the island until we can put together some missing pieces of our investigation." Aron said.

Lynn stood up, putting on black Chanel sunglasses, and pulling her hat low over her eyes. She knew the paparazzi would be circling outside.

"Of course," Lynn said, as she turned to leave Aron's office. Koral held the door open for her and slowly closed it as she watched Lynn walking down the hall toward Susan and Dennis waiting in the reception room.

"Well, what do you think, Aron? Is she capable of murder?" Koral asked, as she walked over to the window in Aron's office and looked out at the bustling afternoon crowd. Watching the mysterious trio get into Lynn's black Mercedes and drive away, she wondered how something so horrific as the murder of an internationally-known rich young lawyer could happen here.

Things like this didn't happen on Grand Cayman. Koral thought the worst thing she would ever come across when she moved here would be investigating people and corporations hiding money in offshore banks that didn't ask questions. Not people hiding bodies inside caves one hundred twenty-five feet underwater.

"I don't think so," Aron replied.

"I don't either. I don't think she had anything to do with this, Aron," Koral told him, turning from the window and sitting down on the corner of his desk. She picked up the plastic bag containing the file label and tossed it across his desk.

"I know, Koral, but something tells me she's involved up to her neck without even knowing it."

Chapter Thirty-Eight

Koral decided she didn't need to check out every marina in Cayman for the mysterious white Cigarette now that Lynn Mallory had come clean about having owned one. She was going with her gut feeling that the Mallory's boat was the one on the North Wall that day. At least it would save a lot of time if she went with that feeling rather than chasing after boats that may or may not have been the one she was looking for.

But who took it out there? She knew one thing for sure. Whoever did take it out to the Wall was the person, or persons, who killed Reese Mallory and more than likely, also killed Jerome Johnson. An uneasy feeling was forming in her gut. Koral didn't like the direction this case was taking. The more she learned about the players in this case, the more dead bodies could turn up.

The only lead in this entire mystery died with Jerome, with the exception of the file folder label found on the floor of his office. Koral was hoping they could lift some fingerprints from the label, other than Jerome's, but unless the owner of the prints had a prior record, was a government employee, or had applied for a residency permit, that would also lead to a dead end. Somehow Koral had to figure out how to make the killer play his hand. She hoped he, or she, would make just one mistake before somebody else ended up dead.

It was getting late and Koral wasn't in the mood to sit at home all evening. She wanted to put this day behind her and start fresh tomorrow. Finding dead bodies wasn't her idea of a good day.

To shake off the willies of seeing Jerome Johnson dead on his office floor and the memory of the sad look in Lynn Mallory's eyes as she identified her murdered husband's dive gear, Koral snagged her friend, Julie Menotti, as soon as she got home and they spent a lively four hours at Peppers dancing reggae and ska with the locals. Julie sipped her favorite Tortuga rum and Diet Coke. Koral stuck to Jack Daniels. In between sets, Julie convulsed Koral with tales of the cheap bastards off the cruise ships who came into the jewelry store she half-owned for engagement rings set with cubic zirconia. "What do they think we are, Wal-Mart?" Julie concluded.

Throughout the evening, Koral didn't think about the Mallory murder, or the Johnson murder, more than twice.

Chapter Thirty-Nine

Ray Durbin and Jeanette Ryker thought they had died and gone to heaven when they'd arrived in Grand Cayman two years earlier. A lot had happened in their dreary, sad lives since then. They had lived like lottery winners for a while, and now they had a new gig in Cayman that would make them even more money, thanks to the cowboy from hell.

As Ray remembered how he had landed in high cotton, he couldn't help but gloat just a little. He didn't look the part of a rich man of leisure, and that was okay with him. He liked flying under the radar. Kept the cops off his back. The only thing he didn't like about not flaunting the fact he could buy whatever he wanted was that he couldn't get hot chicks to look at him twice. Jeanette didn't count as a hot chick. She didn't count as much of anything to Ray except a warm body when he got horny.

After this second job in Cayman, those days would be over. He'd go for a complete makeover, dump Jeanette one way or the other, and focus on getting some eye candy that other guys wished they had hanging all over them. This next job for the big man would be his swan song. He knew how to cover things up, get the job done, and disappear into thin air. He was good at what he did.

Ray's past occasional jobs as a handyman, before the Cayman gig, brought him only enough to eat, pay the rent, and buy beer and cigarettes on a regular basis. The diving work repairing offshore oil rigs had paid substantial bucks, but it was too hard and too dangerous, and it interfered with getting stoned.

When he'd hooked up with Jeanette in a skanky dive on Houston's south side, he never dreamed some rich bold-faced type would be his ticket out of Sleazeville.

He and Jeanette had been living together then for about three months and were enjoying the low-rent version of a night on the town. They were sitting in the No-Telling, a redneck hangout on Telephone Road, when a tall, good looking guy in a suit, tie, boots and a cowboy hat walked up to them and asked them if they'd like to make a hundred thousand dollars.

Ray stopped pulling on a Bud long-neck and cut his eyes up suspiciously at the dude. He looked like he could snap Ray in two with his bare hands. It was the first time Ray had ever seen someone wearing sunglasses inside a bar at night.

"Who are you, Jack?" Ray sneered, taking a drag on a filterless Camel and looking the stranger up and down. "A little out of your neighborhood, ain't ya? Whatcha doing? Slummin'?" Ray laughed at his own slack attempt at a joke.

"Shut up, asshole." The man's face told Ray he'd better do what he was told or suffer some pretty major consequences. "That's not something you need to know. Do you want to make some money or not?"

"For that kind of money, sounds like I'd have to kill somebody," Ray laughed, showing badly stained and crooked yellow teeth.

"Smart man. Let's get a booth and we'll see if you're up to the task," the man told him.

Ray and Jeanette looked at each other, wide-eyed. They slid off the bar stools and followed the man to a sticky tattered booth at the back of the dingy bar. The man sat on one side, and Ray and Jeanette sat on the other.

The man leaned in close and said, "My employer needs someone like you who knows underwater work and who knows how to keep his mouth shut. My sources tell me you did some diving servicing oil rigs off Louisiana. They also say you killed a guy in a bar in New Orleans, but the cops didn't prosecute you when you screamed self-defense. I know better. You killed the guy because he stiffed you on a drug deal. Your friends covered for you and backed the story you told the police. Said the guy pulled a knife and when you struggled with him, he fell on it. Fact is, you stabbed him in the gut while your buddies held him. I've got proof of this in case you're wondering. Some real good pictures that some low-life tourist happened to snap while he was checking out the local color ended up making him some cash when he saw what he had on film and heard I was looking for you. If you don't do exactly as I tell you, this information will be delivered to the New Orleans Police Department tomorrow. I'm sure they would love to re-open your case, and this time, you could get the old needle in the arm. Do we understand each other?"

The man smiled and leaned back in the booth, lighting a Marlboro and blowing smoke in Ray's blank face.

Ray sat there staring at the man, his mouth hanging slightly open, trying to figure out who the hell he was and how he got wind of what had really happened in New Orleans. Better yet, who the fuck had told him? Ray's buddies would never rat him out. They knew better, he thought, but someone had sold him out and now he had a sinking feeling he was getting into something that could get him killed. But look on the positive side, he thought: it could also get him rich.

"Who the fuck are you, man? Who are you working for? Who the hell am I supposed to be killing?" Ray's voice rose with each question.

"Shut up, you little maggot. You do what I tell you. Or go to prison. Or worse. Your decision. It's out of the goodness of my employer's heart that you're getting a shitload of money to help you make your crappy life easier and give you a little incentive to do the job right. You've got one minute to decide, starting now," the man said, looking at his Rolex.

Ray thought about what he could do with all that money. If he did what this guy wanted him to do, he could go wherever he wanted, buy whatever he wanted, and get a girl that was a whole lot better than Jeanette. A hundred thousand could buy him a little class, he thought, smiling to himself and exposing a mouthful of chipped yellow teeth.

"I guess you don't leave me much choice, man. You're on. What do I have to do, and when do I get the money?" Ray grinned.

Jeanette just sat there smiling blankly and nodding her head, thinking about all that money and where she could spend it the fastest.

"You'll be contacted tomorrow. Pack your dive gear and get yourself a passport. You leave for Grand Cayman in two days." The man counted out five one-hundred dollar bills. "This'll get you a twenty four-hour turnaround."

"I got a passport, and a couple of extra ones, if you know what I mean," Ray snapped, folding the cash neatly in the breast pocket of his ratty pearl-snapped shirt. "The kind of specialized work I did on the rigs, I had to be ready to go to Nigeria or Indonesia or wherever the hell they sent me. But this'll come in handy as walkin' around money." Ray laughed, baring his ugly yellow teeth.

The man got up and threw twenty dollars on the table for the beers. "Just be ready to do the job, or I'll be doing you. Believe me, you won't enjoy it. Cowboy's the name. Remember it."

Then he walked out into the hot, humid night.

Chapter Forty

Koral sat in her kitchen contemplating whether or not to keep her date with Julie Menotti to take the dive excursion out to Stingray City.

With everything going on with the Mallory case, she wished they could postpone it for a while, but she didn't want to disappoint Julie. Her vivacious, young, next-door neighbor had moved in a month earlier complete with a cute little black Chihuahua named Cheetah and a Cayman parrot named Buzzard who could talk a blue streak, mostly four-letter words. Koral was certain Buzzard didn't learn those words from her prim new owner. Julie and Koral had hit it off immediately.

A newcomer to the island, Julie was half-owner of one of the high-end jewelry stores near the cruise ship docks in George Town. She'd moved to Cayman when her business partner moved back to Florida to be closer to her mother who was battling cancer.

Koral offered to show Julie around the island and in return, Julie promised Koral a big store discount on any item of jewelry she wanted. Not a bad trade.

When they'd been boogying at Pepper's, Koral suggested that the two of them go out to Stingray City, one of the most popular tourist attractions in the world. It ranked right up there with swimming with dolphins, only you got to commune with stingrays of all sizes.

Generations of stingrays, born and raised with humans constantly swimming and diving around them, and feeding them squid, were as tame as pets. They would eat out of your hand and hover in your lap as you sat on the ocean floor, at a whopping depth, in places of three feet, while letting you run your hands across their smooth skin. The only time you might get stung by one was if you stepped on it or grabbed it by its barbed tail. An act like that might also get you thrown in jail.

Two things you absolutely can't do in Cayman are taking souvenirs from the reefs and harassing sea turtles or stingrays.

Stroking didn't count as harassing. The stingray's white underbellies were the softest thing Koral had ever touched. Besides, the catamaran ride out to the "city" didn't seem long at all, provided the complimentary rum punch held out.

"Koral, are you up?" a woman's voice called out at the front door.

"Why doesn't anyone ever use my doorbell?" Koral said out loud to herself, throwing her hands up in the air.

"Coming, Julie," she called out.

Koral opened the door and Julie bounced in, her long brown hair tied back in a ponytail, and her big brown eyes dancing with excitement. She was dressed for the beach in a green bikini with a colorful floral sarong tied around her hips. She carried a big straw bag over her shoulder and looked about nineteen.

Why does everyone look younger than their actual age except me? Koral wondered. Must be something to do with her lifestyle, which she didn't see changing anytime soon. She was certain that Jack Daniels and Marlboro would go out of business if she banished them from her life.

"I'm so ready to go play with the stingrays," Julie said, tossing her bag in a chair and turning to face a very unamused Koral. "I won't get to take many days off once I start full time at the store," Julie chirped.

"Julie, it's 7:00 A.M. That's 7:00 in the morning," Koral barked. "The boat leaves at 11:00 A.M. Why are you here now?" Koral asked her, exasperation showing in her voice. "How many times do I have to tell you, I don't do mornings!"

Koral knew she shouldn't be so crabby, but it went with the territory, and it wasn't her nature to sugar coat anything.

"I'm sorry, Koral. I just thought we'd get an early start, grab some breakfast at Eats and take off," Julie apologized, her radiant smile disappearing. She looked like a small child getting scolded by her mother. Koral was immediately sorry she had hurt her feelings.

"You know what? That's a great idea," Koral said, giving Julie a big smile.

"I'll take a quick shower, throw on a suit and some shorts, and we'll go do just that," she said, heading for the bedroom. "Make yourself at home and I'll be right back."

Julie's face lit up again. "I'll wait here," she said, plopping down on the sofa and stretching her long, tanned legs out on the coffee table. Just as she picked up Koral's latest issue of *People* magazine, the doorbell rang.

"Koral, want me to get that?" Julie called out. Hearing the water running in the shower, Julie jumped up and headed for the door, tossing the magazine on the table.

Julie never had a chance to find out if she would have liked playing with stingrays. As she opened the door, a strange man with a scrawny goatee, wearing a Panama hat and sunglasses, smiled at her, pointed a gun at her head, and put out the radiant light in her laughing brown eyes with a single, silent shot.

Chapter Forty-One

Dennis Hammond sat on the balcony of Lynn's penthouse contemplating his next move. He wasn't used to being out of control of a situation, and this one was beginning to rage.

He knew when Koral Sanders started asking questions and putting ideas in Aron Ebank's head about him and Lynn, things were going to look very suspicious. Somehow he had to get her to lay off so he could buy some time to figure out what to do. He had waited too long to get Lynn to agree to marry him, and he was determined that nothing was going to get in his way now that he was so close.

Earlier that morning, he told Susan to take Lynn into town for some shopping and have lunch. He needed some space alone to think for awhile, especially after Lynn told him about her private conversation with Ebanks and Koral Sanders. He couldn't believe Lynn had volunteered information about her boat. He knew that goddamn Cigarette would come back to haunt them. Lynn also told him about James Ebanks seeing a white Cigarette out on the Wall the day Reese died, and he knew that trail would lead straight to Jerome Johnson's marina. Sure enough it had and someone had killed old man Johnson. James was probably next, Dennis mused.

Dennis knew that as soon as Koral Sanders found out about Lynn's boat, her suspicions about him and Lynn would reach a full boil. Assuming Lynn had read them correctly after her meeting with them at Aron Ebanks' office, she was in the clear. But he wasn't. All Dennis needed was for Koral to start digging into his past relationship with Reese and Lynn. People who'd known all of them well for years would inflate his attachment to Lynn into an obsession—and the world's oldest motive for murder.

He could see the headlines now, he thought. "Mallory Murdered by Best Friend in Love Triangle." He could sense Koral's dislike of him, and he had to come up with something that would get her off his back and do so without alienating Lynn.

Before those divers found Reese's body, Lynn had seemed close to agreeing to marry him. A romantic trip somewhere with no old memories would have cemented that.

In the courtroom, Dennis Hammond had chewed up top big-city PIs for lunch. He wasn't going to let some island minor-leaguer derail his plans and make him a murder suspect without putting up a fight.

Chapter Forty-Two

Aron was sitting in his office when Dr. Martin Sneed from Forensics knocked on the door.

"Come in."

Dr. Sneed, a tall bird-like man with thinning brown hair and black horn-rimmed glasses, peeked around the door and said, "Chief, I think I've found something that may be important. We were able to lift a fingerprint from that label that was found in Jerome Johnson's office," he said, quickly crossing the room and handing a file to Aron. "We submitted a request for a search through the FBI's Latent Print Operations Unit through their legal attaché and through Interpol and got a hit on it." Dr. Sneed shoved his hands in his lab coat and waited for Aron's reply.

Aron eagerly opened the file to see a thin, mean-looking face with a mustache and goatee staring back at him.

The name below the mug shot was Ray Durbin.

Aron immediately turned to his computer and typed in Durbin's name on the Caymans' customs databank. A few seconds later, Durbin's face filled the computer monitor screen showing he had entered Grand Cayman three days earlier. He looked even more like a nasty piece of work than the photo of him in the file.

Scanning further down the computer screen, Aron saw that Durbin had been in Grand Cayman two years prior almost to the date.

"My God," Aron murmured to himself. Then he smiled at the pathologist and said, "thanks, Martin. You may have given us just what we need to break the case."

As Martin Sneed closed the door to Aron's office, Aron dialed Koral's cell phone. Reaching her voice-mail, Aron left a message to call him immediately. Where in the hell can she be? Aron thought. She was never two feet away from her phone.

This new information was exactly the kind of break he'd been hoping for. At least now they had a starting point. As Aron mulled the information on Ray Durbin over and over in his mind, he didn't see how such a small time crook could mastermind a plot to kill someone like Reese Mallory. Why would he kill Mallory unless he just did it for a thrill? On this, Aron seriously doubted. Someone had to have hired him. But why? Who could possibly have benefited from Mallory's death except his wife and his best friend, who was clearly already maneuvering to be Husband Number Two? But even those two seemed to him to be innocent of any wrongdoing. Aron was certain that Mrs. Mallory had nothing to do with the murder of her husband, and his gut told him that a hot-shot trial lawyer would be too alert to the potential for blackmail to hire a hitman on his partner and best friend. Money couldn't be the motivating factor since Mrs. Mallory had more than enough of her own money to even think of killing her husband for more. And if she wanted to marry Dennis Hammond, surely divorce would be a lot less messy than murder.

Now thrown into the mix was the murder of Aron's old friend, Jerome Johnson. Durbin was obviously careless. He hadn't worn gloves when he went to Jerome's marina office, nor did he notice the label fall off the folder, leaving a precious print behind. A pro would never have made these mistakes. Durbin was a puppet. Someone else was pulling the strings.

The facts were too closely-connected to be two entirely separate incidents. Somehow, Aron had to find the common thread that tied the two murders together.

He felt in his bones that Durbin had to be the person who killed both Mallory and Jerome. It suddenly occurred to Aron that young James Ebanks might be next. He'd been so wrapped-up in Jerome's death that he'd neglected to warn the poor kid and his family. He picked up the phone and dialed the Dive Cayman Dive Shop.

"I realize that James and Captain Ebanks are out on the water," he told the boy's aunt, the dive shop's office manager. "But please get the captain on the radio and have him call me immediately. This is urgent. In fact, it's a matter of life and death."

Aron knew they had to find Ray Durbin before someone else died.

Chapter Forty-Three

Koral stepped out of the shower and wrapped a towel around her as she walked into the bedroom.

"Julie, grab us a couple of Diet Cokes out of the fridge," Koral called out, as she picked up her purse from the bed. Her cell phone was beeping loudly letting her know that she had a message.

"Julie, where are you?" Koral yelled, walking over to the door into the living room. That's odd, she thought, getting no answer. Where would she have gone? Must have forgotten something at her condo, Koral decided.

Koral turned to go back into the bathroom and stopped when she noticed the front door was standing open. Julie knew better than to leave the door open.

"Hello? Julie?" No answer.

Koral's reflexes immediately went on danger alert as she dug around in the clutter in her purse for her gun. Where was the goddamn thing? she thought.

Finally wrapping her fingers around the compact but lethal titanium snub-nose .38 revolver, she threw her purse aside and peered around the door into the living room. An intruder would be minus his balls if she had to use the weapon in the close quarters of her condo. Seeing nothing suspicious, she silently started toward the open front door.

Just as she reached it, Koral saw a sandal on the floor at the end of the sofa. A sandal just like the ones Julie had been wearing. Feeling a knot begin to form in her stomach, Koral peered around the sofa. Julie was lying face up on the floor, a small red hole above her right eye.

"Oh, my God," Koral whispered to herself, slamming the door shut as she pulled the towel tighter around her and ran around the sofa. She knelt down next to Julie's body. A large pool of blood had formed beneath Julie's head and was spreading across the rug. Koral instinctively knew Julie was gone, but she felt for a pulse anyway. Nothing. Koral gently put her hand on Julie's cheek and thought of the bright young spirit that had been so eager to start a new life.

"Goddamn it to hell!" Koral screamed out loud. Who the fuck had done this and why? she thought angrily. Julie didn't know anyone in Cayman. Why would someone want to hurt her?

Koral stood up, her legs and feet covered in Julie's blood as she wondered how she was going to tell Julie's family that this precious girl was dead. And for what? She stood up and clenched her palms until her nails dug into them. Never had anyone invaded Koral's home before, let alone kill somebody in her own living room.

Suddenly, Koral felt nausea creeping up on her. If no one had a reason to kill Julie, then whoever shot her must have mistaken her for Koral. Someone had meant to kill her, not Julie.

Not noticing the towel fall from her body, Koral ran to the dining table, grabbed her cell phone and dialed Aron's number.

After several rings, Aron finally answered. "Aron Ebanks."

"Aron, it's Koral. Get over here right away. Something terrible has happened," Koral said anxiously, as she hurriedly looked around the living room. She hadn't thought to check the closets to see if whoever shot Julie was still there. Not likely, but she knew she still should have checked.

"Koral, what is it? What's happened? Are you okay?" Aron asked, his concern rising with each question.

"No, I'm not okay. Somebody shot my neighbor in my doorway while I was in the shower. The killer evidently thought Julie was me. The only thing I can think of is that somebody thinks we're getting close to finding out something crucial in the Mallory case, and they want to make sure we never solve it. They don't care how many bodies they have to pile up along the way. We just need to make sure we're not added to the pile," Koral said, as she glanced at Julie's body. "And that James isn't. As our eyewitness, he could be next."

Chapter Forty-Four

The only job James Ebanks had ever had was in his uncle's dive shop. He had worked there since he was fourteen, and he loved the freedom it brought him. He couldn't imagine working anywhere else, especially in the confines of an office. Going out on the dive boat every day and meeting people from all over the world gave him an air of education he otherwise wouldn't have had. He always met the most interesting people who filled his mind with visions of faraway countries and cultures. One day, he thought, he might get to visit them. But he would always come back to Grand Cayman.

Nothing could be more beautiful than skimming along the top of the clear aquamarine water every day, taking divers to the hot diving spots along the reef. While the paying customers did their thing, James did his.

He couldn't wait to go beneath the surface to float weightlessly in a silent, technicolor, and mysterious world. He devoured books about the sea and deep diving submersibles like the ones Dr. Robert Ballard used to locate the *Titanic*. He was fascinated by the creatures that lived miles beneath the surface, never before seen by humans, that were photographed by the fearless pioneers of deep sea diving. He wished he had the money to go to college and study oceanography, but for now, he would get his education from the life experiences he logged each day.

James had dived so many times at all his favorite dive spots that the fish were almost pets to him. He even had his special rays at Stingray City and knew them on sight. There was one ray, black with blue eyes, that he named Darth Vader, after the *Star Wars* character. No one believed him when he told them about the blue-eyed ray. Not until they actually saw him. He was a huge and magnificent creature, and the fact that he would let James and the tourists pet him thrilled them beyond words.

James's family had been on Grand Cayman for eight generations, and he couldn't imagine a safer, or more beautiful place to live and raise a family one of these days.

Until that day on the North Wall. Until he witnessed that rich Houston lawyer's murder.

James had lived in fear for the past two years after that awful day. He'd told no one about it, thinking if he just buried it away, it would never come back to haunt him.

He couldn't have been more wrong.

Ever since those divers found that skeleton, people had started dying. James was terrified for himself and his family. What if the killer was after him now? There weren't many places to hide on the island, and he couldn't leave his parents and two sisters to face a killer alone.

After he told the police his story, James felt so proud of himself and bragged to his friends about what he'd witnessed and how he had helped the police. For the first time in his life, he had felt important.

He couldn't believe he had been so stupid.

By now, everyone on Cayman probably knew what he had seen. Word traveled fast on the island, and he knew the killer would hear about him soon, if he hadn't already. He hadn't thought the whole thing through before he came forward with what he knew. Now he had to watch his back all the time.

Keeping the secret for two years about witnessing that murder was nothing compared to having to look over his shoulder for the rest of his life.

He turned back to filling the tanks in his uncle's dive shop. The noise of the compressor erased all other sounds, so when he noticed a form blocking the light from the doorway, he instinctively swung into a deep crouch and scurried around behind the tanks, reaching up the wall for a belaying hook.

"A bit jumpy, boy, aren't you?" he heard his uncle's deep, familiar voice say. "Well, I gather you should be."

"Yes, sir," James stammered, rising. His legs were trembling so badly that he had to hold onto one of the tanks for support. "I'm sorry. I'm sorry I put the family in danger. I should have kept quiet."

"James, don't ever be sorry about doing the right thing," Captain Ebanks said. "All that's necessary for evil to flourish is for good people to keep silent. I'm proud of you for finally stepping forward."

Crossing the tank room with uncharacteristic briskness, he slapped James on the shoulder.

"Now, I've got a little job for you," he explained calmly, looking the boy straight in the eye. "Remember my brother-in-law in Montego Bay?"

James nodded.

"His charter fishing business is doing so well that he could use another boat, and another couple of hands to work it. I offered him the Blue Tarpon for as long as he needs it, along with two of the hardest-working young men I know. You and your cousin will be Jamaica-bound."

"When?"

"Right now. She's gassed up and waiting at the dock in George Town."

Chapter Forty-Five

When Lynn and Susan got back from shopping, Dennis was sitting out on the balcony soaking up the afternoon sun, his Panama hat tilted so that he could just peek out from under the brim. The seventh floor penthouse definitely offered the most incredible view of Seven Mile Beach on the island.

"I think I'm going to take a nap," Susan told Lynn, as she dropped her shopping bags on a chair and headed to the bedroom. "Serious shopping always wears me out," she laughed.

"Me, too. See you in a little while," Lynn smiled, as she walked toward the balcony to tell Dennis they were home.

Lynn opened the sliding glass door and stepped out onto the balcony with its pots of fuchsia bougainvillea and peach hibiscus, pastel umbrellas and matching cushioned chairs arranged in a cozy cluster.

Dennis lifted the hat from his face and gave her a wide smile. "Did you girls buy out the stores or just simply buy the stores?" he teased her.

"Oh, very funny," Lynn said, picking up a towel from one of the chairs and throwing it at him. Dennis sat up and took Lynn's hand, pulling her down next to him. He put an arm around her and gently kissed her.

"What did I do to deserve that?" she asked, grinning at him. She gazed into his dark brown eyes and saw nothing there but love. Could she be so lucky as to have not only one incredible man in her life, but two? Reese would always be a part of her, and she would always keep him in a very special place in her heart, but she knew she was going to have to let him go if she was going to find any kind of happiness with Dennis.

"You didn't do anything. You never need to do anything. You just are," he told her, leaning in and kissing her again, lingering on her lips and causing a stir in him that had been too long forgotten. He pulled back and stared into her eyes, looking for a sign that she wanted him as much as he wanted her.

"Lynn, marry me. I love you, and I've always loved you. I want you more than I've ever wanted anything. I want to take care of you and protect you and love you the rest of my life. Can't you see that?" he asked her, taking her hands and pressing them to his lips. "Nothing matters to me without you."

Lynn quickly tried to find the right words to derail this familiar conversation that never had an ending that satisfied Dennis. But he was wearing down her defenses, and she knew she was just postponing the inevitable, even though it seemed there was always something in the back of her mind holding her back from giving in to his pleas to marry him.

What was it, she wondered, that held her captive to Reese's memory? Or was it something more, something in her instincts warning her to be careful? But careful of what? Surely not Dennis. He loved her and would do anything for her. Why would she be afraid of a man who was so in love with her? Was she coping out by claiming to be true to Reese's memory? Maybe the real issue was fear of risking another loss. She was so tired of all the questions in her mind. Her marriage to Reese had been a dream, but not without its own set of problems. She knew a perfect marriage was not realistic.

"Dennis, you know I love you. I can't begin to imagine what I ever would have done without you these past two years. But now, I have to take Reese home and bury him. I have to bury my life with him, too, before I can even begin to think about starting a new life with someone else."

"You've already started a new life. With me. I don't mean to sound uncaring, but burying Reese's remains is just a formality now. The past two years have belonged to you and me. We've started building something already, and I don't want to wait any longer. Can't you see that? We can get married here in Cayman. What could be more perfect than to get married on the beach, barefoot beneath those two palms where I first kissed you?"

Dennis looked into her eyes, and she could feel herself softening. He was right, and she knew it. Deep in her heart, she knew she would marry him sooner or later. There was no on else in her life. Besides, she had known Dennis for so long, he could anticipate her every thought and move. And she did love him. Maybe not the same kind of deep passionate love she had felt for Reese, but she hoped that would come with time. Dennis was so strong and determined, and so handsome with his dark, Heathcliff looks. She knew she could depend on him and trust him completely. She also knew he worshiped the ground she walked on. So what was holding her back?

"Okay," Lynn said, throwing her hands up in the air.

"Okay? Okay what?" Dennis looked at her quizzically.

"Okay, let's get married," she said, laughing at the surprised look on his face.

"You're serious?" he asked, hardly daring to hope that she meant what she said.

"Yes, I'm serious. Don't you want me now that you've finally worn me down?" she pouted.

"Yes!" Dennis yelled, as he jumped off the chaise lounge and grabbed her, picking her up and twirling her around the balcony.

"Dennis, put me down. You're going to kill us both," she said, laughing as he put her down and took her face in his hands. He kissed her, gently at first, then with an urgency that had been held in for too many long years.

Dennis swept Lynn up in his arms and carried her inside, into her yellow bedroom, kicking the door shut behind them. He walked over to the bed and set her down on the pale yellow satin comforter. His eyes never left hers as he very slowly and deliberately stepped out of his swim suit.

As he stood so close to her, Lynn felt all her defenses disappear as she took him in her hands, guiding him to her. She could feel the desire building in both of them as she stood up and helped him pull her dress over her head, letting her long blonde hair spill down her back. He reached around behind her with both hands and unhooked her pink lace bra, letting it fall to the floor in front of her as he smothered both sides of her neck with soft kisses. All of the pent-up emotions of the past two years were erupting in both of them with a vengeance.

He stared at her perfect breasts for a few motionless seconds before finally taking them in his hands and bending his head to tenderly kiss each nipple, biting softly and caressing them, worshipping each one. He had waited for so long to possess her body, as well as her soul, and he knew that this moment defined their love.

The stirring that was rising up from the depths of Lynn's being was slowly igniting back to life, having been banished for far too long. A heat so intense was consuming her that she felt as if she were outside her body, watching someone else relinquish all resistance to this dance of love.

Dennis stepped back and hooked his thumbs in her pink lace thong, pulling it down slowly and kicking it aside, along with all thoughts of Reese Mallory, as he laid her back on the bed and covered her body with his own.

Holding him tightly in her arms, she wrapped her long, tanned legs around him as his kisses traveled up her face, then lingered softly on her lips. He gathered her up in his arms, as he became more urgent and possessive, and raising her up to meet him, he slipped inside her, moving to a silent melody sung only for the two of them.

As he filled her with himself over and over, Dennis listened to her whisper his name, giving him the prize he had been dreaming of for so long.

Chapter Forty-Six

Aron knocked on Koral's door. "Koral, it's me."

Koral slowly opened the door. She had discarded the towel she had been wearing and changed into her robe. Blood was still on her hands and feet and on the front of the robe where she had wiped her hands on it.

"Koral! Are you all right?" Shock registered on Aron's face as he ran his hands up and down both of Koral's arms, checking to make sure she wasn't injured. The four uniformed officers Aron brought with him quickly filed into the condo and checked each room.

"I'm fine, Aron. I'm not hurt. The blood is Julie's. I knelt down in it beside her. There was blood all over her, and I checked her pulse. I don't know why. I could see she was dead," Koral told him, turning to look at Julie's body on the floor.

Aron took Koral's arm and glanced at Julie's still body. Turning away, he put his arm around Koral's shoulders. "Come with me and let my men do their job," he said, leading her into the kitchen, and away from the horrible sight of Julie's body. The tone of his voice was stern, but Koral knew he was putting on a front for his men.

Aron met Julie when she moved in next door to Koral, and he felt a deep sadness that her young life had been cut short so coldbloodedly. Aron couldn't help feeling a guilty sense of relief, however, that it wasn't Koral who was lying dead on the floor.

Aron pulled out a chair for Koral and sat down facing her at the table. Koral stared at her bloody hands clasped in her lap, and felt her anger rising up again at such a senseless crime.

"Tell me what happened," Aron said quietly.

Koral took a deep breath. She leaned back in the chair shaking her head.

"We were going out to Stingray City today. Julie came over early. I was in the shower, and I guess somebody knocked on the door. She answered it. Now she's dead. That's pretty much it."

Aron had never seen Koral this subdued, and he wasn't quite sure how to handle it.

"Aron, whoever shot Julie was after me, which means he'd never seen me, or Julie and I look so much alike, he thought she was me. But I don't know why anyone would want me dead, other than the fact I'm getting too close to someone on the Mallory case," Koral said. "At least we must be onto something, or someone," she added glumly.

Koral got up and walked over to the refrigerator. She opened the door and took out a couple of beers.

"Want one?" she asked Aron, as she put one back, knowing he didn't.

"Not yet, thanks. But I'll be back later, and we'll sit and talk," he told her.

"I left a message on your cell phone earlier. And don't worry about James. I called Captain Ebanks, and he assured me that the boy would be out of harm's way by lunch. The good captain wouldn't even tell me where he went, just that he'd come back if we needed him for the trial.

"By the way, I have some news about Jerome's murder."

She sat back down at the kitchen table and opened the beer. Koral looked up at him, her interest shifting to tracking down a killer who had now tried to kill her. "What is it?"

"A fingerprint found on that file label matched one in FBI's system. A small-time Houston crook named Ray Durbin came to the island three days ago. He was also here exactly two years ago," Aron told her.

Koral jerked her head up in interest. "Where is he staying?"

"We don't know. On his immigration card, he put down the Westin. However, he isn't registered there. We don't know where he is, and we don't know if he still looks like his passport photo or his mug shot. He may have changed his appearance during the last two years and I'm sure he has several fake passports, but it's just a matter of time until we find him. And we will find him," Aron promised her.

"I know you will. And if I find him first, I'll save you the trouble of a trial."

Nothing would give her greater pleasure than to blow the bastard away, one limb at a time.

Chapter Forty-Seven

The police went through Koral's condo, and Julie's, with all the forensic technology they had on hand but hadn't had many occasions to use. They'd turned up nothing, except Julie's little black Chihuahua and her Cayman parrot. Aron brought both of them over to Koral's and asked her what should be done about them. Koral took one glance at that cute little black dog looking so tiny and so scared in Aron's arms and told him she would take care of both of them, at least for the time being.

As she took Cheetah from Aron and hugged her, stroking her small domed head, Aron said, "I didn't know you liked dogs."

"What do you mean?" she asked him. "Everyone likes dogs."

"What about the parrot?"

"Buzzard is more like a watch dog than a bird," Koral told him. "He picks up words very quickly, and from his vocabulary, he must have been around a lot of sailors before Julie got him. I can't imagine he heard her saying some of that stuff. And his screech will scare the shit out of you, take my word for it."

Aron flinched at Koral's own language. Properly raised Cayman ladies didn't say some of the words Aron had heard come out of Koral's mouth, but he knew he would never change her, nor would he really want to. Koral wouldn't be Koral without her colorful command of Anglo-Saxon no matter who disapproved. He suspected that the bird may have picked up some of his vocabulary from her.

Koral stuck her finger through Buzzard's cage, and he scooted down his perch to nuzzle it. Koral smiled and said, "They'll be fine with me for now."

"Okay, whatever you say. Good luck on your newfound motherhood." Aron grinned, thinking that the three of them would be good for each other. Koral gave him a look as he left closing the door behind him.

She patted a cushion on her sofa and said soothingly to the little dog, "Come here, Cheetah. This is your home now, sweetie." The dog jumped up and curled up on the cushion in a little ball, her big black eyes fixed on Koral. At that moment, Koral knew that the tiny, adorable creature already had her wrapped around her little paw, and "for now" would turn into "for life."

However, Buzzard might be a different story. Belying his name, the bird was quite beautiful with green body feathers, blue under wing feathers and orange cheeks. As she stood his cage in the corner of the living room, he started in immediately.

"Fuck the bastards!" he squawked in avian outrage. "Fuck the bastards!"

"I couldn't agree more, Buzzard," Koral said, bursting out laughing in spite of how terrible she felt. "But you'd better not go hollering like that in the middle of the night, or you'll be parrot soup," she warned him.

After the police finished at Koral's condo and removed Julie's body, she showered and, suddenly bone-weary, lay down for a nap. When she woke, it was almost 8:00 P.M. Damn! She'd slept the day away. She got up, went into the kitchen, fed Cheetah and Buzzard and decided she needed a change of scenery. She got dressed and headed for George Town. She didn't really know where she was going; she just knew she needed to be in the fresh air and alone. She drove to the Blue Iguana and got a table by the water. The place was humming with regulars, mostly ex-pats and local business types. After ordering a conch salad and a Jack Daniels on the rocks, she took a big gulp and thought about how close she had come to being dead.

As Koral sipped her drink, she felt a wave of guilt rush over her. Goddamn it, she thought, if I hadn't been in the fucking shower, I might have been able to save her. Knowing Julie's trusting nature, Koral felt certain that she never looked through the peephole to see the son-of-a-bitch standing on the other side of the door. Koral would have checked to see who was ringing the bell and never would have opened the door to someone she didn't know. She would have told him to get lost or waved her gun at him and scared him off.

Julie never had a chance. Sweet Julie.

Koral finished her Jack Daniels and ordered another one.

"Better go easy on that stuff," a man's voice said.

Koral looked up to see Dennis Hammond and Lynn Mallory standing by the table, obviously all decked out for a special occasion.

"Hi guys. Want to join me?" Koral asked sweetly, smiling at the radiant couple and wondering what had put the glow on their faces, especially his. What a difference a day could make.

"No thanks. We have some celebrating of our own to do," Dennis told her, his smile broadening into a wide grin.

"And what are you two celebrating this evening?" Koral asked. She caught a condescending tone involuntarily lacing her voice. Better watch it, she thought. Don't want to piss them off in case I need more information from them.

"You're the first to know. We just got engaged. We're getting married tomorrow," Dennis smiled, hugging Lynn to him and kissing her cheek.

Koral's face registered complete shock as she fell back in her chair and tried unsuccessfully to hide her amazement. "I guess congratulations are in order," she recovered, hoping her sentiments didn't sound too hollow, as she held up her glass in a toast.

"Thank you, Koral. It's been a long time coming, but I guess I always knew Dennis and I would get married sooner or later. He just made me see that sooner would be better than later," Lynn laughed.

"Yeah, better late than never," Koral chirped, giving them a big smile. You deserve each other, she mused. "Where's your third Musketeer tonight? Didn't she want to join the happy couple?" Koral hoped she sounded sincere.

"Susan left for Houston this afternoon. She gave us her good wishes and wanted to help us celebrate, but she is a psychotherapist with a busy practice," Dennis explained.

Nosy bitch, he fumed. The sooner Koral Sanders got out of their lives, the easier he would breathe. There was something about her suspicious manner that irritated him to no end.

"I wish you both happiness," Koral told them. "Have a wonderful evening." Koral thought she was going to gag.

"You have a lovely night, too, Koral," Lynn said, as she and Dennis turned and headed to their table. Koral stared after them wondering how in the world Dennis Hammond had talked Lynn Mallory into marrying him. Just yesterday, the grief-stricken widow was sobbing her heart out at the police station after identifying her dead husband's wedding band.

Wonder what he did to cheer her up? Koral snickered to herself.

This case was getting more twisted by the minute, Koral thought, as she motioned to the waiter to bring her check.

Chapter Forty-Eight

Ray Durbin sat under an umbrella on the beach at a beat up dive lodge on the east end of the island, sipping a strawberry margarita. This dump was just a temporary stopping place, he thought, as he relaxed in the warm summer breeze. Pretty soon he'd be sitting on the other side of the island where the rich folks stayed. Just as soon as he collected his second hundred thousand from Cowboy, and got rid of Jeanette.

He figured he looked like just another tourist now since he bleached his mousy brown hair, and shaved off his scrawny mustache and goatee. With his oversized sunglasses and a new baseball cap with the Cayman Sir Turtle logo emblazoned on it, even his own mother wouldn't recognize him. He even made Jeanette dye her hair black, which didn't set too well with her. She was a hard-nosed bleached blonde and couldn't wait to get the hell out of Cayman so she could get back to being blonde.

Ray was already counting the ways to spend the money he was going to make on this job. He had finished off that nosy lady PI in her own condo, and no one was around to finger him. He was almost home free.

A shadow fell across Ray's drink. He jerked his head up to see somebody standing between him and the suntan he had been working on the last couple of days. Since the man was backlit by the glare of the sun, all he could see was a silhouette.

The one thing Ray did recognize was the cowboy hat.

"Hey, Cowboy. What the hell are you doin' down here?" Ray asked with a grin, as he jumped up and slapped the man on the back. "Aren't you a little overdressed for the beach, man? That suit and tie must be hotter 'n hell."

"Get your fucking hands off me, you little vermin," Cowboy growled, as he pushed Ray back down in the chaise lounge. "I thought you told me that Sanders bitch was taken care of," he snarled. "I told my people the job was finished. Now, I find out she's still very much alive and still snooping around."

Ray cowered back in his chair wishing he could disappear before the guy made gumbo out of him.

"What are you talkin' about, man? I shot the bitch in the head and watched her die. I saw her die, man," Ray said, his voice going up an octave with every third word.

"Well, then there's a goddamn voodoo queen running around this island because somebody brought her back to life. You better find out what happened and fix it or you can kiss your money goodbye, along with your worthless ass," Cowboy hissed.

"Sure, man, don't give it another thought. I'm on it, and I'll take care of it. Word of honor," Ray groveled. The last thing he wanted was to tangle with Cowboy. He figured he would come out on the losing end if he did.

"See to it, because if you fuck it up this time, you're a dead man," Cowboy warned him, as he disappeared into the sun's glare.

Ray stood staring at a hermit crab scurrying along with beach. He couldn't stop thinking about the threat of his imminent demise at Cowboy's hands should he fail to get rid of that Sanders broad again. When he finally looked up, Cowboy was gone.

What the hell happened at that bitch's house? he thought. Who did he shoot if it wasn't Koral Sanders?

The one thing he did know was that he'd better not screw up again, or it wouldn't matter what color his hair was.

Chapter Forty-Nine

As Susan Alden walked towards customs after landing at Houston's Bush Intercontinental Airport, she was thinking about Dennis and Lynn announcing their quickie wedding plans. She wondered just how much crawling and pleading he had to do last night to get Lynn to finally agree to marry him. She would have liked to have been a fly on the wall. She wondered if he'd applied the famous Hammond tittie trick before or after Lynn said yes. It was enough to make her nauseated. Why she let that bother her, she didn't know. They deserved each other and she wasn't really surprised at all that they were engaged. It had only been a matter of time, she thought.

After showing her passport to the immigration official, collecting her luggage, and going through customs, she walked outside to the waiting limo for the ride home. Settling back into the seat, she lit a cigarette and started to laugh out loud. She could see the limo driver's eyes staring at her in the rear view mirror. He probably thought she was nuts or drunk or both, as if she gave a flying fuck what he thought.

Susan leaned her head back against the soft black leather and closed her eyes. She had given her blessing to Dennis and Lynn almost two years ago when she broke up with Dennis and he started "looking after" Lynn. She knew back in college that Dennis was in love with Lynn and had been since he met her.

But Lynn had only had eyes for Reese. It seemed Lynn always got what Lynn wanted. After Reese died, Susan knew it was only a matter of time until Lynn would have Dennis, too, since Dennis's eyes always softened whenever he looked at Lynn, no matter how much he professed to care about her. So, Susan just accepted the inevitable and got on with her own life.

What she needed now was a diversion and she couldn't think of a better place for fun than her regular suite at the Wynn in Las Vegas.

She grabbed her Blackberry and pushed number one on speed dial. After two rings, a man's voice said, "You took your sweet time calling me."

"Never mind that. Vegas is calling my name, and I want you ready to go when I decide when will that be."

Chapter Fifty

When Koral left the restaurant, she couldn't shake the feeling that Dennis and Lynn's wedding plans had happened a little too conveniently. If she didn't know better, she'd think that Dennis was looking for a wife who couldn't be made to testify against her husband. In the event Koral did get a bead on Dennis involving him in Reese Mallory's murder, she'd have to convince Lynn he was guilty. Of course, the new little wife would be standing by her man and couldn't be forced to tell it to the judge.

Koral really needed to find someone who could fill in some blanks on those two. And she knew just the person to call. She got in her Jeep and headed home, making a mental note to call Susan Alden in Houston the next morning. Susan should have all the answers that Koral needed about Dennis and Lynn. As a clinical psychologist, she'd be certain to have picked up on the little hidden places in their histories. And everyone had little hidden places. Especially people in the public eye who were always trying to shield their private lives.

It was late, almost midnight, and a full moon hung over the quiet, smooth water. Koral never zipped on the plastic sides of her Jeep. She loved driving with the wind blowing in her hair and the sense of freedom it gave her. She even liked to leave the Jeep open when it rained, which was almost every afternoon in the summer.

As Koral drove home down West Bay Road, a pair of headlights appeared in her rearview mirror. The car was right on her tail, which irritated her to no end, so she tapped on her brakes to get the idiot to back off. He didn't. She held her speed for a few more minutes then sped up. The car behind her did the same. She began to get an uneasy feeling as she was approaching a curve in the road that had a rocky drop-off into the water on her side of the road. Just as she reached the curve, the car behind her swerved into the opposite lane and pulled alongside. What was wrong with that nut? she thought. She couldn't see the face of the driver, nor could she tell if it was a man or a woman through the dark window glass. The car moved closer to hers until they were almost touching.

Koral floored the accelerator and swerved over to the oncoming lane of traffic. The next thing she knew, she was thrown forward as the car rammed her Jeep, knocking her back into the other lane, and perilously close to the rocks. The car again pulled up even with her, and swerved hard to the left, this time slamming into her Jeep and sending it careening over the grassy shoulder and rocks. It flipped into the water upside down and as it hit, the air bag gave her a punch to the chest, then deflated.

At least the water was only about four feet deep here, she thought, as the water gushed into the Jeep. She pulled her head toward her chest for a gulp of air as she struggled to keep from panicking. God, her collar bone smarted. She was going to have one colorful bruise from her shoulder to between her boobs, but the damn belt had probably saved her life.

After fumbling to release the seat belt for what seemed like hours, she finally got it unbuckled and slid out the side of the Jeep into the water. Something told her she should stay underwater and swim along the bank until it was safe to surface. Holding her breath that long wasn't easy after the jolt to her chest by the airbag. Her lungs burning, she made her way parallel to the shore and climbed up the rocks. Whoever had tried to kill her a second time would be looking for bubbles.

Chapter Fifty-One

The ringing phone roused Aron out of a deep sleep, something he hadn't had in awhile. Whoever was calling better have a damn good reason, he thought angrily.

He grabbed the clock on his night stand. The glowing digital numbers yelled 1:30 A.M. He knocked the phone off the cradle and caught it before it hit the floor.

"Aron? Are you there?" a woman's voice asked.

"Koral, is that you? What the hell is going on? Where are you? Are you all right?" Aron's questions shot at her in rapid succession.

"Yes, I'm getting ready to tell you, at home, and yes," she replied, answering his questions in the order he asked them.

"That isn't funny. Not at 1:30 in the morning," Aron snapped.

"You think that isn't funny? You should try what I've been through tonight on for size. I hate to wake you up for something as trivial as attempted murder, namely mine, but I really need your help to get my Jeep out of the water in the morning so I can track down the son-of-a-bitch who tried to kill me yet again tonight," she informed him, her voice rising steadily with each word.

She had his full attention now, she thought to herself, as she sat on her sofa, wrapped in a quilt, her wet hair dripping. She pulled the quilt tighter and tucked her legs up under her.

"What in God's name happened?" Aron commanded.

"Would you mind coming over here? I would come there, but as I said, my car is being washed upside down in the West Bay. I need to shower and I'm in a really bad mood. My Jeep is probably totaled, and when I catch the bastard who did this, I'll need a really good lawyer, because I may hit a little high when I try to shoot him in the balls," she said, in full pout mode.

There was that language again, Aron thought, but on Koral, it somehow just sounded natural.

Koral felt better after letting off some steam to Aron as she lit a cigarette and blew smoke toward the ceiling. She knew one or the other of them had better catch the creep who ran her off the road before he had another go at her. The asshole might succeed in finishing the job next time.

"I'll be there in thirty minutes," Aron told her. "Turn off your light and don't open the door. In fact, don't even go near it unless you hear my voice."

He knew this had everything to do with the Reese Mallory case. After Jerome's death, and two attempts on Koral's life, it was no longer just another homicide to him. Now it was hitting too close to people he cared a great deal about, and that just wasn't acceptable.

Chapter Fifty-Two

Nothing irritated him more than being bossed around by a woman. But under the circumstances, he couldn't really complain. After all, she was paying his salary. He knew he could probably get a real job and make less money, but this one was so much fun and right up his alley. The perks weren't bad either. The sex was great, and he sure wouldn't be filing any sexual harassment charges against his boss.

He didn't really like Vegas. He much preferred the warm breeze and tropical climate of Grand Cayman. But he knew the program. Susan said jump and he asked how high. So he would meet her in Vegas when she summoned him, in between any other projects she might have for him. They'd rule at the high-rollers VIP private tables, have wild sex, and then get back down to business.

He walked over to the mirror, and stood there admiring his reflection. His skimpy bikini briefs hid little of the muscled and golden tanned body he had worked so hard to develop. His blond hair, worn a little long, curled around his neck, and his deep blue eyes enhanced his strong jaw, prominent brow, and straight nose. He looked like a Calvin Klein model or a Roman statue—only straight. Either description fit him perfectly. He definitely turned heads wherever he went.

She liked the package. Actually, she couldn't get enough of him. They didn't make love or even fuck; they attacked each other. The only thing she asked of him was to do exactly what she told him. Fair exchange, he thought. For now. A steady diet of this would get old pretty quick. But he would enjoy it while it lasted.

He opened his closet door and selected a pair of black Brioni slacks, black Armani jacket, white Armani shirt, and black alligator cowboy boots. He examined each item closely to make sure they looked perfect. The rich Houston socialite had to have the appropriate escort. He always looked the part of a wealthy Texan, even though he was from Los Angeles.

As he selected two more outfits for the trip to Vegas, he thought how far he had come in just a few short years.

He'd grown up in L.A. in a neighborhood that made the nearby ghetto look good. His family's cheap, rundown two-room apartment wasn't fit for human habitation, but it was all they could afford. The cockroaches were as big as the rats that inhabited the smelly confines of the building. During the night when he was asleep on the putrid sofa, he would wake up screaming when he felt them crawling over his face. He cried himself to sleep many nights thinking that no thirteen-year-old boy should have to live like he did.

He made up his mind that as soon as he could, he would run away from that God-forsaken place. He knew that neither his mother nor his father would ever miss him. To them, he was just an inconvenience. His mother was a worn-out waitress, and his old man was an out-of-work career alcoholic who beat both of them every chance he got. One night his father came home drunk and started slapping his mother around pretty bad. After he had given her a couple of black eyes and a broken arm, he decided to turn on the boy.

Not a good move.

After his old man knocked him across the room with a fist to the jaw, he grabbed a dirty butcher knife off the kitchen counter and ran screaming straight at the bastard, the knife in his outstretched hand. He knocked his father backwards into the wall with a sudden burst of strength that seemed to come out of nowhere. He stabbed him in the chest, and kept stabbing him until he slid down the wall to the floor. With his last breath, his old man told him he'd see him in hell.

He stood over his father's body for what seemed like hours until his mother's whimpering sounds drew his attention to her. He ran to the phone and called 911. Then he left the apartment and never looked back.

He took care of himself after that, living on the streets, and hiding in the underground network with thousands of other runaways. When he turned eighteen, he got a job waiting tables at a fancy French restaurant. One night a good-looking woman oozing diamonds and class noticed him and struck up a conversation. Before the night was over, she offered him a job as a houseboy at her Beverly Hills mansion. Overnight, he was in the money and soon in her bed.

Not long after that he began calling his own shots and decided to give acting a try. He played the stud in a few low-budget porno flicks, but he couldn't handle waiting around to be discovered for legit features, so he left California for Houston to try his hand in a different business. Rich women. It didn't take him long to meet new friends by making the rounds of society balls. With his looks, he knew he would draw the big fish, and he knew just where to dangle the bait.

While he was having dinner one night with some of those new friends at Tony's, in walked the irrepressible Dr. Susan Alden. She scanned the room, and when she recognized the men and women at the table with him, she worked her way across, smooth and slow, stopping at each table to blow air kisses to her adoring public. She was clearly the real deal. When she finally reached his table, she immediately held out her hand and announced, "I'm Susan Alden," not waiting for a proper introduction. After several minutes of small talk, she handed him her business card and suggested they get together for a drink the next night. She told him to be at her house at eight sharp. At eight on the dot, he was ringing the bell at her River Oaks mansion expecting a boring evening of drinks and dinner with the old guard of Houston.

What he found was far from it.

She answered the door in a black negligee, so sheer that he could see that her nipples were bright pink, and that she'd waxed all but a tiny tuft of her pubic hair, Brazilian style. Without saying a word, she took his hand and led him up the grand circular staircase to her bedroom. It was pale ivory and twice as big as that whole ratty L.A. apartment where he'd grown up. Ornately-carved crown moldings circled a recessed ceiling boasting a crystal chandelier. The only light in the room came from candles placed on every conceivable surface, emitting a faint orange scent. The canopy bed held satin covered pillows and had folds of honey-colored silk cascading down the posts. Lying across the satin bed covering were two very attractive and very naked men. Susan led him over to the bed and turned to face him. She slowly slipped the negligee from her body and let it fall to the floor. She held out her hand to him, *and he obeyed. Slowly and deliberately, she undressed him, and then stretched out on the bed between the two men. She held out her arms to him and he joined her. She sat up and straddled one of the men, guiding him inside her, the other one waiting his turn.*

If the porno flicks he'd played in had been anything this good, he thought, the company would have made millions instead of tanking. As he watched in fascination, she made eye contact with him and took his hand, guiding him around in front of her on the bed. She took him in her mouth, doing things with her tongue and lips that he never thought possible.

It was easily the most erotic experience of his life, as he and the other two men shared Susan the rest of the night.

The two of them had been together ever since, in one capacity or another.

In more ways than one, theirs was a strange bedfellows relationship. He really thought she invented his job of special assistant just to keep him around. He'd been vague about his personal history, except for his cinematic adventures, but she'd been smart enough to pick up that he'd do pretty near anything if the money was right. He balanced between being a kept man, a boy toy, and a legitimate employee. But hey, who cared. They didn't make their arrangement public. It was nobody's business. He didn't give a fuck what anybody thought. As long as they both enjoyed it, he was useful to her, and she shelled out the bucks, he'd hang around for the duration.

He hated to trade the beautiful surroundings he enjoyed for the noisy melting pot of Vegas. But they were always quick trips, and he could placate her while checking out the crop of young, rich, gorgeous women. Never hurt to have a replacement on standby when this gig ended.

He had to admit he liked walking through the casinos, where the beautiful older woman on his arm drew envious stares from younger, but less classy types. He had to laugh at that one. Hell, she was only thirty-two. But he was twenty-five. Wealthy older women—young ones, too—all wanted a shot at him. Who was he to deny them?

Chapter Fifty-Three

Koral was sitting on her sofa in the dark, still wrapped in her favorite quilt and holding Cheetah in her lap, when the doorbell rang. The little Chihuahua jumped down and ran to the door barking like a banshee. She was going to make quite a watchdog, Koral decided. Too bad she hadn't been there to make a fuss when Julie was killed.

She was still boiling about her Jeep ending up in the water when that maniac ran her off the road, to say nothing about almost being fish food. If she hadn't acted as quickly as she did, she would have been dead, she thought. That made two failed attempts on her life, and she was getting madder by the minute.

Two loud knocks on the door, and a familiar Caymanian voice shouting, "It's me. Aron!" roused her from her thoughts.

Looking every inch like an Indian squaw, Koral leaned over, put her cigarette out in the ashtray on the coffee table, and got up to answer the door.

She put an eye to the peephole and saw Aron staring back at her. She opened the door, picking Cheetah up before the little dog tore his ankles to shreds. It took all Aron had to keep from laughing at the apparition standing in front of him. He covered his mouth and chuckled as she glared at him, her still-wet hair dripping on the quilt.

"If this wasn't so serious, it would be funny," he said, as she trudged back to the sofa, put Cheetah in her lap, and lit another cigarette. Aron wished she would give up that nasty habit, but of course, she wasn't about to do anything until she got good and ready to do it. He had nagged her for years about it, to no avail.

"Please try to contain your concern," she snapped at him. "If things keep going like they have been, cigarettes won't have a chance to kill me."

She leaned back and propped both bare feet up on the coffee table as Aron sat down in the wicker armchair opposite her.

Koral continued her rant. "Some asshole in a silver SUV with tinted windows ran me off at that bad curve on West Bay Road. I couldn't see who it was, but whoever it was didn't want me to make it home. I can't figure out yet who's trying to hide what, but I'm not going to sit here and wait for them to try to kill me again. First thing in the morning, the bereaved Mrs. Mallory and her newly betrothed are going to sit down with me and start telling the truth. Things are trucking along a little fast with those two. I want you to be there in case I take matters into my own hands and shoot both of them."

Aron sat staring at her, waiting to see if she was finished before he offered his opinion.

"Well, say something. Want a beer?" She got up and padded into the kitchen, Cheetah nipping at the quilt dragging on the floor behind her.

"I haven't had a chance to get a word in sideways yet. First of all, are you hurt? You certainly don't sound it, thank the Lord," Aron told her.

"No, just my pride and a lovely bruise from the goddamn seatbelt." She walked back into the living room and handed him a Heineken. "I don't feel like I've made any real progress on this case, but someone thinks I know something, or am about to find out something, that makes me worth killing. Ever since Reese Mallory's remains were found, people have started dying, and I don't want to be next."

Aron winced at her words. He didn't know what he would do if something happened to her. She was like a daughter to him.

"Jerome and Julie were innocent bystanders in this mess, and now they're dead. For what? For nothing," Koral fumed.

"I've known Jerome for most of my life. He was a good man. And Julie was so young, her life just beginning," Aron said sadly. "In a bad year, we have two, maybe three murders in Cayman. It's almost always a jealous husband or wife, usually drunk. Now we've reached our annual quota in two days."

Koral knew how compassionate a man Aron was and she didn't know how he handled a job like his that demanded such mental toughness. He was more prone to apologize for arresting someone for a minor offense than to come down hard on him. Especially if it was a young person who needed guidance more than jail time. However, he could be tough when he needed to be. Like now.

"Why don't you get dry first of all? Then get some rest. Tomorrow we'll go see Mrs. Mallory and Mr. Hammond and start trying to piece this all together. If you want me to camp out on your sofa with my trusty police revolver, I'll be glad to oblige. I would suggest you ask Sam, but as you know, he had to go to Miami for a couple of weeks for some family matters." Aron wasn't crazy about leaving her alone.

Koral shook her head. "I'll be fine. I'm sure the asshole that ran me off the road will wait for his next chance."

Aron got up to leave. Cheetah jumped off the sofa and attacked his pants leg just as Buzzard let out a loud, "Fuck the bastards!"

"Buzzard, shut up! Cheetah, come here!" Koral demanded. "I'm going to have to get a muzzle for that bird and that dog. Can you believe a four-pound dog can be so ferocious?" Koral asked, as she picked the dog up and followed Aron to the door, her quilt still firmly around her shoulders.

As Cheetah licked her cheek, she hugged the little dog tighter, remembering those pitiful dogs she had helped rescue from that puppy mill back in Houston all those years ago. So many of them had been Chihuahuas, and it still saddened her to think of them.

Aron turned around and gave her a quick kiss on the cheek, something he had never done before in all the time they had known each other. It took Koral completely by surprise. Displays of affection weren't in Aron's makeup.

"What was that for?" Koral smiled at him.

Aron looked at Koral, his face a mask of concern. "I love you like my own child. I just wanted you to know that." He turned and was gone.

Still a little in shock, Koral stood there looking after him and vowed to find out what the hell was going on around here. If anything happened to Aron, she would never forgive herself. She would also personally dismantle anyone who tried to harm him. She had lost all the people in her life she loved and who were important to her. Aron had helped to fill a gaping void in her life.

Like an unwelcome visitor, the memory of losing her father, then her mother three months later, ripped through her heart like a machete. It was bad enough watching her father slowly slip into the dark dungeon of Alzheimer's the last five years of his life, but then stage four prostate cancer killed him three days after it was diagnosed. Koral had barely pulled herself together after she and her mother buried her dad when her mother fell five days after his funeral and broke her hip.

The woman the doctors gave back to her after the thirty minute hip surgery was not her perfectly healthy, independent and feisty mother. Something had gone terribly wrong in the operating room and the virtual vegetable that emerged from surgery was not her mother. They said it was a lack of oxygen to her brain that caused brain damage, thanks to the negligence of the doctors who operated on her.

Three months later, her mother was gone.

It had been agonizing watching her mother's downward spiral to a horrible death. Koral didn't think she would survive the horrific loss of her parents. She had at least been able to prepare herself to lose her father over the last five years, but she could not ever have imagined the fate that awaited her mother. She somehow kept her untethered rage in check as she put complaint filings in motion with the Texas Medical Board and vowed to make the two doctors pay for what they did to her mother by losing their licenses. She also hoped they would drop dead.

Just because her mother was old and unimportant to them, those sorry excuses for doctors played fast and loose with her life and did a rush job in surgery because they couldn't be bothered and were in a hurry to leave town on vacation. They had no idea of the sorrow and heartache they left in their wake by causing her mother's death, nor did they care.

She was going to make them wish they had.

The lawyers told her it could take years for her lawsuit to come to trial, if ever, but she would wait. And she would win. She wanted them to know they were going to be held accountable one way or another.

If she thought she could get away with killing them herself, she would have done it in a heartbeat. But she knew her mother wouldn't have approved of that at all. That's just the way she was…a wonderful, kind and caring person who should still be on this earth. There wasn't a minute of the day she didn't miss her mother and physically hurt at the unfairness of it all.

She owed her mother some justice and she would wait as long as it took.

Just like she would wait for the man who tried to kill her to make his next move.

Chapter Fifty-Four

As Aron and Koral drove along the road into George Town at 9:30 the next morning, they approached the curve where Koral's Jeep lay upside down in the clear turquoise water. The tow truck and crane operator that Aron called were already at work righting it, and pulling it to shore.

"They'll take it to Thompson's Garage and get it back in driving condition within a week or so," Aron told her. "Looks like you'll need a new Jeep. In the meantime, I rented you another one and I'll drop you off to pick it up after we see Mrs. Mallory."

Koral looked at Aron incredulously. "I can't believe you did that for me," she told him. "I could have done that. You didn't need to do it.

"I wanted to. Indulge an old man." He grinned at her.

They pulled up in front of the Ritz-Carlton and left the police car with the valet. They went into the opulent lobby that screamed, "I'm rich," and told the concierge they were there to see Lynn Mallory. He told them to go right up, that she was expecting them, and directed them to the penthouse elevator.

When the elevator opened into the great room of the penthouse, Lynn was standing there to greet them. She was wearing a short green sheath and sandals with her hair tied back in a ponytail looking like a poster child for "Lifestyles of the Rich and

Famous." She looked stunning. She also looked about sixteen. Koral decided she could learn to hate her.

"Please come in," she said, leading the way into the living room where Dennis stood waiting for them.

Dennis walked toward them and said, "And to what do we owe the pleasure of your company this morning, Miss Sanders and Chief Ebanks?" The smirk on his face was just the fuel Koral needed to let him have it.

"Good morning to you, too, Mr. Hammond," Koral replied tersely. "We are going to start at the beginning of this three-penny opera, and we aren't stopping until Chief Ebanks and I are completely satisfied that you have told us everything you know related to Reese Mallory's murder. How's that sound to you?" she snipped.

Lynn stepped between them and said, "Please, Koral, Chief Ebanks, sit down and we'll tell you everything we know. There's no need to get hostile, Dennis," Lynn warned him. "We're all trying to get to the same conclusion here, which is, who killed Reese and Mr. Johnson."

"Don't forget my neighbor, Julie," Koral told her.

"I'm sorry, who?" Lynn asked. She really seemed not to know about Julie's murder, Koral thought.

"My neighbor, Julie Menotti, was shot and killed in my living room last night. The killer thought she was me. Someone also ran me off the road last night. Luckily, I survived. My Jeep didn't. They're pulling it out of the water as we speak."

"My God, Koral." Lynn's face registered complete shock and surprise.

"Did you see who it was?" Dennis was either a very good actor, or he seemed genuinely concerned that someone tried to kill her.

"No, I couldn't see the driver's face. The SUV had tinted glass. But he, or she, won't be so lucky next time. In the past two days, we discovered that Reese's death was not an accident, someone shot Jerome Johnson and Julie, and someone tried to kill me not once, but twice. That all tends to piss me off just a tad. It also seems funny to me that no one has made a move on you two during all this. I wonder why that is? I also wonder if you,

Mr. Hammond, didn't think it would look a little strange that right after Mr. Mallory died, you moved in on Mrs. Mallory?"

Koral couldn't wait for him to take this bait.

"That's absurd," Dennis bristled. "Reese was my best friend, and I have known both Lynn and Reese since we were kids. What was I supposed to do? Stand by and do nothing to help Lynn?" he continued.

Dennis walked over to Lynn, stopping behind her chair and putting his hands protectively on her shoulders.

"Where did that leave Dr. Alden? Weren't you two a couple?" Koral continued.

"We saw each other, but it was never serious. She understood when I explained to her that I was going to have to spend a lot of time with Lynn to help her get through the trauma of losing Reese. We mutually agreed that it was probably best if we just broke it off and remained friends and she agreed. Susan is a big girl. She can take care of herself. She has her own money and a great practice, and no shortage of men in her life," Dennis explained.

It seemed to Koral that Dennis was trying to convince himself more than her.

"So there were no hard feelings at all?"

"Obviously not. I mean, she was just here with us. As you know, she went back to Houston yesterday."

"Right. And now you and Mrs. Mallory are getting married. That's very nice. And quick. I wish you all the best," Koral smiled sweetly.

Dennis glared at her as he kept his hands on Lynn's shoulders.

"If you call finally accepting my eighth proposal quick, then it was quick," Dennis snapped.

Lynn had been quiet, looking out the window, seeming to ignore the heated exchange between Koral and Dennis.

Suddenly, she said, "Chief Ebanks, the other day I asked you if the items I viewed that were found with Reese were all that were recovered, and you said they were. I know his wedding ring was still on his finger, probably because of that broken knuckle, but are you sure they didn't find a gold *ankh* on a chain?" The concerned expression on her face looked genuine.

"No, we didn't. Are you certain Mr. Mallory was wearing it that day?" Aron asked her.

"Yes. As I said when I came down to identify his effects, he wore it all the time. I saw it around his neck when he went into the water that day." She paused and swallowed, lowering her eyes. "I gave it to him the Christmas we announced our engagement. He never took it off."

"I'm sorry, it wasn't found with him," Aron told her.

"Just thought I'd ask again to make sure."

Lynn got up and started toward the bar. "I don't know where my manners are. Could I offer you a drink?" she asked.

"Nothing for me, thank you," Aron replied.

"Not for me either," Koral said.

Lynn went behind the bar and filled two glasses with Chardonnay, knowing Dennis would want one. She walked back into the living room and handed him the glass as she sat down next to him. Probably very expensive wine, Koral thought. They don't do anything cheap around here.

Sounding very official, Koral continued. "Mrs. Mallory, I still need to hear your version of what happened the day your husband died."

Lynn couldn't believe she was going to have to reconstruct that day all over again. Hadn't she done it enough times already? "Koral, I've told this story to every official on this island, and in Houston. Why do we have to do it all over again?" she pleaded.

"Because I want you to. And I'm sure Aron won't mind hearing it again. I'm the only one who hasn't heard the whole story from you in person. So, whenever you're ready." Koral sat back on the sofa and crossed her arms, looking directly at Lynn, her piercing eyes shooting bullets straight through her uneasy target.

Lynn could feel her temper starting to rise, but she knew that would serve no purpose at all. This woman was a thorn in her side, and the sooner she got rid of her, the better. She reached over and squeezed Dennis' hand for support.

She began. "We were all here for a scuba diving weekend. Sid Andrews and Tabby Kirk, Dennis and Susan, and Reese and me. We were going to dive the North Wall that day and had reserved Dive Cayman One. We didn't take our Cigarette boat because we knew the dive boat would be more practical since we all wanted to dive together and not have to worry about the boat."

Of course, you know now that Reese had rented a boat slip at Mr. Johnson's marina to house our boat. I wasn't trying to hide that fact, Koral. It never had any bearing on the case and it just never occurred to me to mention it."

Anyway, the dive boat picked us up at the Ritz-Carlton, and we went out to the Wall. I know James Ebanks said he saw a white boat like ours out there that day, but I didn't notice it. We were all underwater and all together, until we came up. Then Reese wasn't with us. I was coming up ahead of him and thought he was right beneath me. Dennis and Sid and Captain Ebanks' nephew went back down, but they couldn't find him. That's when Captain Ebanks radioed the police and we came back here. That's all. That's the whole story. I don't know what else I can tell you."

Lynn let out a sigh, hoping that would be the end of it.

"So everyone, your entire little group, was on the dive boat when Dennis and Sid went back down to look for Reese?" Koral asked her.

"Yes. Well, everyone who went out there with us."

"Meaning what exactly?"

"Susan didn't go. She wasn't feeling well that day. She woke up with a bug and was sick to her stomach. Not a good idea to scuba dive when you're throwing up. It could be a fatal mistake."

Yes, it certainly could, Koral thought.

Chapter Fifty-Five

It was three days off, but Susan could already see herself in Vegas. Blackjack didn't treat her well most of the time, and she usually lost her ass playing high stakes baccarat. Her luck would start out great then turn to shit. Trying to recoup her losses always put her in a bad mood, which was definitely an understatement.

But the thrill of placing ten thousand dollar bets at the high-roller tables, and the rush she felt when she was winning—nothing could match that, not even the great sex with her valued employee and escort. Of course, there would always be streaks, sometimes hours long, when she was ahead. When those came to an end, as they invariably did, and she was down a hundred grand or more, she only wanted to see Vegas in her rear-view mirror. But it only took a couple of weeks until she started to feel that old familiar pull again. The compulsion was so strong she sometimes suspected she was addicted.

Alcoholics had booze, drug addicts had cocaine, and she had Vegas. To her, the high was all the same, only hers wasn't life-threatening, not even really self-destructive, she told herself. Unless that is, she couldn't cover her markers. Then she would have to start worrying.

She hadn't been home more than an hour when her phone rang. She had just settled down in a luxurious bubble bath surrounded by lavender candles, and was sipping her favorite

Chardonnay. She reached for the phone and pushed the speaker button.

"Hello," she said breathlessly, feeling the effects of the wine and the warm water caressing her skin.

"Susan, it's Lynn. I've been trying to reach you all day," she said. There was an edgy tone to her voice.

God, Susan thought, couldn't Lynn leave her alone for just one day? Talk about dependency issues!

"Lynn, I just got home and I'm really tired and I don't want to talk right now. Can I call you back later?" Susan asked, her feeling of relaxation slipping away. However, something in Lynn's voice told her she'd better not put her off.

"What's going on?" Susan sighed.

"We're still in Grand Cayman and I may have really messed up."

Susan just hated it when Lynn started off conversations like that. She was such a fucking drama queen.

"What's wrong now? Did you call off the big wedding?" she joked.

"No, we're still getting married, but Koral Sanders and Chief Ebanks paid us a little visit today," she explained.

Susan sat straight up in the bathtub, her full attention focused on what Lynn was saying and on the sinking feeling in her stomach.

"Not again. What did they want this time?" she asked, nervously twirling the stem of her wine glass.

"They wanted me to tell them, yet again, the entire story about the day Reese disappeared."

"So, did you?"

"Yes, but when I finished, Koral asked me about the people who were on the dive boat when Dennis and Sid went back down to look for Reese."

"And what did you tell them?" Shit, couldn't the girl put two sentences together and finish a story without a teleprompter? Susan rolled her eyes toward the ceiling, exasperation completely taking over.

"I told them about that trailer trash queen, and I told them everyone in our group was there except you because you weren't feeling well. They asked what had been the matter with you and I told them you had a stomach bug, that you seemed much better when we got back to the penthouse that evening."

Despite the warm bath water, Susan felt goose bumps spring up all over her body.

"Why the hell did you tell them that?" she yelled at Lynn, jumping up out of the tub, and grabbing a towel. She paced the bathroom floor, naked, dripping water everywhere, but who the hell cared.

"Now, they'll think I might have had something to do with Reese's death since I wasn't on the goddamn boat. This is just great. I was sick in bed, but you can bet they'll turn this thing around and before you know it, they'll accuse me of Reese's murder, for God's sake."

Susan was screaming now.

"Susan, I'm so sorry. It just came out before I could think. Surely they wouldn't think you had anything to do with Reese's death. That's just crazy," Lynn told her. "I told them you stayed home in bed all day."

"That's just it, Lynn. You never think," Susan seethed. Jesus, the little energy vampire probably thinks she shits confetti, Susan thought.

"My God, what a mess. I'll be on the next flight out of here. Hell, all I've done lately is run back and forth to Cayman to babysit you and your numb nuts fiancé. I do have a life here, you know, and a practice to run. I've got to get there and straighten this out before they send the whole Caymanian police force after me. I've just about had enough of that goddamn Sanders bitch and her nosy questions, so maybe if I give them a statement, they'll just go away. You and Dennis stay put and keep your big mouths shut for once."

Chapter Fifty-Six

The news that Susan Alden had not been on the dive boat the day Reese Mallory disappeared was music to Koral's ears. This was the first time that anyone in the Mallory party had mentioned that she'd been booked for the boat and had backed out that morning. How that bit of information had slipped through the cracks during the investigation was beyond her. It was going to be interesting to hear Susan's explanation of why she didn't come forward during the initial investigation at the time of Reese's disappearance. Maybe it had just slipped her mind, but Koral didn't think so.

Koral knew Susan had gone back to Houston, so she had to figure out how she was going to handle confronting her with this newfound information. That little tidbit, and the fingerprint belonging to Ray Durbin that was found on the file label, were all the leads she and Aron had to go on, and she was going to make the most of them.

Koral was sure that Lynn had called Susan the minute she and Aron were out of the penthouse to tell her she'd let the cat out of the bag. Now it was time for Koral to make her own little call. She had gotten Susan's cell phone number from Lynn that first day at police headquarters and was dialing it as she and Aron got in their car.

Susan's phone rang five times before voice mail picked up. Koral guessed that Lynn was still talking to Susan and relaying their conversation to her. Either that or Susan saw that it was Koral calling her and didn't answer. Koral was pretty sure Susan was doing back flips about now after hearing that Lynn gave up her little secret. But if she had nothing to hide and could cough up a witness or two who saw her at the penthouse that day, all would be well in paradise. But if not, she'd better start seeing how she might look in stripes.

When Susan's phone beeped to leave a message, Koral said, "Dr. Alden, this is Koral Sanders in Grand Cayman. Please call me when you get this message. We need to talk." Then she left her number.

Koral ended the call and looked at Aron. "What do you think?" she asked him.

"I think she's got to be hiding something. I also think if we find Ray Durbin, we can connect a lot of dots. I just have a gut feeling about all this," Aron told her. "I can't see a lowlife like Durbin having his own motive to kill Reese Mallory."

"I agree," Koral said. "There's something about that woman that hit me wrong the minute I laid eyes on her. You know how you don't like someone before they even open their mouth? Their body language just sends up red flags."

"Yeah, I know what you mean." Aron also knew Koral's intuition had a habit of almost always being spot on.

Chapter Fifty-Seven

Captain Ebanks was just topping off the last of ten tanks for the afternoon dive when he heard the bell above the shop door jingle. He walked into the sales area to see a white man with short bleached yellow hair and bad teeth. He looked more like a commercial diver than a recreational diver—a commercial diver who didn't work regularly.

"May I help you?" Captain Ebanks asked.

"I hope so," the man said with an East Texas accent. "I'm looking for James Ebanks."

"And may I ask why?"

"I owe him some money, five hundred dollars, and I want to pay him back.

The back of Captain Ebanks' neck tingled. There was no way James would have five hundred dollars, let alone that much to loan, and to someone who looked like this man looked. Red flags were shooting up all around this guy and Captain Ebanks knew he had to respond carefully to make sure he didn't tip the man off. He also had to avoid being killed himself.

"He's off the island at the moment, but if you'll give me your address and phone number, I'm sure he'll get in touch when he returns," Captain Ebanks told the stranger.

Keeping his best poker face, the captain turned to get a scratch pad and pen. Before he could turn back, the bell jingled again.

When he looked around, there was no sign of the man. The scruffy little bastard had disappeared.

With a shaking hand, Captain Ebanks reached for the phone to call the police.

Chapter Fifty-Eight

Aron dropped Koral off to pick up the rental Jeep on his way back to his office. She still couldn't believe Aron had taken care of getting her a car while hers was being repaired. That was such a sweet thing for him to do, and very unexpected.

Waving goodbye as he drove away, she walked inside the car rental office. After signing the papers, she went outside to the waiting Jeep and threw her purse in the passenger seat. This would do for a couple of weeks, she thought, as she pulled out onto the road and headed for home. It felt good to feel the wind in her face again.

She was still waiting for Susan Alden to return her call, so she decided to run by her condo to check on Cheetah and Buzzard. She was just turning into the parking lot of the Sundowner when her phone rang.

"Hello."

"Koral, it's Aron. I've got some disturbing news. A strange-looking man just showed up at the Dive Cayman Dive Shop asking for James Ebanks. Said he owed James some money and wanted to repay it. When Captain Ebanks told him the boy was off the island and asked for the man's address, he disappeared."

"Jesus Christ! I'll meet you there." Koral beat the steering wheel with both hands, and screamed out loud. What if James had been there?

Koral calmed herself down as she drove to the Dive Cayman shop. In less than a week, this peaceful island had turned as dangerous as drug-infested Ciudad Juarez. All because a killer was trying to cover his, or her, tracks. Koral felt like she was very close to finding the common thread connecting all the recent murders, and attempted murders, but the answer was still hiding behind a foggy cloud in her mind. Think, she said to herself, starting at the beginning of this whole bizarre mess.

After Reese Mallory's remains were found, the killer must have thought that the police would check on the white boat the Mallorys owned, so the killer high-tailed it to Jerome Johnson's marina to steal the file with the boat information in it. This could only mean that the Mallory boat was the one out on the Wall that day and that Jerome could identify who took the boat out. It was Jerome's bad luck to be in his office when the killer came calling. Otherwise, the killer might have just stolen the file and Jerome would still be alive, especially since Lynn Mallory had sold the white boat after Reese died.

Unless there was another reason for Ray Durbin to have touched that file, he was the actual killer. But Koral's gut told her that he wasn't the one they really wanted. He had no connection with the Mallorys or, apparently, with any of their group. He didn't look like they'd even hire him to clean the pool. So what was his motive? Money? Durbin was a small-time shit-for-brains crook with no aspirations beyond succeeding as a hired scuzzball. Someone had to be paying him, someone high up the ladder.

If Durbin had been hired, there was at least one very interested, very guilty person involved. One who had the ways and means to stay invisible.

Koral didn't want to make the mistake of assuming too quickly that Durbin had wrecked her Jeep and shot Julie, but from the description Captain Ebanks had given to Aron, it sounded like he'd been the one who'd come looking for James.

Durbin hadn't counted on the file label falling off and especially hadn't counted on a fingerprint being found on it. Of course, Durbin couldn't have known about the fingerprint since the police had not made that fact public. Unless someone involved in the investigation had told him.

What was made public was the fact that Koral was working with Aron on the case. The police hadn't come forward with the name of the witness who saw the murder of Reese Mallory, but they'd mentioned that they had one, and the famous Cayman rumor mill had done the rest. Of course, it hadn't helped that James Ebanks had run his mouth off after his interview with Aron and Koral.

When the killer came after her to make sure she was off the case permanently, he, or she, shot Julie by mistake. The big surprise in the middle of all this was Dennis and Lynn announcing their engagement right after the two murders. It could just be a coincidence, but it was still very peculiar.

It seemed to Koral they could be celebrating their success at getting away with all the murders, including Reese Mallory's. Or at least Dennis was. However, she didn't think they would be stupid enough as to draw unwanted attention to themselves with a quickie wedding.

When she was run off the road, she knew Susan Alden was back in Houston, so it couldn't have been her driving the SUV. It could have been Dennis, but she didn't think so. Lynn didn't strike her as a ballsy enough driver. Ray Durbin seemed more likely. Koral needed to find him and get him to talk. He held the answers to this whole sordid mess, she was sure of it.

Koral also realized that her own life was still very much in danger until she found Durbin. The only snag was that she didn't know which rock to look under to find the little insect before he found her.

Chapter Fifty-Nine

Ray Durbin and Jeanette Ryker sat in an out-of-the-way bar on the east end of the island downing margaritas like water. They had been celebrating Ray's success at getting rid of that Sanders bitch once and for all.

"I know I nailed the bitch this time," Ray bragged to Jeanette. "That ragtop Jeep flipped right over and sank in the Car-ib-be-an," he drawled, accenting each syllable.

"Well, it's about damn time, Ray. I can't wait for us to get away from this dump. I hate it here, and I never want to come back. People look at us like we're dirt under their feet. Just wait until we get that money. They won't look down on us anymore," she hissed.

Don't worry, sweetheart, Ray thought to himself smugly. You ain't ever going anywhere else with me once I get my hands on that money. Even a million bucks couldn't clean you up good enough to take out in public.

All they were waiting for to leave Cayman was for Cowboy to pay Ray what he owed him. He'd told them he'd be in touch with them, but so far they hadn't heard from him.

They had been holed up for too long next door to the bar in the ramshackle house that Cowboy had rented for them. He'd wanted to make sure no one from the other side of the island saw either of them. As Ray looked around the bar with its dingy walls and concrete floor, he couldn't wait to start his new life as a rich man.

He watched as the bartender shooed a chicken out of the open doorway. Hell, there wasn't even any glass on the windows. Flies buzzed around his head as he waved his hand over his salt-rimmed glass to keep them away. No more of this shit for me, he thought. From now on, it's classy broads and hotel suites. If he needed a good-looking woman, he'd rent one. He didn't need one hanging around all the time spending his new-found wealth.

"Ray, tell me again what we're going to do when we leave this shithole. I just love to hear you tell it. I can't wait to buy a whole new wardrobe, and become a blonde again," Jeanette gushed, as she downed the last of her fourth or fifth margarita. He'd lost count. God, he was tired of her cackling like a goddamn guinea on steroids.

Ray winced and said, "Yeah, baby, we're going to be rollin' in the dough pretty soon. Then we're gettin' the hell out of this place and never lookin' back." He swallowed the last gulp of his drink.

"Hey bartender, when you can tear yourself away from the chickens, we need another round here," Ray grinned at him.

The bartender, a weather-worn, ponytailed refugee from the upper Midwest, finally ushered the offending chicken out the door, and walked around the bar to accommodate Ray's request.

"Where're you from, man?" the bartender asked casually, as he mixed their drinks.

"What's it to ya?" Ray scowled at him.

"No reason. Just making conversation," the bartender told him, setting the two margaritas with little pink umbrellas in them on the bar.

Ray wiped the back of his hand across his mouth. "Well, we sure as hell ain't going back to the same place we came from." Ray held up his glass to Jeanette in a toast. "No, siree. We're movin' on up, as they say." He laughed and clinked glasses with Jeanette.

"We'll be rubbin' elbows with the rich crowd from now on. Hell, one of those hotsy-totsy rich assholes from Houston must really have a hard-on for some people on this island. They even paid me a bundle to get rid of some of them. Which I did to their satisfaction, yet again. Now, I'm just waitin' fer payday, yet again," Ray slurred, letting out a loud burp.

The bartender studied the two of them, hoping they would leave soon. He needed to make a phone call, and he couldn't do it as long as they were hanging around. From the sound of things, this loud-mouthed bastard would just as soon shoot him as look at him. If the little sleazoid heard who he was calling, there was no doubt in his mind he wouldn't hesitate to kill him.

As if reading the bartender's mind, Ray yelled at Jeanette. "Come on, baby, let's blow this joint. We've got things to do, like get our passports in order, if we can figure out which ones to use." Ray laughed at his weak attempt at humor, showing his crooked yellow teeth in all their glory. He shoved the two empty glasses toward the bartender and jumped to the floor.

Jeanette didn't move as fast as Ray wanted her to, so he yanked her off her bar stool and dragged her toward the door. They were doing a less than perfect job of holding each other up as they finally made it out of the bar and disappeared down the sidewalk.

The bartender reached for his phone and quickly dialed a number.

A woman's voice answered. "Koral Sanders."

Chapter Sixty

"Hey, Koral. It's Charles."

"Hi, Charles. What's up?"

Koral had known Charles King since she first came to the island. He had been a cab driver back then, until he bought the most rundown bar on the East End. He'd given Koral a ride from the airport the day she arrived in Cayman, and they had struck up a friendship. He showed her around the island and introduced her to his friends. More than once, Charles and his friends had been very helpful in nabbing an occasional felon, since everyone knew just about everyone else on Cayman, and the bad guys had the misguided idea that they could disappear on the East End because it was so laid-back and rural.

"A man and a woman just left here after spending the better part of the afternoon drinking margaritas," Charles told her. "It might have been the liquor talking, but he was spouting off about some rich person from Houston paying him big bucks to kill people."

Koral almost dropped the phone. She couldn't believe she might finally be getting a break in this case. "You have my undivided attention, my friend. Go on."

"After those divers found what was left of that Houston lawyer, then Jerome and your neighbor got killed, it just seems to me this is more than a coincidence. I also heard about your accident the other night," Charles told her.

"That was no accident the other night," Koral said. "Whoever it was just wanted to finish the job he screwed up the first time when he shot Julie thinking she was me. More than likely, he's also the person who came by Dive Cayman looking for James Ebanks with some crazy story about wanting to pay back some money. James barely had twenty bucks, let alone five hundred to loan a stranger."

"James is a good kid," Charles said. "Is he okay?"

"His uncle got him off the island right after Jerome was shot. Even I don't know where he is."

"If this guy is the one who's going around popping people, I hope you hang him up by his dick," Charles said. "I've seen this jerk around the past couple of days, and it's been bothering me, like I've seen him somewhere before. He and his trashy girlfriend have been staying in a little house that old man Wilson owns nearby. They pay rent by the day. Doesn't sound like they're planning on staying here long, so maybe you'd better pay them a visit pretty soon," Charles told her. Actually, nothing would please Charles more than to see the rude son-of-a-bitch behind bars.

"Shit!" Charles exclaimed, slapping his hand down on the bar. "I just now remembered where I've seen this guy before. His hair was a different color, and he had a goatee, but it's the same guy. I don't forget a face, especially one as ugly as his. It was a couple of years ago at Jerome's marina. I was getting ready to go out fishing with my cousin Ralph, and this guy was taking a big white Cigarette boat out with a good-looking couple on it. The reason I remember him was that I was wondering how such a classy-looking couple would be with someone who looked like him."

Koral's heart did a little dance when she heard his words. "Charles, are you sure?" She couldn't believe what she was hearing.

"Oh, yeah. I'm sure. That was him. You don't forget a sleazy asshole like him."

"Charles, I love you!" Koral squealed. "Be there soon."

It was getting late, and Koral knew she had to find Aron to tell him what she had learned about Durbin. She also needed to tell him they had to get out to the East Side Bar soon, or the guy could disappear. People who did odd jobs for people with big money had a way of slipping away unnoticed, never to be seen again. Like that trashy girl on the Mallory's diving trip who just disappeared into thin air.

She reached in her purse and made sure her .38 was handy. She also checked out the mug shot of Ray Durbin, and the photo of Susan Alden, and Dennis Hammond with the Mallorys that she'd borrowed from Lynn Mallory.

Best to be prepared, she thought. But who was the male eye-candy? All the men in the Mallory group had been on the dive boat.

Koral knew Aron would be at the dive shop, having Captain Ebanks look through mug shots, so she called his cell phone. It went to voice mail, so she left him a message and told him it was urgent that he meet her at Charles' bar as soon as he could, that she would explain everything when he got there.

At first she thought she should call Sam and ask him to meet her because she thought she might be getting into a dangerous situation with Durbin. Then she remembered he wasn't back from Miami yet. Just as well, she thought. The fewer people around, the better. She didn't want to give Durbin any more chances to harm her friends. She checked her gun again, closed her purse, and headed the Jeep east.

The one puzzling question rumbling around in her mind was who that good-looking couple on the boat with that weasel Durbin could have been.

Chapter Sixty-One

After Lynn picked Susan up at the airport, they drove straight to the penthouse. Susan had calmed down on the outside, but inside she was still furious about Lynn telling that Sanders woman that she had not been on the dive boat. Susan had gotten Koral's message on her cell phone and knew she had to call her sooner or later, but she wanted to have a little "come to Jesus" meeting with Lynn before she did.

The elevator door opened into the great room of the penthouse, and Lynn and Susan walked inside. No matter how many times Susan had seen it or how stressed out she was, she always found the view of the sea from the room breathtaking. It calmed her and helped her to collect her wits for the storm that Koral Sanders was blowing her way.

Susan told Lynn, "I'm going to go unpack and get out of these clothes. Then, you and I are going to sit down and straighten this mess out." She started toward the bedroom and said, "Shit. I forgot to buy cigarettes at the duty-free. I'm going downstairs for a couple of packs."

"I'll call and have room service bring them up," Lynn offered.

"No, that will take too long. I'll run down and get them." Susan put her suitcase down by the bedroom door, hurried into the elevator and said, "Be right back."

Lynn turned as the elevator door closed, and stood staring out the window watching the sun slowly slip below the horizon.

She just wished all this crap would go away and things would be back to normal again. She hated it when Susan was mad at her, and she certainly didn't want to cause a rift in their friendship. She'd dodged that bullet when Dennis and Susan broke up so Dennis would be free to spend time with her after Reese died, and she certainly didn't want to make any waves now.

What she couldn't understand was why Susan was so furious just because she had told Koral Sanders that Susan hadn't been with them on the dive trip that day. What was the big deal about that? she wondered. Susan hadn't been feeling well and wanted to take it easy. Diving when you were nauseated was dangerous. It wasn't as if she was trying to hide anything, Lynn thought.

She turned from the window and noticed Susan's luggage sitting by the elevator door. She decided to do Susan a favor and unpack for her, and then they could relax on the balcony, and talk all this out. Dennis had obviously gone out for some reason or another without leaving a note.

Lynn picked up the Louis Vuitton roll-aboard and took it into the blue guest bedroom. She put it down on the bed and unzipped it, then carefully removed the five colorful casual dresses one at a time. She shook out the wrinkles and laid each one on the bed. One thing was certain, she thought, as she noticed that two of the designer dresses still had the price tags on them. Labels like Valentino, Oscar de la Renta, Giorgio Armani, Roberto Cavalli, and Marchesa were proof that Susan didn't mind dropping big bucks on beautiful clothes.

As Lynn picked up a long black silk La Perla robe, a bent and smeared file folder hidden in the robe fell to the floor. Lynn bent down to retrieve it and had started to put it on the bed when she noticed a small envelope sticking out the bottom. She opened the folder to put the envelope back in it.

Then she saw Reese's name on a piece of paper in the folder. Removing the envelope to look at the paper, she saw that it was the boat slip agreement from Jerome Johnson's marina. Reese's signature was on the bottom.

Lynn felt her head spinning as she realized what she was holding, but what in the world was Susan doing with this folder? This was supposedly stolen when Jerome Johnson was murdered.

She turned her attention to the small white envelope, and with shaking fingers, opened it and emptied the contents into her palm.

A gold *ankh* and broken chain fell into her hand.

Reese's *ankh*. The one that he was wearing when he disappeared.

Chapter Sixty-Two

Ray and Jeanette were busy packing their Walmart luggage in the bedroom of the run-down house they were renting when a loud sound came from the front of the house. They stopped what they were doing and stared at each other for a few seconds. Putting his finger to his lips, Ray dropped the clothes he was holding into his suitcase and stumbled into the small living room, still feeling the effects of a few too many margaritas that afternoon at the East Side Bar.

He stopped dead in his tracks when he saw the figure standing in the doorway.

Cowboy was in his usual suit, tie, boots and hat. Didn't he ever relax? Ray wondered, through his drunken haze. Cowboy's familiar murderous scowl covered his face. The front door was in splinters where he had kicked it open.

"What the hell's wrong with you, man?" Ray yelled at him, waving his arms around. "Can't you knock like other people?"

Jeanette peeped out of the bedroom door and tiptoed into the living room. She took one look at Cowboy and ran to hide behind Ray, grabbing him around the waist, and whimpering like a puppy.

"Get off me bitch," Ray screamed, pushing her back against the wall.

"Shut up, you little snake," Cowboy warned through clenched teeth. "How many more times are you going to fuck up? I've given you chance after chance and you just can't get the job done."

"I don't know what you're talkin' about, man. I did everything you told me to do," Ray screeched, sweat beginning to pop out all over his face. "That loud-mouthed kid who was on the dive boat left the island, but that wasn't my fault."

"If you're doing such a near-perfect job, then why is that Sanders bitch still running around breathing?" Cowboy glared at Ray as he began to pace the floor slowly, back and forth, between them and the door, while Jeanette continued to claw at Ray for protection.

"She's not! I ran her off the road and saw her car fly into the water, upside down, with my own two eyes. I waited, and there were no bubbles. She didn't come up. She drowned, man! The bitch is dead!" Ray felt like he was going to pee in his pants. Cowboy wasn't someone he wanted to fuck with, and he knew for a fact Cowboy wasn't here to have afternoon tea. Much to Ray's dismay, Cowboy was obviously not there to give him his $100,000, either. This was not working out well at all, Ray thought dismally.

"News flash, dick brain. She must have grown gills because she sure ain't dead. Did it ever occur to you to double-check when you do a job? Matter of fact, she's hot on your trail. Which brings me to the main reason for my visit. We can't have you flapping your mouth about me or my employer, can we now?"

Cowboy almost laughed out loud at the look of stark terror on Ray's face which had drained of all color. He let out an exaggerated sigh and reached inside his jacket, pulling out the biggest 9 mm Glock semi-automatic that Ray and Jeanette had ever seen. Then he pulled a silencer out of his opposite inside pocket and began to screw it on the gun.

Jeanette screamed when she realized what was about to happen, and backed up against the wall, pulling Ray back with her.

"You know, Ray, you really lost your edge these past couple of years. You used to be good at what you did, but you've gotten careless. The way you handled the Reese Mallory deal was pure poetry, but now you've lost your touch. Gotten sloppy. Not a good thing in our business," Cowboy grinned, as he finished locking the silencer in place on the gun.

"Come on, man, what the hell are you doing?" Ray cowered against Jeanette, covering his face with his arms, and trying his best to get behind her.

She was having none of that as she pushed him away, and tried to run for the splintered front door, her ample bosom bouncing up and down, causing her spider and web tattoos to engage in a macabre dance.

Whoever said a moving target was hard to hit had never met Cowboy. He whirled around, aimed, and fired two quick shots, hitting Jeanette square in the back of her head before she hit the floor.

Ray looked on in horror as Jeanette fell flat on her face to the floor, a pool of blood forming around her boot-polish-black hair. He let out a little yelp as Cowboy turned back to face him, waving the big gun in front of him.

"You want to make a run for it, too, you little fucker?" Cowboy smiled.

"No, no, please. Don't. Just give me another chance, and I'll do it right this time. I promise," Ray cried. "I'll make sure she's dead this time. I will. You'll see," he pleaded.

"No can do, friend. You had your chances. I wish I hated this part of my job. But I don't. Bye now."

Before Ray could duck, Cowboy raised the gun, pointed it at his head, and fired two quick shots, one hitting above each of Ray's bloodshot eyes. Ray slammed back into the wall, and slid down it, a trail of blood and brains following his body to the floor.

Standing over the two dead bodies, Cowboy shook his head and laughed. "If you want something done right...."

Chapter Sixty-Three

Dusk had settled on the horizon by the time Koral got to the East Side Bar. She parked the Jeep, jumped out, and hurried inside.

Charles really needed to get this place fixed up, she thought. He had the money, she knew, so what was he waiting for? It was a mess. She had to shoo a couple of chickens off the walkway just to get inside the door. The chickens definitely had to go. Even though she had nothing against chickens, they certainly weren't an attractive accessory, and they definitely didn't make for a very inviting place to sit and have a drink.

Charles was behind the bar arranging bottles of various brands of liquor when Koral stepped inside. She jumped up on a barstool after giving it a couple of quick swipes with her hand. Couldn't be too careful with all those chickens running around, she thought.

"Hi," she said breathlessly, as Charles leaned on the bar and put a couple of Black Jack on the rocks down in front of her.

"Cheers," he said, picking up one of the glasses.

"What a man," she told him, as she picked up the glass and let the smooth liquid do its job. "You always know how to put a smile on a girl's face. Especially today," she grinned.

Charles was such a sweet guy and could be a really handsome man, she thought, as she studied him while she sipped her drink. He just needed to cut off about a foot of his hair, shave, and maybe take a bath every couple of days. Put a Tommy Bahama shirt on him, and a pair of Dockers shorts, and he would be passable as a date. She didn't even know if he owned a pair of shoes other than his ever present flip-flops. Not that she was looking for a date, especially with Charles, since he was at least fifteen years older than she was. For that matter, she didn't know if she could ever let a man get close to her again. Not after losing Mike the way she did. That pain would never go away, and she didn't intend to get hurt like that again if she could help it.

"And what put you in such a good mood?" he smiled at her, taking a sip of his drink.

"You did, and I hope you're going to put me in an even better one," she answered cheerfully.

Koral spread some pictures out on the bar in front of Charles, and pointed to the mug shot of Ray Durbin.

"Look at this picture and tell me if it's the same man you said was in here today. I also need to know if he's the same man you saw taking that white Cigarette out at Jerome's that day two years ago."

She could hardly contain her excitement at the prospect of finally locating that bottom feeder Ray Durbin.

Charles picked up the mug shot of Durbin and said, "Yep, that's the guy I saw take the boat out, all right. Right down to his scroungy moustache. Except his hair is blond now, and he doesn't have any facial hair."

As he handed the picture back to Koral, he happened to see the other picture on the bar, lying beneath the one of Durbin. The one of Susan Alden with Lynn and Reese Mallory. He picked it up and studied it a few seconds, frowning as if he knew the people in the photo, but couldn't quite place them.

"I've seen this woman before," he said, thoughtfully. Then he flicked the picture with his fingers as recognition hit him. "She's the good-looking woman I told you about who was with the other dude and this guy in the boat that day.

Koral looked up at Charles, her eyes wide with disbelief.

"Which woman? There are two in the picture." Koral held her breath.

Charles laid the picture down on the bar and pointed to Susan Alden.

Chapter Sixty-Four

Koral didn't know what to do first. She could hardly contain herself. She decided she'd better check out the house where Durbin was living to make sure he hadn't fled the island yet. There wasn't time to wait for Aron, so she had to make a major judgment call, one she hoped she wouldn't regret.

She called Aron at work. His secretary told her he had been in a meeting with government officials since he'd returned to his office, and probably would be tied up for a while longer. Shit, Koral thought. The Ministers of Tourism and Economic Development are probably reaming him out about the skyrocketing murder rate.

Koral thanked her and called Aron's cell phone again, leaving a message about what she had found out, and what her next move was going to be. She knew he would heartily disapprove of her trying to apprehend Durbin alone, but she couldn't take a chance on him getting away while she waited for back-up. She also didn't know how he had planned to get off the island. If whoever hired him had a private jet waiting, he could easily slip through their fingers.

She almost took Charles up on his offer to go with her to Durbin's house, but decided against that. With all the other casualties of this case, she didn't want anything happening to Charles. She had chased down bad guys alone before and knew what she was doing. Charles didn't. She told him if he heard gunshots, or if she wasn't back in fifteen minutes, to call the police immediately.

As she walked out of the bar, Koral took her gun out of her purse as unobtrusively as possible, and stuck it in the waistband of her skirt, covering it with her shirt. She then stopped at her Jeep and locked her purse in the compartment under the seat. Taking a quick look around, she started walking down the sandy path beside the narrow two-lane road flanked by brightly-painted houses of yellow and peach.

As she approached the run-down cottage where Durbin was supposedly staying, she thought how odd it seemed for a terribly neglected house to be among all the neatly kept ones on the street.

Figures, Koral thought. A dirt bag would live in a place like this, which was in dire need of repairs and yard work. Just like his miserable life was in need of repairs, or better yet, permanent retirement, she thought. In the midst of the well-kept homes, and yards with flowers blooming in the beds, Durbin was a one-man neighborhood blight.

She almost felt personally responsible for getting him out of Grand Cayman and into prison to make sure he never came back to disrupt the tranquility of the island.

As she got closer to the house, she noticed the front door of the house was standing open, barely supported by one hinge. The frame next to the knob was splintered, as was the whole bottom panel. She could hear flies buzzing inside. Best not go in there without checking things out, she thought, as she cautiously crept between the neighboring house and Durbin's and took her gun out of her waistband. There were open windows on either side of Durbin's cottage, and she cautiously made her way toward one of them. Sinking down in the dirt in the flower bed, she inched her way up to the window and peeped inside.

Durbin and a woman, whom Koral presumed was his girlfriend, were lying dead in the floor. Koral's heart began to beat a little faster as she hurriedly backed away from the window, almost falling, and ran back down the sidewalk to the bar.

She bolted in the door as Charles came out of a back room, and hurried over to her.

"Are you all right?" he asked, a worried look on his face. "You look a little pale."

"Yeah, I'm fine," Koral said, a little out of breath. "Just not used to seeing this many dead bodies in such a short period of time. Durbin and his girlfriend are dead," she said, mostly to herself.

She realized that Susan Alden couldn't have killed Durbin and his girlfriend. Susan wasn't even on Grand Cayman. She was in Houston.

Someone else had committed these murders.

But who?

And what was Susan Alden doing on the white boat with Durbin? Giving her the benefit of the doubt, Koral thought maybe Susan was an innocent bystander in all of this. Maybe the handsome man with her and Durbin on the boat was the "higher up" leader of this ever-widening web of mystery. But who was he and why did he want Reese Mallory dead?

Chapter Sixty-Five

Lynn was standing in the middle of the blue bedroom holding Reese's ankh and chain when she heard an accusing voice behind her.

"What the hell do you think you're doing?" Susan demanded. "Are you going through my things?" she asked incredulously, crossing the room and eyeing her clothes spread out on the bed.

Susan stopped as her gaze drifted down to Lynn's hands holding the ankh and chain. Then Susan saw the file folder on the bed.

Susan slowly turned to face Lynn. Her beautiful face was contorted with contempt, her hateful tone unmistakable.

"So, now you know," she sneered.

Lynn sank onto the bed, and looked up at Susan in disbelief.

"Why? How? Did you kill Reese? How did you get his ankh? He was my husband! He was your friend!" she screamed at Susan, as her disbelief turned to rage.

Susan's lip curled back like a tiger's poised to attack. "Oh, please don't take that holier-than-thou attitude with me now. It won't work anymore. Sure you loved Reese. We all did. I, however, loved him more than most. At least I would have given him children."

"What are you talking about? What do you mean you loved him and would have given him children?" Lynn stood up and glared at Susan, her heart beginning to race.

Susan shoved her back down on the bed.

"Sit down," she ordered, venom dripping from her words. "I'm not nearly through yet. I'm just getting started."

Lynn obeyed, fear beginning to replace bravado, as she watched Susan morph into someone she didn't recognize.

Susan walked slowly over to a chair, never taking her eyes off of Lynn, circling her prey. She pulled the chair around to face Lynn on the bed and sat down, leaning over within inches of Lynn's face.

"Yes, we killed Reese, or rather my friend did. And we'd do it again," Susan hissed, throwing her head back, and laughing uncontrollably.

Lynn jumped up and grabbed for the phone on the stand by the bed, screaming at Susan. "You're crazy and I'm calling the police right now. You'll pay for this if it's the last thing I do!"

"Put the phone down now, or it will be the last thing you do," Susan snarled.

Lynn stopped and turned around to see Susan pointing a gun at her. Slowly, she replaced the phone.

My God, she's going to kill me, too, Lynn thought.

This whole thing just couldn't be happening. She wondered where Dennis was now when she needed him most.

Then the thought hit her that Susan was probably going to kill both her and Dennis. She felt panic rising and knew she had to do something, but what? How could she do anything with a gun pointed at her? She knew she had to keep Susan talking, or Susan might lose it and kill her just for the fun of it.

"Why, Susan? Why did you have Reese killed? What could you have possibly gained from his death?" Lynn stood as still as she could, even though her entire body was shaking. She thought of all the catty remarks Susan made at other people's expense, all the putdowns. Lynn had always thought Susan had a dark side, but so did a lot of people. However, this was way beyond anything Lynn could have imagined. From the looks of things, Lynn knew Susan wouldn't hesitate to use the gun on her for even the slightest wrong move.

"The term you're looking for is 'sociopath,' if you're wondering where to peg me," Susan purred. "That means we pretty much don't give a fuck about anyone, or whether they live or die. And we're very good at getting what we want, whatever it takes."

She straightened her shoulders and leaned back in the aqua slipper chair, using the gun to motion Lynn to sit back down on the bed.

"Would you like to hear the whole sordid, steamy story, my precious Lynn? Sure you would. Sit down and listen carefully. I don't want you to miss a single word, especially when I get to the sex part," Susan said, watching the disbelief on Lynn's face as she emphasized the "sex part."

"It probably never occurred to you that there is a real world out there. Real people with real problems live in it. I hear them every day. Day in and day out, they come to my office, and pour out their fucking trivial little problems to me about their trivial little lives. It finally got to be such a downer that I decided a diversion once in a while would help me put the gory details of their dreary existences out of my mind. So, I started going to Vegas and gambling a little. Very little at first. But, oh, it was a rush. When I started winning, I began gambling more and more until finally, I had lost so much, I knew I could never recoup my losses. Daddy cut me off and said I would have to take care of my money problems myself. Dear old Dad. Never could count on him in a pinch.

"That's where Reese came in. But you already had him lock, stock and barrel. Or so I thought. He came to see me one day, on a professional basis. It seems he was very disturbed because you didn't want to have any little Reeses running around, and he did. He told me he was thinking of leaving you because you just wouldn't even consider his feelings in the matter. Imagine that. Someone actually thought of leaving precious Lynn Saferty Mallory. You couldn't let that happen, could you? Who could you lean on? Certainly not yourself. And how would that look to your society friends? They would all think you were shallow and superficial, someone so cold and uncaring as to not want to have children. And with a man like Reese. My God, woman, were you nuts? Every woman I know would walk across hot coals to have a man like Reese. And you had him but weren't willing to compromise to keep him.

"Poor Reese needed some advice. So I gave him some. Sex, that is, with a little advice thrown in." Susan drove the last words home and delighted in watching Lynn's face twist with pain at hearing them.

"Oh yes, we had a very pleasurable rainy afternoon on my office sofa. Reese was more than happy to make love to a woman who had feelings and knew how to love him the way he should be loved. Unfortunately, straight-arrow Reese's character and morals overrode his sexual urges, and he went home to his dear, precious Lynn to work things out. Fucking fool. That was a big mistake. It didn't help him or my bank account at all. I lost all feeling and respect for him then. That made it easier to execute our little masterpiece.

"The estate my parents left me when they died so tragically was practically gone. Of course, it wasn't all that much to begin with since Daddy and Mommy dear did love to live well. Wish I had known that or their yacht would have blown up in Cayman a lot sooner. The way Daddy talked, he was loaded. Unfortunately, he was usually loaded with scotch."

Lynn's face registered total shock as the impact of Susan's words sunk in about the boating accident.

"You had your parents killed? My God, Susan, how could you do such a thing? What happened to you to make you like this? You aren't the Susan I knew at all. You're a monster," Lynn shouted at her.

"Oh, shut the fuck up, you sad little creature, and let me finish. I hate to be interrupted when I'm telling a good story," Susan shot back at her, frowning and rubbing the gun's barrel against the side of her head.

"Anyway, where was I? I have to get this story straight. Oh, yeah. I was going to have to sell the house, my Porsche, my stock, everything to pay my gambling debts. Reese's fortune would have taken care of all that, and so much more. It would have been pocket change to him. But no, he ran home to his pretty little princess.

"That's when Plan B was hatched. If Reese wasn't in the picture any longer, I knew exactly what Dennis would do. And he did. He couldn't get to you fast enough. He's so goddamn predictable. He's so unbelievably dense at times, too. I kept telling him not to screw things up with you, to be patient and give you time to get over Reese, and when the timing was right, to ask you to marry him. Evidently, it worked. I gave myself a big pat on the back for that one. Things were right on schedule.

"But then, they found Reese, and that Sanders bitch started nosing around. Then, that stupid boy had to go and open his big mouth about seeing the white boat on the Wall that day. Some people just don't know when to keep their mouths shut. Jerome Johnson could have identified me since Ray Durbin, my friend and I were the ones who took the boat out to the Wall. I had to go with Ray to good old Jerome's marina, because Ray wasn't authorized to use your boat and I was. Because someone had to handle the boat while Ray was underwater, my friend and I played the dazzling couple. And Jerome, of course, had to be dealt with immediately.

"Ray messed up again by not getting to that Ebanks boy before his family got him off the island, but at least he wasn't around to provide further details. He could be taken care of later on.

"My friend is great when he does a job himself, and he's a piece of work in the sack. If only he were better at picking subcontractors. He found Ray through some connections in an offshore workers watering hole in Houston. Ray isn't long on brains, but he knew how to do what was needed to make sure Reese didn't come back from that dive trip. You didn't have the pleasure of meeting Ray, but you probably met his girlfriend, Jeanette, that day on the boat. Couldn't miss her with those tacky tattoos on her tits. She served her purpose though, which was to divert anyone on the dive boat from zeroing in on the white Cigarette while Ray was taking care of business underwater.

"I told my friend to have Ray bring me Reese's ankh to prove that he had finished his assignment. I knew Reese wouldn't part with that touching love trinket voluntarily. I brought it and the folder with me just in case things didn't go as I planned. I could always plant them in your room and make sure the police found them, especially after you told me you asked that Chief Ebanks about the ankh the other day at the police station. They might wonder how you got it if Reese had it on when he went diving that day. But things have worked out beautifully without all that fuss.

"I keep getting ahead of myself here. I certainly don't want to leave out any juicy details. I got sidetracked about the ankh. Let's see…. Oh, yes. When Ray screwed up killing the Sanders bitch twice, and started spouting off his stupid mouth at that dumpy bar, he had to be removed from the scene as well. And ol' Jeanette clearly had to go. Ten minutes with the cops and she would've sung like a cockatoo on crack. Ray was also supposed to take you off my hands, but now I'll have to take care of that myself.

"But, of course, you haven't heard about Ray and Jeanette's demise yet, have you? Koral Sanders hasn't paid you a visit today with all this news, but she will. You can count on it.

"The only kink in the plan is that you and Dennis aren't married yet. But you will be tonight as soon as he gets back. This is where it gets really good. Are you ready? I have a minister stopping by tonight to perform the ceremony. He should be here any time now. I can be your maid-of-honor. Isn't that rich? When Dennis gets back, you can surprise him with the news that you two are getting married right here, tonight. And guess what happens after you're married? We'll take a little boat ride across the North Sound, out to the Wall. You'll be joining Reese tonight, my dear."

Lynn looked at Susan with horror. How could she have woven this plan over two years and still passed herself off as a normal human being? Lynn found it incredible that someone she thought she'd known since childhood could turn out to be such a monster in disguise.

"You heartless, murdering bitch." Lynn wanted nothing more than to choke the life out of Susan at that moment, "You won't get away with this."

"Watch me, sweetheart. And one word of warning out of your sweet little mouth when Dennis gets back, and both of you are dead. Got it?"

Lynn's mind suddenly turned to Dennis again, and she asked Susan, "What are you going to do to Dennis? Please don't hurt him, Susan," she pleaded. "He's never done anything to hurt you."

"Oh, right! He didn't hurt me at all, did he? Hello! He didn't break up with me so he could be with you, did he? Ding, ding, ding! My friends didn't all look at me with pity because they all knew he dumped me for you, did they? He didn't humiliate me in front of the whole fucking city of Houston, and all those goddamn social barracudas, did he? They just couldn't wait to start talking about me behind my back. You think that was fun for me to hear those goddamn hens clucking? Oh no, Dennis didn't hurt me. He destroyed me! But don't you worry, golden girl, I'm going to have the last laugh.

"You ain't heard nothin' yet. Just wait until you hear the end of the story," Susan whispered.

Chapter Sixty-Six

Susan let out a deep sigh after her tirade, then continued.

"Now for the *Pièce de Résistance*. Are you ready for this one? Here's my parting shot. Saved the best for last.

"Dennis is now going to know how it feels to lose someone he loves. He played fast and loose with my feelings, but now he's going to get some of that back. But I'm not about to harm him physically, dear, just send him to night-night land for a little while. Right after he marries you, he'll feel a bit woozy and have to lie down long enough for you to go play with the fishes. Then later, he'll wake up, I'll be here, and you'll be gone. I'll tell everyone that you said you needed some air and went out to the beach right after the wedding, never to be seen again. We'll tell everyone that you must have still been so distraught over Reese that you just walked into the sea and never came back. Toodles! Dennis will be heartbroken and I'll be right there to comfort him, along with all your zillions, which you will leave to him when you write a little codicil to your will. Right now.

"Now get up and go sit down at the desk and write what I tell you. And remember, not a word to Dennis when he gets here or I'll kill you both where you stand. And if I have to do that, I have the evidence to make it look like you found Reese's ankh hidden in Dennis' briefcase, along with the file folder. So, you shot him when you thought he had killed Reese and then turned the gun on yourself. Are we on the same page now, precious? Do I make myself perfectly clear?" Susan smiled, sheer madness reflected in her eyes.

Lynn's mind was reeling from everything Susan had told her. How could she not have seen all this happening? All these years Susan had everybody fooled. She had meticulously planned this and was very close to carrying it out. After all, she'd gotten away with murdering her parents, and no one had suspected a thing. Surely someone had helped her do that, Lynn thought. But who? She couldn't possibly have done it alone.

Lynn was desperate to warn Dennis when he came back, but if she tried to do anything, there was no doubt in her mind that Susan would kill them both like she threatened.

Lynn looked at Susan, and nodded her head that she would do as Susan told her, then asked, "Who is this friend you keep talking about?"

"You'll meet him soon enough. He'll be here in a few minutes. He's very handy to have around, for a number of reasons. Now get moving." Susan motioned with the gun for Lynn to move to the desk. Lynn obeyed, her feet feeling like dead weight as she walked over to the desk and sat down.

She opened the desk drawer and took out a piece of Ritz-Carlton stationery and a pen. As she looked at the gold embossed lettering on the paper, she thought of her life with Reese and how perfect it had seemed on the surface. In reality, it had jagged edges, too, just like ordinary people's marriages.

"Now write exactly what I tell you. You, Lynn Mallory, being over the age of twenty-one years and of sound mind, do hereby write this first codicil to your Last Will and Testament leaving your entire estate, and all that entails, to your husband, Dennis Hammond. Then, sign and date it. Dennis will be touched. He'll just think you are so in love with him that you just couldn't wait to make him the beneficiary of everything you own." Susan's expression was dead serious. "And it will be completely legal. No witnesses or notary necessary if it's written in your own hand. And very hard to break. But you know that, since you're a hot shot lawyer," Susan snickered.

After Lynn finished writing, Susan grabbed the piece of paper representing one of the largest fortunes in the country, folded it up, and put it in the pocket of her dress. Lynn sat very still, her hands clasped in her lap, as Susan sat down on the bed.

"Now we wait," she announced, a slow, evil grin beginning to spread across her face.

Lynn couldn't stand it any longer. She had to know. She turned toward Susan and asked, "You were never my friend, were you?"

"Jesus, Lynn, ya think?" she laughed, waving the gun around in the air. "I didn't hate you. I just wanted what you had. You were always the one who got everything. The great men, all the attention, homes all over the world, the rich and powerful friends, everything. You tell me. I had a little money, but nothing compared to yours. We were well off, yes, but then I found out that my father had pissed it all away."

The sound of the elevator door opening caused Lynn to jump. The amused look disappeared from Susan's face as she got up, and walked quietly to the door of the bedroom.

A big smile formed on her lips as a tall, blond, blue-eyed Adonis walked into the room. He was dressed in a suit, tie, boots and a cowboy hat.

Susan walked slowly over to where the man stood, and snaked her left arm around his neck. She lifted the gun with her right hand so that it still pointed straight at Lynn's chest. The man put his arms around Susan and kissed her as if only the two of them were in the room. When Susan untangled herself from his embrace, she turned to Lynn, breathless, with a smoldering look on her face.

"Lynn, meet Cowboy."

Chapter Sixty-Seven

After Dennis left the penthouse, he went straight to the Tiffany & Co. Boutique in the lobby of the Ritz-Carlton Hotel. All of a sudden, it occurred to him as he was talking to Sid at his office in Houston that he had not bought Lynn a wedding ring.

Dennis told Sid that he and Lynn wanted him and Tabby to fly to Cayman for the wedding and stand up for them.

Sid could hardly wait to call Tabby and tell her the news. He told Dennis they wouldn't miss the wedding of the year for anything, even though it would be the smallest wedding of the year he'd ever attended.

With a five-carat pear-shaped diamond engagement ring and wedding band of smaller oval diamonds nestled in a black velvet box in his pants pocket, Dennis decided he would surprise Lynn with the rings tonight at dinner. God, he had waited for this for so long, he thought, and now it was finally happening. Everything was falling into place.

As he rode the elevator to the penthouse, he ran his fingers through his dark hair. His Tommy Bahama shirt was the color of Lynn's eyes, a beautiful aquamarine, and he decided he looked pretty good, actually not bad at all. He also decided that he was the luckiest man on earth.

As the elevator door opened and Dennis walked into the great room, he saw Lynn's white Chanel bag on the sofa table. He knew she was home since she never went anywhere without that bag. It weighed a ton, and he wondered how she carried it without help. She told him once that she could be marooned on a desert island, and that if she had that bag with her, she could survive for years. There was no telling what all was in it. It was a woman thing, he decided.

"Lynn, are you home?" Dennis called out, as he noticed the balcony door was half open.

"On the balcony." The answer came so softly, he almost didn't hear her.

He took the velvet box out of his pocket, and walked over to the balcony. Stepping outside into the warm evening, Dennis saw that Lynn wasn't alone.

With her were Susan, a tall handsome blond man, and a man who was obviously a minister, Dennis thought, since he was wearing a white clerical collar and holding a Bible.

"Hi everyone," Dennis said. Puzzled, he walked over to the group, put his arm around Lynn and kissed her on the cheek.

"Susan, what are you doing back here?" he asked her. "You just left. We didn't know you were coming back so soon."

Turning to the blond man with her, he said, "Hi, I'm Dennis Hammond, extending his hand to Cowboy.

"This is my friend, Cowboy, and don't you dare laugh," Susan grinned, as the men shook hands.

"Wouldn't think of laughing. It's nice to meet any friend of Susan's," Dennis said.

"The pleasure's all mine," Cowboy drawled, a slow smile spreading across his face.

"Have we met before?" Dennis asked him.

"I don't think so. I would remember meeting a famous lawyer such as yourself," Cowboy told him.

Susan decided she'd better put an end to their conversation before Cowboy said something he shouldn't in front of the minister. Having to kill a man of the cloth wouldn't be a good move.

Susan quickly grabbed Dennis by the arm, dragging him away from Cowboy, and said, "Dennis, this is Reverend Oscar Harvey."

Dennis shook hands with the minister and smiled. "Okay, Reverend Harvey, I give up. To what do we owe the pleasure of your visit this evening?"

The minister opened his mouth to speak but never had a chance to answer Dennis.

"We have a big surprise for you, Dennis dear," Susan chirped. "Lynn called me to tell me you two were getting married tomorrow and asked me to come. Of course, I wouldn't have missed this for anything, so I jumped on a plane, which I've been doing a lot lately, and here I am. When Lynn picked me up at the airport, we had a bunch of girl talk about weddings on the way back here, which got us all in the mood. We decided that since it's such a lovely evening and we're all here, she wanted to surprise you and get married tonight. So we called Reverend Harvey, and he graciously agreed to perform the ceremony. It's very impromptu, but that just makes it more fun. So what do you say? Want to have a wedding?" Susan smiled her most sincere smile.

Reverend Harvey just stood there grinning, and waiting for everyone to decide if indeed there was going to be a ceremony.

Lynn hadn't said a word through all of this, and Dennis noticed the look on her face was not one a blushing bride should be wearing. She actually looked like she was going to be sick. He was surprised that she didn't speak up when Susan started talking about having the wedding tonight.

"Lynn?" Dennis stared at her with a confused look on his face.

Lynn looked at his handsome face and knew that if she didn't do exactly what Susan said, that she would kill them without hesitation. She couldn't let herself even imagine that happening. She smiled at Dennis and hooked her arm through his.

"I think we're going to have a wedding," Lynn replied, trying her best to look happy.

Reverend Harvey looked relieved as he reached into his jacket for the papers to be signed.

Dennis glowed. "If my fiancée says we're going to have a wedding, then that's exactly what we'll have. I just happen to have a couple of rings right here," Dennis said, taking the black velvet box out of his pocket.

Wanting to do this the right way, he got down on one knee in front of Lynn and held the opened box up to her.

"Lynn, will you marry me?" Dennis asked her, looking up at her with that endearing, disarming smile.

She looked at the exquisite rings, attempting a smile that didn't quite reach her eyes. Susan shot her a warning glance, and Cowboy patted his jacket pocket to remind her there was a gun in it. He'd already shown it to her and told her she'd better behave herself.

"Well, what do you think?" Dennis asked Lynn. "Do you like them? Is the diamond too small?" he laughed.

"I love them," she managed weakly, as she cupped his face in her hands.

He took the two rings out of the box and took her left hand in his. "Let's make sure these fit before the ceremony," he said, as he stood up and looked at her with nothing but love in his eyes. He couldn't believe he was actually going to marry the woman he had loved for years. He slipped the engagement ring on her finger, and it fit as if it had been made for her.

Lynn looked at Dennis, her eyes filling with tears.

"What's wrong?" Dennis asked, a stricken look on his face as he stood up.

"Nothing. Nothing at all. I'm just so happy and I love you so much," Lynn told him, as she put her arms around him and tried to act normal. She wouldn't be able to live with herself if she did anything to cause Dennis to be hurt or, God forbid, killed at the hands of this madwoman.

Suddenly, Dennis said, "Oh my, God! I just talked to Sid and told him we were doing all of this day after tomorrow. We have to wait for them."

"Oh, they won't care if they miss the ceremony," Susan teased him. "They just don't want to miss the partying afterwards. You know them. They'll be just as happy toasting you at a post-wedding bash tomorrow. Why wait? Don't you want Lynn to wake up in the morning with a new name?"

Thank God, Susan's argument seemed to work on Dennis, Lynn thought.

"Okay, but you're going to be the one to call them, not me," Dennis laughed. Susan laughed with him, but for a much different reason.

"Don't you worry about Sid and Tabby. I can take care of them," Susan said.

Lynn's mind was racing. There had to be some way to get out of this. But there stood Cowboy, with that faint hint of a pistol under his elegantly tailored jacket. If she made a move, she and Dennis, as well as Reverend Harvey, would quickly and surely be dead. She decided she had no choice than to wait for an opportunity, a flaw in whatever Susan had planned for after the ceremony.

Chapter Sixty-Eight

Koral's cell phone rang as she was driving back to George Town after leaving the police at the house where Ray Durbin and his girlfriend had been murdered.

She was frantic to talk to Aron and to get to Lynn Mallory's penthouse as fast as they could. Now that she knew Susan Alden was behind all the murders, she figured that Lynn and Dennis were in a boatload of danger. She also knew that Susan was the only one who knew the identity and whereabouts of the person who had killed Durbin and his girlfriend. She was also absolutely certain that killer was on Susan's payroll.

"Koral Sanders," she answered.

"Koral, it's Aron. They just informed me at the station what happened at the East End after you called it in. Are you okay? Give me the details. I've been in meetings almost all afternoon. What's happened?"

Finally, Koral thought.

"Aron, take a breath," she fussed at him, halting his barrage of questions. "My God, your meetings are long! I'm fine, but you aren't going to believe what's happened in the last few hours. Meet me in the lobby at the Ritz-Carlton. I'm on the way there now. We've got to find Lynn Mallory and Dennis Hammond. I think Susan Alden is behind the murders—all of them."

"What? Are you sure?" Aron asked her.

"No doubt about it. She didn't commit them herself. She hired someone to do her dirty work. Charles at the East Side Bar called me today and said Ray Durbin and his girlfriend had been in there drinking all afternoon. Durbin was running off at the mouth about some rich person from Houston hiring him to kill someone. I went out there and showed Charles a photo of Durbin, and he identified him. He also said he remembered seeing Durbin taking a white Cigarette out of Jerome's marina the day Reese Mallory disappeared. He said a good-looking couple was with him. I had a photo of Susan and the Mallorys with me. When Charles saw it, he pointed to Susan Alden and said she was the woman in the boat with Durbin. That's why Susan said she was sick and couldn't go out on the dive boat. She was with Durbin taking care of the boat while he was underwater taking care of Reese Mallory. She sent Durbin to kill Jerome and steal the Mallory folder because she knew he could identify her, and she sent him to kill me to get me off her ass. He also fit the description of the sleazeball who came looking for James. Susan kept her own hands clean, of course. She was in Houston. She went back yesterday, so the scary thing here is that someone besides Durbin is taking orders from her, and we have no idea who that is. Susan had this planned from the beginning, starting with Reese Mallory's murder. I just need to find out why," Koral told Aron. "I don't see what she hoped to get out of it, but it must be something big."

Koral only hoped they got to Lynn and Dennis before Susan did.

"That's great work, Koral. I'll meet you at the Ritz. Be careful." Aron told her. This was going to be a long night, he thought. He just hoped no one else would die before it ended.

Chapter Sixty-Nine

Lynn and Dennis stood in front of Reverend Oscar Harvey on the balcony of the penthouse under a canopy of stars twinkling in the clear night sky. Moonlight bathed the smooth surface of the water while a warm tropical night breeze rippling through the palm trees completed the perfect romantic setting.

Looking up at Dennis, Lynn wore a strapless white eyelet sundress that she had changed into for the ceremony. It was the closest thing to a wedding dress that she had brought with her from Houston.

It couldn't have been a more blissful night for a wedding, Dennis thought, as he held Lynn's hand and vowed to love, honor and protect her for the rest of his life.

Dennis seemed to lose himself in Lynn's eyes as they said their vows, but he couldn't help but think that they didn't quite sparkle tonight like they had yesterday.

Her long blonde hair swirled around her in the gentle wind, making his heart race. "My God, you look like an angel floating down from heaven. I've never been happier in my life," he whispered to her.

As Dennis slipped the glittering diamond wedding band on her finger, Reverend Harvey pronounced them husband and wife. Dennis kissed his bride while Susan and Cowboy applauded softly.

Lynn felt a swirl of dizzy nausea. "Stay in control," she commanded herself. "It's your only chance."

Shaking hands with everyone, Reverend Harvey wished them a long and happy life together. Slipping him an envelope containing three hundred U.S. dollars, Cowboy escorted him to the elevator. When Cowboy rejoined them on the balcony, Susan turned to the table laden with champagne flutes full of Dom Perignon that she had ordered up from room service. She handed Lynn and Dennis one, then she and Cowboy held theirs up in a toast to the happy couple.

"To my breathtaking bride," Dennis said, as they touched glasses and downed the bubbly gold liquid. Susan watched closely as Dennis drank half of his champagne. Shouldn't be much longer til night-night time for the groom, she smiled.

When Dennis kissed Lynn, Susan almost retched. At least she wouldn't have to witness such disgusting displays of affection much longer. Revenge truly was delicious.

Poetic justice, she thought. Nobody humiliates me and gets away with it. Soon sweet stud muffin Dennis would be eating out of her hand, not luscious Lynn's, for years to come.

Her very rich hand, she giggled. Susan could almost taste their victory.

"Wow," Dennis said, putting a hand up to his temple. "That champagne must be extra potent," he slurred. "I feel woozy."

Lynn glared at Susan.

"Come on, darling," she told Dennis, "I'll take you to the bedroom. Lie down for a few minutes and you'll feel better." As Lynn put her arm around him, Dennis fell to his knees.

"Dennis!" Lynn shouted. Dennis looked up at her, everything a blur, as she tried to help him up. He grabbed at her, almost pulling her down with him, then fell face down on the floor of the balcony.

"Don't worry about him, cutie pie," Susan snipped, as she walked over to Dennis and leaned close to his face to make sure he was unconscious. Lynn thought she saw Susan stick something in the pocket of his shirt, but couldn't be sure. Maybe she was just patting his chest in a mock show of concern.

"He'll be fine," Susan assured her. "He'll just sleep for a few hours. By then, you'll be gone, I'll be back here to comfort his aching head and heart, and we'll be planning a nice memorial service for you on the beach where you disappeared. Right down there. Isn't the view perfect? *Fait accompli. Au voir. Adios. Auf Wiedersehen. Tah-tah.*"

Susan threw her head back, letting out a cackle that made Lynn's skin crawl.

Suddenly, Lynn felt an anger welling up in her that she had never felt before. How could someone manipulate lives the way Susan did? How could she murder people with no remorse? Impulsively, Lynn stood up and walked over to Susan. She slapped her as hard across the face as she could. Susan's head snapped back as her hand flew to her cheek where Lynn hit her.

"Well, my goodness. Who would have thought you had that in you. Ice princess Lynn in touch with her anger, I see," Susan laughed, rubbing her face. "But it's a little late in the game, sweetheart. You're history."

"Cowboy, escort Mrs. Hammond to the car, please," Susan told him, walking toward the elevator.

Cowboy grabbed Lynn's arm and pulled her along with him to the open door. The three of them got on the elevator, and stood watching Dennis' still body on the balcony floor as the door closed.

Lynn was terrified that was the last she'd see Dennis, but she felt a chilling certainty that she would be seeing Reese again tonight if help didn't come. Soon.

Chapter Seventy

Aron arrived at the Ritz-Carlton ahead of Koral. He parked the police car in front of the hotel and showed the valet his badge, telling him he'd be right back.

"Excuse me," he told the concierge, who was busily tending to some important task behind his desk.

"Excuse me," Aron said again sternly. "I'm Chief of Police Aron Ebanks. I need to see Mrs. Mallory at once. It's urgent."

The concierge turned around and said, "I'm sorry, Chief Ebanks, you just missed her. She left with Dr. Alden and a gentleman just a few minutes ago."

"Dr. Alden? Are you sure it was her?" Aron was astonished that Susan Alden had come back to Grand Cayman after leaving just yesterday morning.

"Oh, yes, sir. I know Dr. Alden. She's been here several times."

"Did you know the man with them?"

"No sir, I've never seen him before."

"What did he look like?"

"Tall, blond, handsome."

"What was he wearing?"

"A suit, tie, boots and a cowboy hat."

Aron had no idea who that could be. This was a new player in the game.

"Do you know where they were going?" Aron asked.

"No sir, but Dr. Alden said they were celebrating Mrs. Mallory's and Mr. Hammond's wedding that took place here this evening in their penthouse."

"Their wedding? Tonight?" Aron couldn't believe Lynn and Dennis had changed their plans and gotten married tonight. He wondered what the big hurry had been.

"That's right."

"Wasn't Mr. Hammond with them?"

"No sir, he wasn't."

That's very odd, Aron thought. If they were celebrating, it seemed to him that the groom would be with them.

"Which way did they go?"

"They headed toward town in a black Mercedes."

Aron thanked the concierge and hurried out the front door just as Koral's rented Jeep wheeled into the driveway. Aron rushed over to her and jumped in the passenger side.

"Let's go," he told her.

"Where? Aren't they here?" Koral asked him. "No. Mrs. Mallory headed toward town a few minutes ago with Susan Alden and some man. From the description the concierge gave me, I have no idea who the man is. The concierge said they were celebrating. Mrs. Mallory and Mr. Hammond got married here tonight," Aron told her.

Koral looked at him in amazement. "You're kidding, right? Married? And Susan Alden is in Cayman? What did the man look like?"

"No, I'm not kidding. I'm dead serious. Mrs. Mallory and Mr. Hammond got married and yes, Susan Alden is here. A tall, blond, good-looking man dressed in a suit, tie, boots and a cowboy hat was with them. And the odd thing is Mr. Hammond wasn't with them. I have no idea where he is unless he is in the penthouse or left ahead of them without the concierge noticing. If we hurry, we might be able to catch sight of their car and follow them," Aron said. "There aren't too many black Mercedes on the island."

The moment the words came out of his mouth, Aron knew he would be sorry he told Koral to hurry. She didn't need any encouragement to drive like a maniac.

"Hold on," Koral told him.

Floor boarding the Jeep, she screeched out of the driveway and into traffic. She immediately started passing the cars in front of them, scaring the slow-moving drivers and Aron half to death. At least with the chief of police in the car with her, she didn't think she'd have to worry about getting a speeding ticket, or getting hauled off to jail for reckless driving.

Koral had just passed the last car blocking their progress when she caught sight of the black Mercedes about a hundred yards in front of them. Thank goodness the traffic had slowed them down, she thought.

"There they are," Koral said, as she pushed the Jeep a little faster.

Aron got on his cell phone and called the police dispatcher telling her to stay on standby and be ready to send back-up to their destination when he relayed it to her.

Then he told the dispatcher to send some officers to the Ritz-Carlton and see if Dennis Hammond was in the penthouse and still breathing. Aron had a sickening feeling that Mr. Hammond might already have become Susan Alden's next victim.

Koral followed the Mercedes down West Bay Road into George Town and onto Church Street, then Harbour Drive. She slowed down as it turned into the parking lot of Jerome Johnson's marina.

Koral stopped the Jeep when she saw the Mercedes parked close to the walkway leading to the boat slips. In the darkness, she saw a man get out of the driver's side and open the back door for Susan and Lynn. The man's face was hidden by a cowboy hat. The trio started walking toward the dock leading to the boat slips. Koral turned off her headlights and began inching the Jeep closer to where the Mercedes was parked. She stopped and turned off her motor.

Watching the scene unfolding in front of them, Koral asked Aron, "Do you think we should try to stop them by ourselves?"

"Absolutely not. If those two murdered five people so easily, possibly six if Dennis Hammond is dead, do you think they would hesitate to shoot us on sight, no questions asked? As soon as they saw us, they would know we were on to them.

We'll follow them if we can, without being seen. I'll call dispatch and give them our location," Aron told her. "We have to wait for reinforcements before we do anything."

"Look, they're getting in a boat. We have to follow them, Aron." Koral knew if they didn't do something fast, Lynn Mallory Hammond wouldn't be alive much longer.

The three people on the dock stopped in front of a boat slip where a huge, red Cigarette with three engines was rocking gently in the water. Koral wondered who owned that little forty-two foot toy.

The tall blond man stopped for a moment under a security light on the dock walkway and listened for any sign if they were being followed. As he slowly turned and scanned the area to make sure they weren't being watched, he took off his hat and ran his hand through his hair.

Koral gasped when she saw his face revealed in the light and quickly covered her mouth with her hand.

"Oh, my God!" she whispered to herself, as a rush of recognition washed over her.

"What's wrong?" Aron whispered back to her.

"I know that man."

Chapter Seventy-One

Koral tried to catch her breath, feeling as if her heart might stop at any moment.

She remembered the night she met the handsome blond man in the cowboy hat.

She'd treated herself to a solo dinner at the Blue Iguana Restaurant. She'd been thinking about Mike and when she did that, it made for a long and emotional day for her. She was ready to just chill out and relax at a table for one by the water. God, she was tired of losing people she loved.

Especially someone who was so young and full of life.

Especially someone she was in love with.

Especially Mike.

There wasn't a second of the time they spent together that she had not committed to memory in that little place in her heart reserved for him. She remembered everything they shared and all the glorious nights making love on the beach and on the yacht he captained. Memories. They were capable of making you burst with happiness or ripping your heart apart from profound pain.

Unable to stop herself, she could feel her mind rewinding and her heart replaying their brief love affair all over again. All of the emotions of her past seemed to rush up at her and it was all she could do to keep herself together. She had to stop thinking about Mike and how hard it was when she lost him.

Shit, she thought, is this how my life is going to play out? Find someone I love, then poof, they die. Guess I'd better not let myself love anybody else. Getting involved with me is life-threatening.

She had just finished her Jack Daniels on the rocks and ordered another one. She didn't normally drink that much that quickly, but tonight she was feeling especially low, and the smooth liquid just seemed to go down easy, deadening the pain just a little.

She leaned forward and propped her elbows up on the table, resting her chin in both hands, forgetting everything her mother ever taught her about good manners. The waiter brought her drink and sat it down in front of her. She had to smile as she thought about how she and Jack Alford used to sit for hours at the Almond Tree and drink Black Jack and talk about the problems of the world. And they usually knew how to solve them. When Hurricane Ivan hit the island in 2004, it had taken the Almond Tree with it when it left. God, she missed that place. And Jack. He had since left the island when his work permit of seven years expired. She wondered if he would ever come back again.

She wondered if anything would ever be the same again.

She looked around at all the tables full of couples gazing romantically into each other's eyes, and thought about how long it had been since a man held her in his arms.

Then her gaze stopped on a gorgeous man with blond hair, and a muscled physique sitting alone at a table across the deck. His Tommy Bahama shirt was the color of the sea with a palm tree design and Koral was willing to bet it matched his eyes perfectly.

My God, she thought, what woman in her right mind let him loose by himself? And at night?

She was still staring at him when he suddenly looked her way, and their eyes met and held for a moment. Then he smiled, nodded his head toward her, and held his glass up to her in what she took to be an invitation. She was thanking the Black Jack for giving her just enough of a who-gives-a-shit attitude to give him one of her "come fuck me" looks. As if reading her mind, he got up and started walking toward her.

Anonymous sex on the way.

Oh shit, she thought. I've gone and done it now. Showtime.

Koral just sat there watching him in all his blondness, as he stopped at her table. He asked her if he could join her, and she said yes without hesitation. She was right. His eyes were the most incredible shade of blue she had ever seen. They talked and laughed and drank champagne for the next two hours. God, she had gotten so drunk, which she never allowed herself to do, well almost never, but she was having fun for the first time in ages.

The next thing she knew, he was waking up in her bed the next morning, or was it afternoon? They had made love all night and half of the next day. Then, he told her he had to leave to take care of some business in Houston. He took her phone number and her e-mail address and promised her they would see each other again.

But they hadn't.

Until tonight.

"He was here a couple of years ago. I met him at the Blue Iguana one night and we had drinks. He said his name was Cowboy. He told me he worked for some rich socialite in Houston. Personal assistant or something like that."

Koral hoped her explanation to Aron would suffice, and he wouldn't question her further. She decided Aron never needed to know the rest of that story.

The realization of who Cowboy really was hit Koral with icy certainty.

"He's Susan Alden's hitman."

Chapter Seventy-Two

"But what about the lowlife on the East End?" Aron asked.

"Cowboy hired him, and Cowboy got rid of him. And his girlfriend. She was the one on the dive boat with the Mallorys that day."

"Then Cowboy was the man with Susan Alden on the white boat that day."

"Yep," Koral nodded. "The stunning couple out for fun in the sun."

The puzzling thing to Koral was why Susan wanted Reese dead. If Koral could just figure out a way to get Lynn away from them, not only would she and Aron probably be saving Lynn's life, but maybe Lynn would be able to shed some light into that murky little corner of this puzzle.

The trio didn't seem to be in a very big hurry as they stood next to the boat. Lynn trembled visibly as Susan boarded the boat and Cowboy nudged Lynn to go ahead of him. As soon as she stepped into the boat, Susan pushed her down into the back seat. Cowboy jumped in and stood behind the wheel.

A few seconds later, the huge engines roared as Cowboy fired up each one. While they were idling, he circled the cockpit, and tossed each of the four docking lines ashore. Returning to the controls, he put the engines in reverse as Susan sat down next to Lynn in the back seat and began to tie Lynn's hands behind her back. Not a good sign, Koral thought, watching the big boat begin to move backwards.

As the Cigarette backed out of the slip, Koral realized that she and Aron had to do something fast, or they'd lose sight of them and Lynn would be history.

Spotting a smaller silver Cigarette berthed a few slips further down, Koral motioned Aron out of the car. "We can't wait for backup," she told him. "We'll lose them."

The silver boat was several feet shorter and only had two engines, but they were big ones. It would have to serve their purpose. None of the other boats Koral saw nearby would even come close to being fast enough to catch the big Cigarette. As long as they kept the big boat in sight, they might have a chance to rescue Lynn.

"Come on," she motioned to Aron, as she bent down low and ran toward the dock.

Against his better judgment, Aron got out of the Jeep and lumbered to catch up to Koral. The big boat was leaving the marina at idle speed as they hurried down the dock and jumped into the smaller one. Koral immediately got down on her hands and knees and flipped over onto her back, sliding up under the dashboard of the boat's control panel.

"What are you doing?" Aron asked, a disbelieving look on his face.

"I learned long ago that knowing how to hot wire cars, and boats when necessary, would come in handy. This is one of those times. Don't ask who taught me," she told him, while she worked furiously under the dashboard.

Finally finding what she was looking for, Koral pulled the colony of wires down from under the steering wheel.

"Aron, give me your little flashlight," she told him. She knew he always carried it in his pocket, and he took it out and handed it to her. She put it in her mouth, holding it between her teeth, to shine it on the jumble of wires. It only took her less than a minute to find the right ones. She touched them together, and the big engines screamed to life.

She quickly got to her feet and slid into the driver's seat, taking the steering wheel with one hand and the throttles with the other.

Aron was always amazed at Koral's talents, but this was a new one.

"Aron, toss those back docking lines off," Koral ordered, as she untied and threw the front lines to the dock. Aron complied then looked around for a life jacket. If she drove a boat the way she drove a car, he figured he might need one.

"Aren't you going to turn on the lights?" he yelled.

"Can't risk it," Koral shouted back. "They won't hear us over their own engines, but they'd sure see us if we lit up."

She began to back the boat out of the slip, all the while keeping an eye on the running lights of the red Cigarette as it reached the end of the row of docks and idled for a minute before turning toward the open sea and the cut in the reef leading to open water.

Koral hoped that they could close some of the distance between them unnoticed before Cowboy kicked the boat into high gear. She knew her wake was rocking the docked boats, but she couldn't worry about that right now.

When she was clear of the docks, she revved up the engines and slowly sped up, almost knocking Aron off balance. Koral glanced over at him to make sure he was alright. She motioned to him to sit down and hold on. The big boat was disappearing quickly into the night and Koral could barely see its running lights. She pushed the throttles forward and the high-powered engines came alive. In a matter of minutes, Koral had settled into the disappearing wake of the big red boat with the full moon guiding them like a beacon in their chase.

The wind whipped Koral's long brown hair around her face. Never had a scrunchie when you needed one, she thought.

"Where do you think they're headed, Aron?" she yelled, over the roar of the engines.

"It's my guess they're headed to the North Wall."

Chapter Seventy-Three

Now that he was satisfied he could give his men a pretty accurate reading of where Susan and Cowboy were headed, Aron ducked into the cabin of the boat and called on his radio for police reinforcements. Noticing a spotlight hanging on a hook, he made a mental note. It might come in handy.

"Dispatcher," a woman's voice said.

"This is Chief Ebanks speaking." Even in the cabin, Aron had to yell to be heard over the engine noise. "I need officers in boats and helicopters sent out to the North Wall immediately. This is an emergency. We are in pursuit of two murder suspects who have a female hostage with them. Inform all officers that the suspects are a man and a woman in a forty-two foot red Cigarette boat and that Koral Sanders and I are in pursuit in a smaller light-colored boat. The suspects are armed and extremely dangerous. Advise all officers to use caution and stay in radio contact at all times with their positions."

"Yes, sir," the dispatcher responded.

Aron climbed up from the cabin, grabbing the handrail on the dashboard for support. The force of the wind almost knocked him back, and he struggled to keep his eyes open while holding onto the rail for dear life. He stood beside Koral as she pushed the throttle of the boat to full speed across the dark sea. Even running wide open, they were still a couple of hundred of yards behind Cowboy and Susan.

The full moon had graced them with light to guide them, but it also meant the suspects could see them if they looked hard enough. In the distance, the running lights of the boat they pursued were clearly visible. Aron hoped their own craft would remain unseen until the police reinforcements arrived.

Lynn Mallory's life depended on it.

Chapter Seventy-Four

As Cowboy pushed the big Cigarette's throttles down, the boat rose out of the water like a bucking horse coming out of a chute. Then it leveled out across the smooth surface of the Caribbean.

Lynn sat in the back seat, her hands tied and her long blonde hair flying out behind her. She sensed her hopes for rescue fading by the minute. How could everything be ending for her in this beautiful paradise where she and Reese, and now Dennis, had made so many memories? She hoped that her death would be quick, but knowing Susan and the mountain of envy and hate she had built up over the years, that might be too much to ask.

Susan sat beside Lynn, smiling happily, as if she were on a Sunday outing. Her head was leaning back against the seat. Looking at Susan's face in the moonlight, Lynn thought, she's absorbing my fear like a sponge and loving every minute of it.

Lynn wondered how in the world she hadn't picked up on Susan's carefully hidden hatred over all these years. Surely there had been instances that should have sent up red flags, but she obviously had been too naïve or too wrapped up in convincing herself that her world was perfect to see what was happening. She would never think one of her best friends would be capable of such horrific crimes. Lynn had always been so careful about the people she allowed inside her most trusted circle.

Now, one of them had killed her husband, as well as several other people, and was going to kill her.

Lynn was trying to figure out where Susan and Cowboy were taking her, but in the dark it was hard to get her bearings. They had been following the beach, and suddenly they were turning as they rounded the western tip of the island.

With a sickening feeling, Lynn realized they were headed to the North Wall.

This was where she was going to die.

Chapter Seventy-Five

The concierge at the Ritz-Carlton looked up as the front doors opened and five policemen rushed into the lobby.

"What's going on here?" the concierge demanded.

A middle-aged officer stepped out of the crowd of uniforms and said, "I'm Lieutenant Forth. We need to get into the Mallory penthouse."

The concierge didn't move.

"Now!" the policeman yelled.

The flustered concierge pointed to the elevator leading up to the penthouse and the policemen piled into it. When it reached the top, the elevator doors opened into the Mallory's living room and the policemen exited quietly, their guns drawn. Even the trained men silently gasped and gave a low whistle at the luxury surrounding them.

Lt. Forth snapped his fingers at them and motioned for them to check each room as he walked toward the open door leading to the balcony.

At first glance, Dennis Hammond appeared to be dead. Lt. Forth rushed over and knelt down, pressing his fingers into Dennis' neck to check for a pulse. It was faint and uneven, but it was there. He turned Dennis over and grabbed a chair cushion to put under his head. Dennis took a shallow breath and his eyes fluttered open.

"I found him," Lt. Forth called out to his men, grabbing a pillow off the chaise lounge to put under his head. "Call an ambulance."

"Is he alive?" one of the policemen asked, as they all gathered around Dennis on the balcony.

"Barely. His pulse is very weak. It looks like whoever drugged him almost gave him a lethal overdose. Is anyone else in the penthouse?" Lt. Forth asked.

"No, sir. It's empty," one of his men told him.

"Call Chief Ebanks and tell him Mr. Hammond is alive. Then find out where that ambulance is. If we don't get this man to the hospital fast, he may not make it."

Chapter Seventy-Six

Cowboy was in his element behind the wheel of the powerful boat, with his blond hair slicked down on his head by the wind and his shirt open to his waist.

He casually scanned the water looking around for signs of other boats in their path. They were so close to the prize and he certainly didn't want to hit something in the dark and die before they could enjoy the rewards of all their hard work.

When Cowboy looked back, he saw a faint shape a good distance behind them. Maybe a boat, maybe a piece of junk floating on the water. He also saw the lights of what looked like a helicopter flying low. He squinted, thinking his eyes were playing tricks on him, as the shape on the water became clearer. It couldn't be her, he thought, out here in the dark, chasing him, and to his amazement, gaining on him.

"Son-of-a-bitch," Cowboy smiled, grabbing a pair of high-powered binoculars from beneath his seat. He slowed the engines so that he could hold them steady enough to see. Even though he couldn't tell who the people were in the boat, he knew it had to be Koral.

He remembered the night two years ago that he spent with Koral.

She was one hot chick. Not only great-looking, but smart, too. He actually hated to have to leave her the next morning. He told her nothing about himself, not even his real name. When he walked over to her table at the Blue Iguana that night, she didn't seem care if he had a name or not. Looks alone named the game that night.

Koral told him she was a private investigator, and a damn good one according to her. She had been demonstrating that the past few days and seemed hell bent on proving that point tonight. He had been so careful to avoid running into her while he was in Cayman this time. He knew if she saw him, the results would be a disaster.

Private investigating wasn't all she was good at doing. The sex had been incredible. He really hated that he wouldn't ever see her again after their night of, as she called it, fantastic anonymous sex; but in his business, he couldn't afford to make long-term commitments. And he certainly couldn't let someone who worked with the police discover what that business was.

Most importantly, if Susan ever found out he'd screwed around on her, she'd cut off his balls and feed them to him for breakfast—whole.

How Koral had tracked them down, and how the hell she had followed them all the way out here without him seeing her boat, he didn't know. He and Susan had been so careful. He pushed the throttles forward, but the smaller boat kept gaining on him.

"Son-of-a-bitch," he swore.

Susan saw Cowboy looking behind them with the binoculars and was on her feet in a second. Turning around, she saw the arsenal of boats that seemed to come out of nowhere and a couple of helicopters flying above them.

She moved up beside Cowboy and screamed in his ear, "Who is that?"

"I'll give you three guesses," he yelled back at her.

Susan's face twisted with rage. All of their perfect plans were falling apart in front of her eyes, and someone was going to pay.

"That fucking bitch! I'll fucking kill her," Susan screamed, as she unsteadily walked the few steps to the back of the boat where Lynn sat. She grabbed Lynn by the front of her dress and pulled her to her feet. Lynn struggled against the ropes binding her wrists behind her as Susan started to drag her to the cockpit of the boat where Cowboy stood.

Lynn strained and turned to see what Susan and Cowboy were looking at behind them. Bright lights were burning from several boats racing through the water, boats she hoped knew she was in this one and would reach her in time.

"I'll take the wheel," Susan yelled to Cowboy, over the wind and engine noise. "You throw the princess overboard. Make sure no one ever finds her." She handed a rope to Cowboy with an anchor tied to the end of it.

Lynn jerked away from Susan's grip when she saw what was happening and fell hard against the side of the boat. Turning the steering wheel over to Susan, Cowboy shifted his focus to Lynn.

He bent down and grabbed her feet to tie the anchor rope around her ankles. Lynn began fighting for her life, kicking at him as hard and fast as she could. She knew if he got that rope tied to her feet, she wouldn't have a chance in hell. That thought made her kick all the harder, catching Cowboy in the face with one well-placed heel.

"You little bitch," he yelled, grabbing the side of his face.

"Hurry up," Susan yelled at him, turning around to see what was happening.

"I can't get this goddamn anchor rope tied. She won't stop kicking," Cowboy yelled at Susan.

"Forget the anchor. Just throw her overboard. They'll never find her in time in the dark," Susan screamed back at him.

"No!" Lynn begged him, as she lay on the floor of the boat trying to scoot backwards away from him.

"Sorry, baby, I don't make the rules." He grabbed her around her neck and jerked her to her feet.

Lynn started screaming as loud as she could, and Cowboy began to laugh.

"Who do you think is going to hear you, sweetheart? You're shit out of luck. Kiss your pretty little tight ass bye-bye, and give our regards to Reese."

Cowboy lifted Lynn up with one smooth swing, and then she was airborne.

Chapter Seventy-Seven

Lynn smacked the water at high speed, almost knocking her unconscious. Her arms felt as if they were being jerked from their sockets as she rolled over and over, skimming over the water like a flat rock. She finally stopped rolling and struggled to get her head above the surface, kicking her feet furiously. She moved her body around taking a quick inventory to see what might be broken. Nothing seemed to be, thank God.

But that was the least of her worries.

With her hands tied behind her back, she knew she would drown in a matter of minutes if one of the police boats didn't run over her. The wind had picked up, and the water had begun to get rough. She knew she couldn't tread water continuously with her legs alone, and with fatigue replacing the adrenalin rush, she knew it was just a matter of minutes until she sank below the surface. Choking and trying to float on her back, she started screaming and kicking her feet up to splash the surface of the water. She could feel her body sinking with every movement, but she wasn't going to give up without a fight. She hoped to God that someone in one of the boats following them had seen her being thrown overboard.

As Lynn felt herself begin to drift down, the water almost covering her face, a sudden peace came over her, like angels were rocking her to sleep in their arms. It was as if they were telling her it was all right to let go, and they would take care of her.

If she couldn't keep afloat, then she wanted death to come quickly. She decided she would just swallow one big mouthful of water, and that would be it. She would go straight down into the abyss that shrouded the North Wall, into Reese's waiting arms.

Just as her head went beneath the water, Lynn heard a loud muffled roar, then felt something grab her hair, pulling her back up.

Up to glorious air. And life.

Chapter Seventy-Eight

With the helicopter's search light guiding them, Koral and Aron had the speeding Cigarette boat in sight and were gaining on it. They could see three people in it struggling.

"We've got to keep our eyes on them in case they decide to lighten their load," Koral yelled at Aron. Riding the smooth V in the wake of the big boat, they could see everything going on inside the cockpit.

The words were barely out of her mouth when she saw a squirming bundle being thrown over the side. She knew it had to be Lynn.

"Did you see that?" she yelled to Aron.

"Yes, I did. Can you go any faster?"

They knew Lynn would be dead if they couldn't find her in the water and soon. That was going to be a problem since the helicopter with its powerful searchlight, and the police boats, hadn't slowed down, but kept in pursuit of the big Cigarette. They were focused on chasing it down, not on whatever or whoever, went overboard. It was up to Koral and Aron to find Lynn before she drowned.

They began to scan the water as Koral slowed the engines, but she and Aron saw nothing. Let the police boats handle Susan and Cowboy, Koral thought. They couldn't possibly catch the powerful Cigarette, but the helicopter could keep it in sight and radio its position ahead.

"She'll be dead if we don't find her soon. Hell, the toss from the boat at that speed could have killed her," Koral yelled to Aron.

Trying to see a body at night in the water is like trying to catch a hummingbird with fish bait, Koral thought. She slowed the boat again, close to idle, and then she heard it.

A faint sound, a woman's voice calling out.

"Listen," Koral said, her eyes wide, willing herself to see better in the darkness.

"What is it?" Aron asked her.

"Did you hear that?"

"I didn't hear anything."

"There it is again."

Koral swung the boat around and followed the direction of the voice she heard. She grabbed the spotlight Aron had retrieved from its hook in the cabin and shined it on the water in front of them. She idled along, tracking the voice. About thirty yards in front of them, she saw it. A head bobbing in the water.

"There she is!" Koral shouted, pulling back on the throttles.

She scrambled down into the cabin and grabbed two orange life jackets. On her way back up, she threw the spotlight's strap over her shoulder.

Koral yelled at Aron. "Take the wheel and go after them. Call one of the police boats and tell them to come get us. We'll be fine. You just catch that boat."

Then she was gone over the side.

Aron saw Koral swimming toward Lynn, but he couldn't see Lynn in the dark. Where was she?

"Koral, can you see her?" Aron called out.

"I see her. Get going and don't worry about us. Just hurry and send someone back to pick us up." Koral sounded more hopeful than she felt and hoped Aron would get a boat back to them fast. Thank goodness the life jackets had locator lights on them.

Aron checked the boat's GPS so he could send help to Koral and Lynn, pushed the throttles to full speed, and sped off in pursuit of the two killers.

He could still see the helicopter's lights chasing the big Cigarette out over the open sea and wondered where in the world

Susan and Cowboy thought they could run to escape. From the looks of things, they were headed straight for the reef that guarded the North Wall.

Unless a person knew exactly where the cuts were, that could be a deadly course.

Chapter Seventy-Nine

Aron radioed the dispatcher as he headed after Susan and Cowboy. He told her to have two of the police boats go back to pick up Koral and Lynn and gave her the GPS reading. He knew it was going to be hard to find them in the dark, but he had confidence in his men and in Koral. Thank goodness the two life jackets Koral jumped overboard with were equipped with battery-operated locator lights which would give the police something to look for in the darkness, in addition to using their high-powered spotlights.

Aron also said a silent prayer that this night would not end badly.

Koral watched Aron push the boat forward, disappearing into the night, as she quickly scanned the water's surface looking for any sign of Lynn, hoping she was still alive. She thought she saw something about ten yards away from her, but then it was gone. Then, it appeared again and Koral made out the shape of a head.

"Lynn!" Koral yelled, as loud as she could manage. No answer.

Swimming and kicking as hard as she could, Koral started toward the form in the water. She could see it beginning to slip beneath the surface and just as it went under, Koral made a dive for it. Grabbing a handful of hair, she jerked Lynn's head above the water, holding her tightly until she could get the life jacket under her. Lynn was barely conscious, sputtering and coughing, but alive.

"Hold on, Lynn," Koral urged her, while she fumbled to untie the nylon rope binding her wrists behind her, which was all but next to impossible under water. "You'll be just fine. The police boat will be here soon and pick us up." She hoped she sounded more confident than she felt. She didn't know how long she could keep both of them afloat with the current taking them further out into the open Caribbean with every wave. Those GPS coordinates Aron gave his men wouldn't be accurate too much longer.

Koral was trying to reassure Lynn as she struggled to get her into the life jacket after she finally got her hands untied. She was out of breath herself and getting chilled. Even eighty-three-degree water could numb you eventually, and cool thermo clines threaded through the currents along the North Wall.

"Koral, is it really you?" Lynn finally sputtered, her voice weak and barely above a whisper, as she cut her eyes around to see who had come to her rescue.

"Yes. Don't talk. Just be still. You're okay."

"Koral, it was Susan. She did all this."

"I know, Lynn. Just be still and concentrate on staying awake. Please. Save your strength."

"But I have to tell you. In case I don't make it, you have to make sure she's punished." Lynn began to cough as she tried to get the words out. The waves were getting rougher by the minute and kept filling her mouth every time she tried to speak.

"You aren't going to die, Lynn. I sure won't let that happen after everything I've done to save your eighteen-carat life," Koral assured her, trying to inject a little levity into this sorry situation.

"She killed her parents. She had that man Cowboy rig their yacht to explode. They were here in the Caymans when it happened. She killed all those people here, too."

Something snapped to attention in Koral's mind when Lynn mentioned something about a boat explosion in the Caymans. Surely that couldn't have been the same explosion that killed Mike. Surely not. But she hadn't heard about another incident like it, so it had to have been that one.

My God, she thought. Susan killed Mike along with her own parents.

Now Koral had an even better reason to catch that bitch. Susan had robbed her of a future with Mike. But unless that police boat came soon, Koral figured she wasn't going to catch anybody. The police were going to find two dead bodies floating somewhere between the North Wall and Cuba.

Chapter Eighty

Susan stood next to Cowboy at the wheel of the Cigarette as they sped into the darkness toward the North Sound. She could see the lights of the police boats in the distance behind them. The helicopter was still overhead following them.

"Turn off the running lights so they can't see us," Susan yelled to Cowboy. "If they can't see us, they can't find us. We can circle back to the marina or ditch the boat somewhere along the beach, then get the hell out of here before they know we're gone."

She wasn't about to give up yet, not after all that planning and all those years of waiting they had endured. Besides, Lynn was floating down to the bottom of the sea at this moment, a journey that may take a while given the eight-thousand foot depth.

Susan's mind was on getting back to the penthouse, picking Dennis up when he came out from under the powerful sedative she slipped into his champagne, and having the pilots get Lynn's jet ready to leave all this chaos behind. She would tell the pilots that Lynn had stayed behind to take care of some business and would meet them later. Then, they would break the news to everyone that Lynn was dead. They would tell everyone that Lynn had been despondent for some time, and the pressure was just too great for her. She had simply walked into the sea. No one needed to know which sea that was or where. They would think about that when the time came.

By morning she and Dennis would be on a beach in South America and soon, all of this would be forgotten and Cowboy could ride off into the sunset. No one could touch them. Susan knew exactly how to handle Dennis. And all of Lynn's money. Susan wanted it all. The money, Dennis and a wedding ring. So, bye bye Lynn.

"I hope to hell you know what you're doing," Cowboy told Susan, as he flipped off the running lights. All he could see in the darkness was darkness. Even with the full moon, it was difficult to maneuver the speeding boat's path when he wasn't quite sure where he was.

With the sea so choppy, Susan and Cowboy didn't notice the waves breaking over the shallow reef marking the top of the North Wall warning intruders to beware until they were right on top of it. The big boat hit the jagged coral, lifting it up and airborne. It flew through the air like a 747 taking off and turned on its side. As the underside was ripped apart by the coral, the three full gas tanks ignited.

The fireball exploded in brilliant orange and red flames, engulfing the boat. Behind the bar at Kona Kai, bottles of liquor rattled together. Children in West Bay shouted to their parents to come watch the fireworks. In minutes, there was no trace of the boat.

It was as if it and its occupants had never existed.

Chapter Eighty-One

Lynn stood on the balcony of the penthouse drinking in the mauve and melon-orange sunrise. Her blonde hair was blowing gently as the warm breeze wrapped her in its welcome embrace. She was thinking how thankful she was to be here to enjoy anything after what had almost happened to her and Dennis.

"The sunrise only wishes it were as beautiful as you are," a man's voice said behind her.

She smiled without turning, as Dennis put his arms around her and began massaging her shoulders, still sore from her ordeal. She leaned back into him and closed her eyes.

"I thought everything was over night before last. I thought you were dead, and there was no doubt in my mind that I was going to be dead, too. If it hadn't been for Koral and Chief Ebanks, we wouldn't be here," she said softly.

"Well, I did wonder if I'd died and gone to hell when I woke up at three o'clock with a barbiturate hangover," he laughed.

"I really owe Chief Ebanks and Koral a lot," Dennis added. "I don't know what I would have done if anything had happened to you. I also owe them an apology for acting like such a jackass."

"I still can't believe what Susan did," Lynn mused. "How she planned this for years is just beyond me. I just want to put it out of my mind, but I can't forget it. All those people she killed, all the lies, the way she and that horrible man died, it's been so surreal."

"There is one good thing she did," Dennis said, running his hand over her hair and brushing it back from her face.

"What?" Lynn looked up at him in shock.

"She did force us to get married."

Lynn laughed and said, "Remind me to send her a thank you note. That's what brides do, right?"

"It is. And speaking of brides, I would like very much to kiss mine now."

"We did sort of get interrupted, didn't we?"

Dennis gathered Lynn in her arms and kissed her just as the phone started ringing. They both giggled and Dennis said, "We may never get to do this the traditional way."

He went inside to answer it and came back out to the balcony with it in his hand. "It's for you."

Lynn took the phone and said, "Hello."

"Lynn, it's Koral."

"Hi, Koral. You were first on my list to call this morning. Dennis and I would love for you and Chief Ebanks to come to dinner soon. That's such a small thank you for everything you did for us, but it's a start. We can never repay you for saving our lives," Lynn told her.

"Saving lives. That's what we do best," Koral joked. "We just happened to be in the neighborhood and wondered if we could drop by for a minute. We're in the lobby."

"Certainly. Come on up."

"What did Koral want?" Dennis asked her.

"They're coming up for a minute."

When the elevator door opened a couple of minutes later, Koral and Aron stood there with a huge wrapped package.

"Come in," Lynn said, walking over and hugging each of them.

"Hello, Mrs. Mallory. I mean Mrs. Hammond," Aron corrected himself with a smile.

"We just wanted to drop this off for you," Koral said, handing Lynn the package.

"What is it?" Lynn asked her.

"A wedding gift, of course. Maybe in Dennis' case, a peace offering," Koral joked.

Dennis said, "I do hope you'll forgive me for being such a jerk. I'm really a nice guy."

They were all laughing as the elevator door opened, and Sid and Tabby stood there looking a little surprised at the odd gathering in front of them.

"Sid! Tabby! What are you doing here?" Lynn squealed, as she rushed over to greet them with a big hug.

"Well, the concierge told us we could come on up. We heard there was a wedding taking place. Did we miss anything?" Sid asked.

Lynn turned around and looked at Dennis, Koral and Aron who were all trying to keep straight faces. They burst out laughing while Sid and Tabby stood there looking puzzled.

"Boy, do we have a story to tell you," Lynn told him, taking his and Tabby's arms.

They were all still laughing as they went out to the balcony to enjoy the glorious Cayman morning.

Dennis stood watching them and thinking how perfectly everything had worked out, even with a couple of unexpected turns.

He deserved an Academy Award or two for his performance, if he did say so himself, and his little band of puppets had performed like clockwork, most of the time. Susan had been an easy mark a couple of years ago with her hunger for money and prestige, and she'd bought into his plan just as he knew she would.

When she met Cowboy that night at Tony's and brought him into their scheme, the two of them had made the perfect pair. She wanted Cowboy's body and he wanted her connections. When Cowboy hired that lowlife Ray Durbin on Susan's orders to kill Reese, the players were all assembled. All Dennis had to do to manipulate Susan was to dangle Lynn's millions in front of her and promise to marry her once Lynn had written the codicil to her will leaving everything to him.

But just like Ray Durbin, Cowboy and Susan hadn't held up their part of the plan by not succeeding in getting rid of Lynn. Now, he had to devise another perfect scheme, but that would have to come later when all of the fallout from the past few days had died down and no one suspected him of anything, especially so soon after marrying Lynn.

Who knows? he thought. I might even keep Lynn around for a while to enjoy what I've worked so hard for all these years. She was definitely worth keeping in his bed for a while. That face and that body would please him for quite some time. When the new wears off, she can easily be replaced, he thought, that crooked smile Lynn loved so much spreading over his face.

Dennis knew nothing could be traced back to him. His hands were clean in all of this. He'd made sure of that. No trail, paper or otherwise, would lead anyone to his door. Cowboy had done all the dirty work taking his orders from Susan, and Susan was the perfect diversion. She was psychotic and he knew it. All she had to do was be herself and everyone would think she was the mastermind of his brilliant plot if any questions arose. He had planned everything so Susan would be the visible one at strategic times, not him.

He had coached her perfectly on everything to say to Lynn if Lynn discovered their treachery before they had carried it out. He made sure Susan knew that absolutely no suspicion could be cast on him or the entire plan would fall apart and Susan would lose her chance at everything she coveted most.

All these years, everyone had written Dennis off as Reese's mild-mannered best friend who had always been secretly in love with Lynn. Some had even felt sorry for him. Screw them, he thought. Well, what do you think of me now? he laughed, a smug grin spreading across his handsome face. I have it all now…finally.

If, or when, anything ever happened to Lynn, he was set to inherit everything she owned, no questions asked, and she didn't even know it.

Dennis thought of the codicil Lynn had written which he had safely tucked away from inquiring eyes in a safe deposit box. Lynn thought the codicil had gone up in flames with Susan on the boat, but Susan had slipped it in his shirt pocket after she drugged him at the penthouse, before she and Cowboy took Lynn out on the boat. To make sure it wasn't destroyed while they were disposing of Lynn, Susan left it exactly where he'd told her to leave it in his pocket. Before the police got to the penthouse and found him "unconscious" on the balcony, he had already hidden the codicil away and resumed his position on the balcony for them to "rescue" him after he had finished off the drug-laden glass of champagne. He knew he had to make the situation look genuine or the lack of drugs in his system when they checked him at the hospital would show up and screw up everything.

The boat hitting the reef and exploding with Cowboy and Susan on it was unexpected and just icing on the cake. Now he didn't have to worry about disposing of them, however, he really was going to miss all the great sex with Susan, especially those foursomes like the one at her house when she first brought Cowboy into the picture. Now, that was a night.

If that bitch Koral Sanders had kept her nose out of his business, Lynn would already be history and he wouldn't have to be plotting yet another "accident."

Oh, well, he thought. That's what I do best.

Epilogue

Cowboy floated on his back on the surface of the water, the darkness and the full moon his only companions.

Blood was pouring from a deep gash on his forehead and his skin screamed where the fire had burned it when the boat exploded. The saltwater made the pain almost unbearable, but he would survive it, like he had survived everything.

He floated in the water for what seemed like hours. The current was carrying him back toward the beach. He knew if he could just let the current do the work for him, he could save his strength and find his way back to safety. The waves rocked him gently as if they were soothing his wounds. Then, as the first rays of dawn began to creep over the horizon, he turned to see a deserted stretch of beach lined with palm trees swaying in the warm breeze of morning.

As soon as his feet could touch the sandy bottom, he dragged himself up out of the water and fell exhausted onto the white sand. The gash over his eye had stopped bleeding and was gaping open. The burns on his arms stung like a million bee stings. The pain gave him the strength he needed to get to his feet and walk unsteadily toward the grove of palm trees.

When he reached the trees, he noticed a small yellow house close by, seemingly deserted, except for a dog lying on the back porch and some chickens in the yard. He made his way to the house hoping the dog wouldn't bark and alert anyone inside.

He knew he was on the sparsely populated north side of the island. He just hoped there was a car nearby so he wouldn't have to hitchhike into town.

As he walked up to the dog, it began to wag its tail, and he gave it a pat on the head. Satisfied he wasn't going to be announced by the dog barking, he climbed the steps to the back door and turned the knob. The door opened and he stepped inside.

No one was in the house, so he made himself at home while he searched for medicine and bandages. Finding what he needed in the bathroom, he cleaned and bandaged his head and his burned arms.

In a bedroom closet, he found some dry clothes. They looked a little too large for him, but anything was better than the torn wet ones he was wearing. He took a black long-sleeved shirt and a pair of jeans from the closet. They weren't a perfect fit, but they would do. He also noticed a straw cowboy hat on the closet shelf, almost identical to the one he lost earlier, but much cheaper. He took it down and put it on. Also a little too large, but what the hell. It was just what he needed to keep his face hidden and look like one of the locals, he decided.

Might as well rest for a while, he thought. His ordeal last night had taken all his strength. He couldn't risk being seen in the daylight anyway, so he waited until dusk before venturing outside. The owners of the house must work long hours, he thought, since no one had come back all day.

He remembered the small blue car he had seen earlier in the front yard and decided it would do just fine to take him into town. He was almost home free, he thought.

Just as he reached to open the front door, it flew open and a pretty teenage girl stood there staring at him with a surprised look on her face. She opened her mouth to scream. He grabbed the front of her shirt and pulled her inside, turning her around with one arm around her neck while his hand covered her mouth.

"If you promise not to scream, I'll take my hand away," he said.

She whimpered and nodded her head. As soon as his hand moved, she began to yell with everything she had. He quickly circled her neck with both of his hands, forcing her to her knees, and watched the terror in her eyes as he slowly began to squeeze the life from her body.

He couldn't have known she was nineteen years old and getting ready to be married to her high school sweetheart. He couldn't have known she had two brothers and a sister who adored her, as did her doting parents. He couldn't have known she was two months pregnant. And he wouldn't have cared if he had known all these things. It was his nature.

As her life drained away, a spark seemed to reignite in him. He was thinking of the people he had to find as he dropped the girl's body and it crumpled at his feet.

He went outside and looked to see if there was anyone around. Seeing no one, he walked quickly to the car and slid behind the wheel. It was his lucky day. The keys were in the ignition.

As he drove past the airport and down Seven Mile Beach, he was mapping out a plan in his mind. Everyone thought he was dead, and that was the way it was going to stay. The dead can't kill, which meant no one would ever be looking for him again. He could go anywhere or do anything he wanted. He was officially dead.

That was a good thing since he had some payback to attend to and it wouldn't be pretty. Koral Sanders better be watching her back. Nothing had been done to try to find him and Susan after the boat explosion. Everyone just assumed they had died and left him out there to save himself. He never saw Susan again and knew she didn't make it. He figured hell was going to be a lot hotter with that little firecracker lighting fuses in it. He had to smile at the memory of their time together.

He slowed down as he began to approach a row of condos along Seven Mile Beach. He saw the Sundowner and turned into the parking lot. He sat in the car for an hour watching people come and go. When he was satisfied he could get into the condo he wanted without being seen, he got out of the car and walked toward the building.

He stopped in front of her condo and expertly opened the door with the thin tweezers on a Swiss army knife he'd found in the pocket of the pants he took from the dead girl's house. As he entered the condo, he heard a fierce high-pitched yapping and a furious avian squawk: *"Fuck the bastards!"*

Another fifteen seconds of this and every neighbor in the place would be running outside. Backing out and shutting the door softly, he spotted an alcove with a broom, a rag mop and bucket and a pile of rust-stained rags. It was screened from sight but offered a clear view of *the door. He could wait there unobserved. He could wait there as long as it took. He was patient. Very patient.*

The End